BEFORE SHE KNEW

(Inspired by actual events)

CR HIATT

AMB

Kim -
I hope you enjoy!
CR Hiatt

Copyright

CONTENTS

Author's Note

Before She Knew is a work of fiction inspired by actual events. The names, characters, places, and locations depicted have been changed to protect actual identities.

PROLOGUE

I KNEW HE wasn't in love with her, with either of them. It was only lust. But lust is a powerful aphrodisiac that can turn into an obsession. Could it also turn him into a killer? Did he lure me to my hiking spot, entice me toward the edge, and then push me off the cliff into the powerful waves of the ocean down below?

PART ONE:

CHAPTER 1 - KATIE

Present – April 2020

I FELT HER watching me the minute we walked into the bookstore… and then I saw her. The same woman that showed up at every book signing I had within the last six months. Every location I scheduled, she popped up. I could never get a good look at her; she remained in the shadows, away from those attending the reading or there to get a book signed. She always made her presence known just enough to let me know she was there. I started referring to her as My Stalker. Each time I tried to get close for a better look, she slipped away.

I almost caught up to her at my last appearance during a local fair on Cape Cod. The weather was beautiful; perfect blue sky, not a cloud on the horizon, and the invigorating smell of the salty sea air drifted inland from the ocean waves as they crashed into the shoreline. The locals were enjoying themselves wandering through the rows of canopies and tents filled with homemade crafts, nautical-themed gifts, baked goods using the cranberries from the infamous bogs, and the unique Cape Cod décor and colorful fishing lures that sold like hotcakes when tourists flocked to the New England coast.

Mobile kitchens and a brewery company, offering various new beers, lined up along the pathway leading into the park. Laughter echoed from the kids, teens, and carefree adults when they reached the top of the Ferris wheel, while others admired the *Budweiser* Clydesdale horses on display.

I had my canopy set up. My editor and publicist, Olivia Stewart and Madison Ryan—also my BFFs— were there for support. I did not know what to expect or how large the crowd would be so I bought several boxes of books to sell knowing I would eat the cost if they didn't. I draped a banner across the front of the canopy, had bookmarks, postcards, and business cards to give away, and offered cookies, brownies, and candy as an enticement to stop by. It was like a fun social gathering with friends until I saw her.

My Stalker was in the crowd.

She was some distance away. Her eyes were watching me while she hid the rest of her face behind the cotton candy her mouth was devouring seductively in a manner I found discomfiting. When she caught me looking, she lifted her cell phone, and the flash went off.

She was taking pictures of me.

There was only one reason she would need a flash with the sun shining in the middle of the day; to purposely taunt me.

After several minutes, I don't know what happened maybe I snapped from her continued and unsolicited attention over the past few months. There were still two customers in line waiting to get their books signed when I saw another flash. I couldn't help myself. I jumped out of my seat and started fast-walking toward her.

Flustered, Olivia and Madison tried to smooth things over at the booth while I worked my way through the crowd; following her, hoping to find out who she was and why she kept surfacing at every appearance. Did she have a problem with my books?

She reached the parking lot, and I thought it was my chance to catch up to her since pedestrians were blocking the entrance. I followed her through the maze of vehicles and gained ground until she unexpectedly jumped over the temporary orange safety fence put up for the fair. Then she hopped into a dark SUV parked on the other side and sped away before I could read her license plate or get a close-up of her face.

That was two weeks ago.

Today's book signing was more professional and not exactly my comfort zone. The store was huge, privately owned, and the manager was a graduate of Harvard; someone who preferred prominent individuals in journalism or politics, celebrities, and authors whose works made the NYT's bestselling list.

"You'll be fine," Olivia said to me for the umpteenth time since we left home that morning.

"Of course you will," Madison added. "Just be yourself, and ignore that she's here. No repeat performance like the fair."

Even though My Stalker has never done anything to harm me, physically, it was still unnerving that she was always there. Toying with my psyche and purposely getting under my skin, leaving me to wonder why.

Ignore her, they said. Be yourself, they said. If only it were that easy.

I wasn't famous, definitely wasn't a celebrity, and my books haven't made the major publication lists, yet. I have had two books achieve bestseller status in one of my categories, which meant I received dozens of emails and messages from readers. Considering there are millions of books published, I deemed that quite an accomplishment. Though I doubt a Harvard graduate looking for books to make the *Oprah* or *Reese Witherspoon* Book Clubs would agree, the book store manager was giving me a chance all the same. Still, I couldn't help but wonder how I managed to get a stalker with very little notoriety.

"I can see the wheels spinning in your head, Katie, stop overanalyzing," Olivia scolded me.

I smiled and looked around at the crowd of people, an even mix of locals and tourists, from what I could tell, and of course My Stalker.

"I'm just not sure this location is the right audience for my book," I said, feeling a moment of insecurity, which was probably one of My Stalker's intentions each time she showed up.

It was common knowledge that Provincetown, Massachusetts, normally referred to as P-Town, was a tourist and artist destination known for its beaches and harbors. They also recognized the location as a top vacation destination for the LGBTQ community. Today's appearance was for a book I wrote depicting a female spy in a game of cat and mouse with the assassin who killed her partner. One reason it continued to garner attention, without a major publishing firm behind me, was because of the allure of romance between spy and assassin during the chase. I didn't think it was artsy enough to appeal to the touristy town.

Madison ignored my doubts. "The manager seemed to think there would be interest or she wouldn't have set up the signing. Tourists are looking for escapism reading material. You're letting *her* get under your skin."

"You're right," I said, trying to brush my pessimism aside.

"And remember," Madison added, "the manager agreed to the signing because she was interested in seeing the way we draw readers in, which she discovered via our website, the book page, and the marketing material we sent her. By the looks of it, our system is piquing interest."

I glanced toward the front of the store where customers were lingering. Instead of just the traditional signing where I would read a few chapters, take questions and then sign books, we added visual displays to draw in customers as they walked through the door. I hired a production crew who put together a two-minute film teaser that revealed the action in the book and introduced the female hero and male villain via two local actors similar in appearance described in the book.

When we arrived at the store, Olivia and Madison set up a film projector and screen. Then they programmed the projector so the trailer would play continuously for customers to view upon entering. It detailed the book and synopsis before the teaser started and during the credits. As they strolled through the store, they would also see other illustrated artwork depicting action scenes, and large 3-D versions of the characters displayed throughout. And of course, I placed an eye-catching banner over the area for the signing. Each graphic highlighted a cover of the book to, hopefully, be engrained in their psyche.

"They do seem to show interest," I replied, "not a huge audience, but better than I expected." I relaxed when I noticed several of them detour over to the book display table set up near where I started my animated reading of chapters hoping to reel in buyers. I was also happy to learn some specifically came for the signing after seeing the dates on the author page.

"Marketing 101," Madison repeated what she told me the first time we attempted it.

After some success, the three of us had teased each other that we had our little niche going and as long as it brought in steady sales, we didn't care about the bestseller lists for the major publications.

While reading my designated chapters, I glanced around to see if I could get a sense of the audience's interest. At one point, I almost lost my focus when I got confused by the unexpected actions of My Stalker. She was intentionally trying to distract me, which was unusual. Normally, she watched and studied me, or pulled out her camera to take a picture or film me.

I still couldn't get a good look at her face. She kept bobbing up and down behind shelves of books and a tall palm tree plant, waving her arms flamboyantly. Remembering how I embarrassed myself at the fair, I forced myself to tune her out. It wasn't easy. I lost my place at one point and left out a few words. Thankfully, the audience didn't seem to notice, or if they did, they didn't mention it.

After the reading was over, refreshments were served and the floor was opened for questions. A line formed for me to sign books, not a long one, but enough to make me feel the trip was worth it.

According to Madison, every signing was worth it, even if only one individual was standing in line. I didn't understand that logic, but since marketing was her forte, who was I to disagree?

A young adult female slowly raised her hand in the crowd, egged on by the group she was sitting with. "I read this book when it was released and was wondering if you'll be publishing another one soon?"

"Thank you for your support. I hope you liked it."

She nodded. "I was cheering for the assassin, not that I wasn't supportive of the female spy tracking him. She was the hero, after all; I just sympathized with the assassin because of how they forced him into his role."

I smiled and noticed how enthusiastic she was now that she had the floor. I found myself wondering how far she had come to attend the signing. Was she here on vacation, or was she one of those that specifically interested in the signing?

"I've received quite a few emails saying the same thing," I said to her. "And yes, I am working on another book, hoping to release it soon, thank you for asking."

"What's it about?" another woman chimed in without being called on.

"I wish I could tell you, but my publicist swore me to secrecy for the time being."

I winked at Madison, and a few people in the audience laughed.

"Seriously though, I can't tell you the plot, but I am gearing toward a psychological suspense before publishing the sequel in the spy series."

I was down to the last few customers waiting for a signature when I got the unsettling feeling My Stalker was willing me to look her way. It was like déjà vu, and a sensation I've had several times over the last year; even before I was aware I had a stalker. It affected me so much that I did a little research on the subject. The term was scopaesthesia, though it was easier just to say my gaze-detection system was working.

I scanned the faces in my small crowd, and then perused the rest of the store, making sure to cover the area where she tried to distract me earlier. She was no longer there. Other than a couple who stopped by to check out the book on the display shelf, noticed the picture on the inside page, and then glanced in my direction to confirm it was me, there wasn't anyone watching me that intently.

Yet the feeling was still strong.

I was trying to shake it off when an employee of the store approached me with a quizzical look on his face. "I'm sorry to interrupt, but someone called the store for you." He held out a portable phone.

I accepted the phone, as confused as he was. Who would call the store for me?

"Hello?"

"JR Harris," a voice said, but I couldn't make out whether it was male or female, "or should I say, Katie Parker?"

It sounded like they were holding something over the phone to disguise their voice. It was someone who knew JR Harris was a pseudonym. They also knew my actual name. I don't hide it, I just don't advertise it.

"Yes?"

"Why do you lie to the world?"

"Excuse me?" I said. "Who is this?"

"Why do you pretend to be something you're not?"

"I don't understand what you mean. Tell me what you mean."

"I've been watching you … and I'm not going to stop."

The last comment gave me an unsettling feeling. I assumed it was My Stalker? What was I lying to the world about, using a pen name? It's common practice. There was no response, and the line went dead seconds later.

I handed the phone back to the employee, a curious frown visible on my face.

"Is everything okay?"

I forced a smile. "Everything's fine. Thank you."

Intuitively, I glanced around the store again, and then toward the front window a good distance away from where I sat. That's where I saw My Stalker, outside, blatantly watching me, and then purposely duck out of sight when she saw me look her way. I couldn't see if she had a phone in her hand? After several seconds she didn't present herself again, so I tried to brush the words aside and returned my attention to the next customer in line. I promised Madison I wouldn't cause a scene as I had at the book fair signing.

A minute later, I heard screeching tires followed by the persistent blare of a car horn; ordinary actions on busy streets in a big city, but P-Town? I looked outside again: My Stalker had purposely stepped off the curb into the ongoing traffic and forced the driver of a white Jeep to slam on the brakes to avoid hitting her, totally indifferent to the near accident she almost caused.

When she reached the opposite side of the street, she paused and glanced back toward the bookstore. Even though I couldn't see her clearly from where I was in the store, I couldn't help but feel her overt gaze that seemed to laser itself through the front window and latch onto me.

My body involuntarily shuddered.

Why is she stalking me?

What is her goal?

I looked over at Olivia and Madison; they were chatting with the manager of the store discussing the invoice and numbers of books sold for today's appearance, oblivious to what was going on outside on the street.

Rather annoyed now, I finished signing for the remaining customers, thanked them for their support, and reminded them to watch my author page for news on the release of the untitled book I was currently working on. I tried to shut out the thoughts racing through my mind, but the voice on the phone kept breaking through: *Why are you lying to the world?*

I joined Olivia and Madison where they were restocking the display shelves so the store could keep selling after we departed. Then I grabbed the car keys from Olivia and slipped away to collect the 3-D artwork, disconnected the projector, and folded up the portable screen to carry them out to the car.

Truthfully, I wanted an excuse to see if My Stalker was still lurking nearby. I looked up and down the street but didn't see her. Part of me felt like I was just mixed up in one of my fictional plots, so I pushed it out of my head and rejoined the girls.

"That went well," Madison said, straightening the books on the shelf so that the spine was visible and readers could see my pen name among all the other books displayed.

"As usual, you were right," I responded, keeping what happened quiet for the time being.

Olivia folded up the empty book boxes after we stocked the displays. "Better than I expected as far as sales go."

Madison added, "A lot of customers might not have attended the reading portion, but there were sales from watching the video and seeing the 3-D cutouts, probably out of curiosity."

I took a step back to view the shelves. I can't explain the feeling I had seeing my title lined up with other authors' books, some famous names, and others I'd never heard of before today. Every author knew what I was talking about. The manager had said if the signing reached a certain number of sales, the store would allow the book to remain upfront. As an indie author, I welcomed the opportunity, but I also knew if the book failed to produce, another would quickly take its place.

Olivia turned to me, smiled, and said, "We should do the same type of promo for your next book tour. How's that outline coming, by the way?"

"It's getting there," I said, even though I wasn't as far along as I had hoped.

"Keep plugging away," she said. "As you told me, if you want to remain independent you have to keep putting books out to keep the momentum going."

"I do keep saying that, don't I?" I had an entire folder filled with ideas for stories that I created and could develop them into a plot for a book, but none of them were calling out to me. I could easily have written another spy book, but I wanted to attempt psychological suspense since they were currently the rage, and notes in my journal reflected it could happen—especially with all the gaze-detection episodes I've had lately. I'm trying to write to market this time.

Olivia gave me one of her mischievous grins. "Just remember what Madison and I have been saying for months now."

I shook my head and rolled my eyes, knowing exactly what she was going to say. They've been trying to get me out of my comfort zone of writing mysteries or thrillers that focused on crimes or terrorist attacks and wanted me to push the envelope.

"Yes, I know," I said, laughing and repeating the mantra they've been sharing with me for a while now, "sex sells."

"Exactly," they said in unison.

Even though I knew they were teasing and would never advise me on what I should write in my books, I could never have guessed that sex would be prominently featured in my next plot, or that I would wind up being the basis for the main character.

CHAPTER 2 - KATIE

Present – April 2020

ANYONE WHO HAS ever driven to P-Town—which is at the final tip of the Cape Cod Peninsula—knew there wasn't much to see along Highway 6 or 6A unless you exited off the two-lane road and toured the seaside villages along the way. Once we were on our way home with no visual stimulation to keep us entertained, I took that time to tell Olivia and Madison what happened at the signing; My Stalker trying to distract me, the phone call, and how she nearly caused an accident in front of the store.

Ordinarily, I wouldn't make too much of My Stalker's actions because I didn't like to give them more significance than they deserved. Olivia and Madison have been with me on some of the occasions when she showed up, but she usually just watched from the crowd or took photographs. Today, her behavior was strange and more aggressive.

From the driver's seat, Olivia looked at me through the rear-view mirror. "I assume you think she's the one who made the call?"

I returned her gaze from the back seat. "Besides *Gibbs* on *NCIS*, who is it that always says there are no coincidences?"

"Touché."

"I couldn't tell if the caller was a male or female, but it's a little too convenient that she was there at the time of the call. And who else could it be? *Why do I lie to the world*? What does that even mean? What am I lying about?"

"You got me on that one. But if she did make the call, why do you think she used your real name and your pseudonym?"

"I don't know, to let me know she's aware of my real identity?"

Madison said, "That sounds ominous. Maybe she doesn't understand that authors use pen names?"

"She's not very educated then; pen names are common."

"Was the woman today the same one who showed up at the fair?" Madison asked.

"The same."

"Describe her for me, again."

"She never gets close enough for me to see her face clearly, which means I can't guess age. I'd say several inches taller than me; dark hair, almost black. She's always wearing skin-tight ripped jeans and today she had on a low-cut tank top. She's not shy about showing skin. She also spends a lot of time in the sun or a tanning booth; even at a distance I could tell it was a fake tan."

"She keeps showing up at book signings, which means she's following the author page to see the schedule," Olivia said. "Maybe she posted something on the page in the past."

"It wouldn't hurt to look."

Madison opened her cell phone and clicked on the Facebook page for my pen name, JR Harris, and scrolled through recent posts and comments. "I don't see any odd posts in the last few days, or profiles fitting the physical description. I'll have to do a more thorough search on the computer when we get home."

Olivia glanced toward Madison "What about messenger or the email account listed on the books?"

"I'll have to check those when we get home, too," Madison responded. "There are too many emails to have them sent to my phone."

"Maybe it has nothing to do with the books?" I said, even though it was more of a question than a statement. "Why would a reader ask me why I was lying to the world?"

"I don't know," Olivia said, "but why does she keep showing up at book signings if it's not about the books?"

"Maybe *Gibbs* was wrong. Maybe now and then there is such a thing as a coincidence."

"Bite your tongue," Madison said with a chuckle. She swiveled around and looked at me in the back seat, musing. "Is there any way for a reader to be on the author page, learn your proper name and then go to your personal page?"

"I don't think so. I don't have my actual name listed anywhere on the author page, but it's not like I'm hiding my identity, just publicizing the pen name for branding. Either way, if a reader knew my name and went to my page, they wouldn't learn much about me. I don't put private information on there. If they were nosey, they could observe what I like or comment on, which might lead them to interpret certain things about me or possibly discover who a friend might be, but they wouldn't learn anything about my personal life. If that's what she's doing, it's still stalking."

Olivia said, "That's why I don't go on Facebook much; so many deranged people putting personal shit on there. It's creepy."

We were silent for a couple of minutes, doing what women do; analyzing.

"Maybe we're overthinking it," Olivia finally said, speaking in a teasing tone and trying to lighten the mood. "Maybe the woman is just following you because she thinks you're hot."

I inwardly groaned.

"It *was* the LGBTQ beach community," Madison added, picking up on Olivia's humorous thoughts and trying to put me at ease with the light-hearted jokes.

"She's been stalking me for months," I reminded them.

"We're just trying to ease your mind," Olivia said.

"I know," I said, smiling back at her through the mirror. "It would have been crazy for someone to drive down to the tip of the Cape just to taunt me at a book signing, but if that was the case, it's probably a good thing she hasn't approached me. I wouldn't have known what to say if she attempted to hit on me."

All three of us laughed, which was Olivia's intention when she steered the conversation in a different direction.

At the sudden sound of static on the radio, we realized we were moving out of the Provincetown area, and the local channel disappeared. Olivia scanned the stations and stopped when she found one with mellow music and turned it down low so the soft tunes could play in the background.

I leaned over to the right passenger seat to sort through my laptop case, trying to find my journal. If trivial or not, I had been keeping track of each time My Stalker made an appearance, starting with the dates of occurrence, where I was when it happened, and anything relevant. I wanted to add what happened at the bookstore while it was still fresh in my mind.

Not long after, my thoughts were interrupted by the sound of someone revving a motor on the left-hand side of the vehicle.

"What the hell," Olivia said, peering through the exterior mirror on the driver side of the vehicle, "some jackass is trying to play chicken with us." She grabbed the steering wheel tight with both hands at ten and two, preparing for defensive driving.

Madison braced herself in the front passenger seat, unclear about what was going on.

I swiveled around to look out the back window. "What the—"

An individual on a motorcycle was speeding up alongside the SUV, purposely taunting us and getting dangerously close. There were no other vehicles on the highway at the moment, and like me, Olivia always drove the speed limit, giving the bike the ability to remain steady with us on the two-lane road. The motorcycle was a Harley Davidson, but with all the weaving back and forth, it was hard to register the model, and I couldn't make a description of the rider either. I assumed male by the height and the all-black leather attire; chaps, work boots, and jacket and the helmet had a built-in face mask of all black glass.

The rider was about a foot away from the fiberglass of the SUV when he suddenly lifted his right-booted foot and kicked the passenger door where I sat.

The jolt took us all by surprise.

"Sonsabitches!" Olivia yelled, not holding back on her anger, using one of her favorite curse words. "Is the scumbag trying to run us off the road?" She unintentionally swerved to the right. The tires hit gravel, and the wheels skidded before she could veer back onto the highway.

"Should I call 911?" Madison asked, her voice rattled by the motorcycle rider's actions.

The rider revved the engine again, and I could sense the evil mirth inside the mask.

The motorcycle suddenly slowed down, allowing us to move ahead, giving us hope the game was over. Our relief was fleeting; the motorcycle veered to the right to get behind us and the rider cranked the gas to continue the torment.

Fearing what he might do, I kept watching through the back window. The rider kept weaving from left to right, enjoying the dangerous sport he was playing; knowing it was difficult for Olivia to see him through the side mirrors with the constant movement.

After a couple of miles, he obviously got bored with those maneuvers, cranked the gas again, and sped back up alongside us.

"He's not stopping," Madison said frantically. "I am calling 911."

Not wanting to join in his fun, Olivia eased off the gas and allowed the vehicle to slow down. Then she turned the steering wheel to the right, allowing the

SUV to veer off the highway until all four wheels were rolling over gravel and debris. Not as easy for a motorcycle to follow on two wheels, though he could keep the pace alongside us.

I'd had enough of this jerk. I could see he didn't have a weapon but was merely using his motorcycle as one. I noticed a bag of tennis balls on the opposite passenger floor; Olivia probably bought them to play with her yellow lab puppy. As silly as it was, I grabbed them, then rolled down the window and leaned out, trying to get a better view of the bike.

"Katie, what are you doing?" Madison yelled. "Are you crazy?"

"At the very least, I want to annoy him."

I was a pitcher on the softball team during high school, but it wasn't easy trying to throw a fastball through the open space of a car window. I aimed at the helmet.

He ducked, but the motion caused him to wobble a little, so I fired off another, and another. At one point, he eased up on the gas while he struggled to avoid the balls, but I quickly realized all I was accomplishing was making him mad.

While the window was open, he maneuvered the motorcycle so that he was opposite the passenger door where I sat. If he had a gun, he could have killed me right then, but he just stared at me through his mask for what felt like an eternity, only it was probably only a few seconds. He was trying to frighten us. I didn't want to give him the satisfaction, so I stared back even though his eyes were behind his face mask. My intuition clicked in and I realized this wasn't some random motorcyclist.

"Now we'll have witnesses," Olivia finally said, looking up ahead at another vehicle coming in our direction in the opposite lane.

The car was still too far away, but Highway 6 was only a two-lane highway. If the motorcycle rider continued the game, the oncoming vehicle would become part of his game. Instead, he kept his focus on me, positioned the gloved fingers of his right hand like that of a gun, and mimicked pulling the trigger before he cranked the gas, then high-tailed it ahead of us.

"Crap, I couldn't get the plate number," I said, trying to control the involuntary shiver.

Olivia slowly pressed down on the brake, trying to stop the vehicle and avoid skidding out of control.

Once we parked, I leaned forward in my seat and touched both of their shoulders. "Are you two okay?"

"What the fuck was that?" Olivia shouted, letting loose with a few more f-bombs to ease her anxiety. "Did he gesture using a gun at you?"

"Yes, *she* wanted to scare us."

"Well, it worked," Olivia said, and then she stared at me through the mirror when she realized what I said. "Wait, you think that could have been a female? Her?"

I didn't want to admit what I was thinking; it would make it real. "No coincidences, remember."

"Deep breaths," Madison said after finishing up with the call. She attempted 911 only to realize she had to call local since we were on the highway, and they couldn't track where we were. "Someone should be here shortly."

"Unfortunately, we've got nothing definitive to tell them," I said, annoyed I couldn't get a plate. "I know it was a Harley, just not sure of the model."

"Probably just some idiot out for a joy ride and getting kicks by trying to terrify a car full of women," Madison said.

Olivia and I shared a look; both of us thinking the same thing, but not wanting to scare Madison. "I don't think so," I said to myself as I leaned back in my seat.

A Massachusetts State Trooper finally arrived. We told him what happened; without the model of the bike, license plate, or a better description of the rider, it didn't help. We asked if he passed a motorcycle on his way toward us, but he only turned onto the highway about a mile up ahead. He would put a call out to others, but the chances of finding the perpetrator were slim. A lot of Harley riders wore leather chaps and helmets with face masks when it was chilly, and this was a common highway for them to enjoy. There was no damage to the car. The kick unnerved us, but it didn't leave a mark. At least there was a report filed, even though it wouldn't amount to anything.

After we calmed ourselves and continued on our journey, I couldn't shake the feeling that it wasn't a random deal. Olivia felt the same, but we didn't want to say it to the officer. With nothing to back it up, we'd just look like paranoid females. It came back to that theory of: did we believe in coincidences? We were physically fine, just another attempt to mess with my psyche, so I noted it in my journal.

The rest of the trip was quiet except for the discussion of whether or not to tell our husbands. We agreed not to. Since nothing came of it we didn't want to get them all riled up and have Madison's husband decide he would chaperone us from now on. That would put a damper on our gal time. For the time being, we would keep everything quiet and just head home, have some dinner, and enjoy a night by the fire, along with a stiff drink.

CHAPTER 3 – MY STALKER

Before – September 2017

LUST CAN HAPPEN in a matter of seconds when you first meet someone. It's an immediate physical and sexual attraction that develops in your mind without even forming a thought that you might be interested in the first place. A primal desire that you need to fulfill and it can turn into a full-on obsession if you don't have control over your emotions.

That was how it started for me the first day I met Jake Parker. He aroused me the minute he rolled up to the station for a training class, seated on a Harley Davidson wearing his leather chaps, a vest over his uniform, and a pair of work boots.

Tanned and muscular, he looked strong and lethal.

And damn, the visual thrill sent a wave of heat up and down my body and I wanted him that instant.

He maneuvered his motorcycle into the small parking area next to the Chief's SUV with confidence that some riders lacked. He had complete control of the bike. His moves were smooth as if he and the bike were one. I immediately sensed the magnetism, and I couldn't help but fantasize about him controlling me.

The guys I worked with and hung out with did nothing for me. They were either married with kids and had the type of personality that made them jump when their partners called, or they didn't care about their looks and didn't have a clue how to treat a woman like me.

Sure I let them take me to bed, even carried on with a couple for a few months, but all I got out of it was the satisfaction of knowing they'd be at my beck and call. They were whipped, all because of the type of sex I had to offer. That filled me with a sense of power and satisfied my desire to dominate, but not my physical needs.

"That's only something you fabricated in your head," the psychiatrist insisted when I explained my feelings during a mandated appointment after my Chief insisted I seek help. The psych informed me I suffered from *Histrionic Personality Disorder* and attributed it to my inability to have normal relationships.

I scoffed and argued my points during the session. *"HPD... what the hell is that; some lame diagnosis so you doctors can capitalize on the pharmaceuticals? Every day you're coming up with new ones. When I was a kid, there was no such thing as a peanut allergy or ADD."*

"Histrionic Personality Disorder is not new, and you're not alone; there are over four million individuals who suffer from the ailment."

After that statement I didn't just scoff; I laughed out loud. *"What pharmaceutical company is getting rich off this one?'*

"You can dismiss what I'm telling you, but unless you follow the treatment, things will only get worse. Your recent actions at work reveal you're already exhibiting severe symptoms: your need to be the center of attention, your provocative attire at inappropriate places, and obsession over

relationships your mind tells you are intimate when they are not…"

I tuned out what the psychiatrist had to say, especially when I met Jake Parker. He was all alpha male, and I knew things would be different with him. From the moment of introduction, I wanted to make him mine.

He was presented as our training instructor for the day. I was leaning against the Chief's SUV shootin' the shit with a few others when he stepped off the bike and removed his sunglasses. He looked directly at me with his smoky blue eyes and held my gaze as he walked toward me, ignoring the men as if he and I were the only two there. My hair was down and I was in my turnout pants with a white tank top, nipples showing through the cotton fabric because of the slight breeze.

He noticed, and he knew that I noticed him noticing.

I ran my tongue across my lips sending an invitation that we would be taking this lust further … at least that was how it played out in my mind.

In reality, he stepped off the bike and marched toward the chief without even glancing in my direction. They shook hands and carried on a conversation for several minutes, and others joined in the chat like old friends. Eventually, the chief introduced us, informing Jake that I was fairly new and still had a lot to learn. He smiled, said he trained a few newbies in certain skills, and suggested I look him up if I had questions. He was professional, but of course, I took that as an invitation, ignoring the psychiatrist's words that echoed in my ear.

From what I could tell there was mutual respect between all of them. That told me the guy was highly regarded in the world of first responders. For my chief to show that kind of adulation meant Jake Parker was one of the good ones—something I wanted to discover for myself and made me want him all the more.

There was only one small problem with my fantasy that would need to be dealt with: perfect and wholesome Katie—the description given to me by a co-worker who met her—and informed me that she had been Jake's wife for two decades.

CHAPTER 4 – MY STALKER

Before – September 2017

JAKE TURNED OUT to be the instructor for the entire week instead of just one day, like I assumed. Being in his company for several days in a row, I assumed I'd lose interest as I did with so many others that I found to be boring the more time I spent around them. That didn't happen. My obsession grew stronger, and my physical need was off the charts.

After the last class, a group of us went out for beers at a nearby pub. It was there that I made my first move. The others had already gone home. Jake was lingering until I finished my beer, trying to be polite, which I was purposely taking advantage of.

"You offered to help me out with training if I needed it; was that a legitimate offer?" I leaned towards him so that he had an ample view of my breasts. I was in street clothes; tight jeans and a tank top with no bra. I only wore a bra when I was on duty, and only then, because some whiney-ass wife complained about her husband being in my presence at the firehouse.

He had a few beers and was feeling no pain, so I caught his eyes wandering before they settled on my face. Men were all the same. They were visual creatures, and I knew how to manipulate them in that regard.

"Yeah, it was legit. How can I help?"
Back to Mr. Professional.

"Well, I was thinking if you're sincere that maybe you could train me privately; one-on-one so that I could pass the muster and show the guys I work with that I have what it takes. You know how hard it is for women to fit in until we prove ourselves."

I noticed a shift in his body while he thought about my offer and worried that I might have come on too strong and scared him away.

"Money is no problem. I will pay you for your time. Whatever rate you normally charge is fine."

He shook his head. "It's not about the money. I'm just not sure how much time I'd have for private training. My schedule is pretty hectic as it is, and Katie—"

"Katie? That's your wife?" Of course, I already knew she was his wife. I already learned so much about his precious Katie.

He nodded. "Yes. Katie's cool about all the hours I put in. She doesn't nag. I just don't know how I'd explain that I'm taking on another full-time gig."

Good lord, he made her sound like a saint. She never nags; made me want to puke.

"It doesn't have to be full time and we could work around your schedule," I offered, trying not to push too hard. I shifted around so I was facing him. He could see the tanned nipples through my top—I never wore a bathing suit in the tanning booth.

He eyed me speculatively. I could tell he was sizing me up, trying to figure out if I had an ulterior motive.

"You can stop by after you get off work or you're on your way home, something easy like that; just an hour of your time. Well, just think about it. I'll give you my card. You can text me anytime."

"That might be workable," he said, once I eased off the pressure.

I reached into my bag, pulled out a card, and leaned across his frame to tuck it into his pocket. My nipples brushed his arm and sent a tingling sensation through me. I could tell it caused a reaction in him, too.

"I'll check my schedule and get back to you," he said, and then pushed himself off the seat. "But for now, I need to head out. Katie's expecting me. You all set?"

I thought of letting him walk me out just to see how he would say goodbye, but the better way to play it would be to leave him wanting. "You go on ahead. I have a friend stopping by after work, so I'll just wait here."

He paused for a moment and then nodded.

He didn't need to know I just made that up. Just letting him know I had other options, and that it wouldn't matter to me, personally, if he didn't agree to train me. I knew how to play the game; I could take all the time necessary. I always got what I wanted in the past.

"Good meeting you this week," he said as he dropped some cash on the bar to pay for both of our drinks and a tip. "I'll let you know if I have time available."

I watched him walk out the door and waited until I heard the motorcycle leave the parking lot before I left the bar. By the time I stopped for a few supplies at the grocery store, bought myself a bottle of liquor, and arrived home, Jake Parker had already sent me a text: *Hey, I'd be happy to train you if it's acceptable that I stop by early in the a.m. after I'm off a twenty-four-hour shift?*

I made him wait a good thirty minutes before I replied: *Early a.m. is great ... just send me your schedule so I know what days, and I'll give you the address.*

Ten-four, he responded.

I wondered if I should push my luck and send him a sexy pic, or remain professional like he was, until after I started the training, which I knew would turn into something else. No man had turned me down yet. In the end, I merely sent a thumbs-up gif along with my address. Before I planned my seduction, I needed to know more about Jake and Katie Parker.

CHAPTER 5 - KATIE

Present – April 2020

THE SUV FINALLY turned into the Bella Beachside Community, a private seasonal community during spring, summer, and fall where the three of us have cottages with the Atlantic Ocean as our back yards. Olivia drove through sections A - F and turned right into section G—the Grove.

She pulled into her assigned parking spot, stepped out, and opened the back of the SUV, where a hand-carved African tribal art sculpture took up most of the space. When we arrived early in Provincetown, she went to check out the antique store next to where we were holding the book signing and made the unusual purchase, believing it would be good décor for the small beach community.

I stepped out and joined in to help her remove it. Together, we followed Madison over the thick sand toward a tree stump that would serve as its resting spot.

"What happened to its hair?" Madison asked, looking up from where she was screwing a chain to the stump so we could wrap it around the sculpture and secure it to the spot.

Olivia laughed. "The woman who sold it to me said she had it sitting outside and the birds kept pecking at it to make a nest. This was all they left behind."

Dark brown and fine, wool-like material was woven into its head which gave it the appearance of hair similar to that of a troll, only now, there was barely an inch left after the bird's nesting attempts. Its sculpted arms and legs were crossed as if sitting in a tribal warrior meeting which was perfect for the tree stump centered between the cottages and, according to Olivia, would make a perfect mascot each year.

We positioned the sculpture on the stump making sure its bottom was evenly balanced and wouldn't tip over with a strong gush of wind that could sometimes occur during a nor'easter or hurricane season.

"Jake has a mop head that you can use to replace his hair," I offered, "as long as you don't mind the dreadlock look."

Madison gave us a knowing smile. "I can already envision the caustic remarks from Ted."

That comment made me laugh, remembering various sarcastic statements her husband, Ted, has made through the years. The group always joked that comedian, *Jeff Dunham*, replicated an older version of Ted when he created his puppet: *Walter, the grumpy old man*.

Madison shook her head and grimaced. "Yes, that's my husband, Mr. non-politically correct."

"He's all yours," Olivia and I both said in unison.

~~

I excused myself, grabbed the Tupperware bin filled with book signing equipment from the SUV, and headed toward my cottage to change into some warmer clothing. It was only April and chilly, especially with the fog and breeze that was always prevalent near the water.

"Hey, Kat," my husband said, using the nickname he gave me when he stepped inside the sliding glass door and yelled up to the bedroom where I was changing. "Do you have a minute to go over the schedule since I'll be leaving in the morning?"

"Be right down, changing into some warmer clothes."

"Need any help?" he teased.

"I said changing into warmer clothes, not undressing."

"You're no fun."

He was sitting at the Island counter with his laptop open when I entered the kitchen, and our six-year-old Golden Retriever, Bailey, was lying by the patio door.

"Madison is prepping the dinner so thought I'd get this out of the way since I have to leave early tomorrow. How'd your signing go?"

"Not bad," I said, making sure I said nothing about My Stalker as the three of us agreed. "There were more sales than there were bodies at the reading, but it was good."

"Good, glad it went well."

I grabbed a bottle of water out of the refrigerator, took a quick drink, and then sat down next to him and opened my phone.

He positioned the laptop so I could see it, and then typed in a few details. "We're coming to the hectic time of year, schedule-wise."

I laughed. Jake's schedule has always been hectic, even before he and I met over two decades ago. He had two twenty-four-hour shifts each week at the firehouse, but he was also an instructor which meant he had training classes, sometimes two to three days a week, other times taking up a four-day weekend that he spent out of town. His department also held bi-weekly training for those on dive and tech rescue teams, and he was an officer on the district tech team.

"Yeah, I know, I'm always busy, but for the next two months I don't even have two days off in a row."

"No worries," I said, used to it after all these years. "I'm finishing up the outline for the new book, so that's probably good timing. Oddly enough, I take longer to put together an outline than I do writing the actual book."

"Well good, you'll finish the book quicker with me out of your hair."

"That's the plan. Olivia's keeping up the heat so I do."

He motioned toward the current date on his laptop calendar. "Okay, so you know I leave tomorrow morning for the first responder ride in D.C., which I told you before."

When I met Jake twenty-two years ago, it didn't take long for me to realize that he was an adrenaline junkie. He could never work a nine-to-five job, dinner at six, and then expect him to relax for several hours. It wasn't in his psyche. Aside from his regular commitments, he added another hobby to the mix to keep from getting bored on his days off, which was why he was leaving on a trip in the morning. For the last two-and-a-half years, he got involved in a First Responder Charity Ride (FRCR), a motorcycle ride that raised funds for first responders wounded or killed on duty.

When he started with the charity I didn't mind; I thought it was just a local ride that would take up a few hours on a Saturday or Sunday, and it was for a good cause with funds going directly to the first responder, or family. That didn't last.

The popularity of the charity took off and first responders in several states started rides in their cities using the good name of the original charity. Now, there was a ride scheduled every month. Each one lasted the entire weekend; a meet and greet on Friday, the ride on Saturday, clean up on Sunday, and then the traveling time back and forth for those out of state.

Steve Taylor, a retired Marine, started the charity and asked Jake to be on the board of directors. Needless to say, his time at home for the last few years has been extremely limited.

I pulled up the calendar on my phone. "Yeah, I have the ride noted, you leave at 9 a.m."

"I think I forgot to mention the water rescue training coming up after the local ride here in Boston."

I shook my head. "Nope, don't have anything down for water rescue."

He ruffled through some paperwork. "We've got some guys coming in from out of state, so it looks like we'll be training all that week, so I'll be getting a hotel during that time."

"So it's an academy class?" When he works for the academy and the class is two or more hours away, they put the instructors in a hotel so they don't have to drive back and forth.

"No, this is for the department, so I'll have to pay for my hotel."

I raised my eyebrows at that. The hotel fees were starting to add up. He was spending money for a hotel this weekend, then again for the local charity ride because he had friends coming in from out of town, and now for local training, too. I thought of commenting, and pointing out it was too much, but I didn't. If he didn't get a hotel room they'd probably train most of the day, the guys would want to critique what they did while having a beer and dinner at the pub, and then they'd get home late only to have to wake up early. Expensive, but safe... and more writing time for me, I mentally reasoned.

"Then my normal work schedule and a couple of rope rescue classes, but those will be done by early afternoon. Oh, and then we have the union meeting to discuss the back pay issue."

"You just had to run for union president," I teased.

"Billy asked me to."

Billy was his younger brother who was also a first responder, only he didn't inherit the adrenaline junkie mentality that Jake did.

"What are those days you have highlighted in red?"

"Those are the dates for the local charity ride," he said.

"The ride was already noted in my calendar, just not the two days before the weekend."

"Yeah, sorry about that; Steve said we're expecting thousands of riders to come in for the weekend so he asked me to help set up since I'm on the board."

I shook my head. "Good thing you've got a while before retirement; you'd go stir crazy if you didn't have something to do."

He ran his fingers through his hair, momentarily discomfited by the idea of retirement, and then a mischievous smile formed on his lips. "I won't retire until I have to, and then we'll just get a motorhome so I can drive you around to all your book signings. While you and the gals are inside entertaining the masses, Bailey and I will tour the sights."

"Yeah, okay," I teased. "After an hour of wandering, you would get bored and come into the bookstore looking for me to take Bailey so you could check out the pubs in the area."

"That's why I told you we need to make her a service dog; then she can join me in the pub."

"That's something you would do. Are you going to print that schedule out, or just send it to me on the phone so I can add it to what I already have?"

"I'll send it to your phone." After a minute, he stood up, brushed his lips across my cheek, and playfully tapped the back of my butt; a new form of affection he developed the last few years.

Bailey saw both of us move and assumed that meant it was time to play, so she was up on all fours with her tail wagging, looking back and forth between us to see who was going outside first.

"I'm going to take a quick golf cart ride to the package store before dinner," he said while he waited for his laptop to shut down. "Need anything?"

"No, I'm all set, you taking Bailey with you?"

"Do you think she'd let me go without her?"

I laughed. "No."

He loaded the laptop back into his black bag and walked into the bedroom. On the way back out, he grabbed the key to the golf cart off the hook hanging by the kitchen closet door.

"Are you sure I can't get you something; another bottle of wine?"

"No thanks, we're all stocked up on what I need for the weekend."

Bailey followed him out the door and ran toward her basket of balls, thinking it was time to play, only to stop in her tracks when he didn't follow her. A minute later, I heard the golf cart and glanced out the window to make sure he didn't leave without her. She hurried to catch up and climbed into the passenger seat, looking more like a human than a dog. She was so addicted to the golf cart that she would sometimes hop in and whine until one of us picked up on the fact that she wanted to go for a ride. Residents could drive the carts all around the private community, just not along the beach or out on the major roads.

When you turn left out of The Grove, you pass side streets designated A through F and then wind up back at the front entrance where the office was located. Two miles away to the right, you'd come to the small town grocery store. Continuing to the end of the four-mile road, there was a recreation hall with a sports field on one side for baseball or soccer, and a swimming pool, tennis court, basketball, volleyball, bocce ball, and horseshoes on the other side.

Beachside Community didn't allow package stores inside the gates, so Jake would normally park the golf cart by the office and walk across the main street to the store. I heard the distinct sound of the horn Jake added to the cart as it rambled down the road; the alarm tone from the show Emergency.

~~~

While he was at the store, I took the time to review the calendar dates he gave me and organized my writing schedule. There were pros and cons to his absences. Cons: even with a schedule, it was hard to keep track of when he was coming and going. His time away meant I would be responsible for the upkeep of the homes: lawn care, repairs necessary after weather-related incidents, and the usual shoveling of snow after one of the unpredictable New England blizzards. Pro: his time away gave me the uninterrupted computer time for research and the privacy necessary that went into writing a book or screenplay, not to mention the inevitable social media work essential during the marketing phase of the project. I could work from anywhere as long as I had my laptop, a printer, and access to the internet. April 1st of each year we packed up the truck and trailer, and then transported the necessities down to the seasonal beach cottage and remained there until the last weekend in October.

Olivia, Madison, and their husbands, Jim and Ted, owned cottages in the beachside community for three years before we arrived, but they weren't full-timers. They only came down on weekends and holidays because of their schedules and family commitments. It didn't take long for the six of us, five when Jake wasn't around, to become inseparable. As my editor and publicist, Olivia, Madison, and I spent a lot of time together during the last several years, especially when the seasonal community was open. When they weren't at their cottages, we communicated via texting, Facebook, or Dropbox for editing and marketing.

When I returned with the mop head, Olivia and Madison were at the grill checking on the homemade pizzas. Madison always enjoyed cooking, and since Olivia and I didn't care, she took on the duty of pre-planning meals for the group on weekends. Unfortunately, she worried so much about making sure we were all fed that she had a habit of waking up at four a.m. to put ingredients together for whatever meal she planned for that day.

Jake had returned from the package store and was now carrying pizzas over to a table set up by the fire pit. Jim and Ted were already seated around the fire, drinks in hand, and commiserating over their stressful week dealing with faulty equipment or customers who struggled with communication.

"Chow's on," Jake said, placing the pizzas down on the cutting boards. He grabbed two slices for himself and devoured them in his usual eating habit learned at the firehouse, trying to finish a meal before an alarm sounded, forcing the firefighters to leave the food behind to get cold. He joined the fire department as a volunteer when he was a teenager, so it was a waste of time to advise him to slow down.

"Does everyone have what they need?" Madison asked. As the eldest daughter to seven siblings, she was always trying to take care of everyone else before worrying about herself, but if not for her, we would order takeout.

Olivia and I gave up on cooking regular meals a long time ago because of our partners' erratic schedules; Jake's unusual schedule as a first responder and her husband owned a construction business whose time was contingent on customers constantly phoning in last-minute requests. We never knew when they'd be home, and too many times the meals wound up in the trash.

"We're all set," Olivia said, motioning the seat next to her, "so come, sit down and enjoy."

Madison took her seat, and there were a few moments of silence while we all filled our palettes.

"Delicious, as usual," Olivia said, and I agreed, taking turns on the two slices I chose with different ingredients.

The six of us had diverse tastes, but Madison always tried to accommodate each of us; even Jake, who had peculiarities where food was concerned. She placated him this time by making his favorite meatball and sausage pizza.

"How'd the signing go?" Jim asked in between mouthfuls.

Olivia glanced at me and smiled. "The signing itself was great, but Katie's admirer showed up again."

"Admirer?" Jake said, glancing at me for confirmation with a questionable look in his eyes that said: why didn't you tell me?

I glared at Olivia. I hadn't mentioned anything to Jake about having a stalker and we all agreed not to mention the motorcycle forcing us off the road.

"She's teasing; it was just a woman who keeps showing up at my appearances; probably a disgruntled reader."

"She?" Jake teased, with a shit-eating grin on his face. "Steppin' out on me, are ya?"

"Ha ha ha, aren't you funny?"

"I can be," he said with a gleam in his eyes.

I observed him for a moment; it was good to see him happy and bantering with the group like he used to. Between work, classes, and the motorcycle trips over the last two years, he hasn't been around as much to sit by the fire with the group. I've told him many times that it wasn't just me he left every time he went on one of his trips.

"Jake, are you going to be around tomorrow?" Jim interrupted. "My father's coming down and we're planning on doing a clam boil."

"No, sorry I'm going to miss it."

"He's heading out for one of his rides," I added, which earned me a frown from Jake.

He didn't always like admitting to the group that he was leaving for a pleasure trip. Jim and Ted were more family-oriented and thought he was a bit on the selfish side regarding his motorcycle trips. It would never occur to them to take a trip without their wives taking part.

"I have to leave here around nine to meet up with the other guys going on the ride," Jake said, trying to be a little more forthcoming. "A few of the charity board members are going to help and asked me to join them."

Bailey noticed Jake finished eating and walked toward him, sat down by his feet, and put her paw on his knee, waiting and hoping for the last piece of crust she was sure he was going to share. He gave in to her and then tossed his paper plate into the fire pit.

"How long is the ride, Jake?" Madison asked.

"Depends on the guys I'm with. If it was just me I could haul ass there, do the weekend ride and then head back after a night of rest."

Olivia glanced over at me; I assumed to gauge my reaction. As my editor, she knew I had been working on the outline for my current novel. With Jake away, my only interruption would be Bailey staring at me to hit the ball or take her for one of her walks. She also knew Jake had been going on a lot of charity rides lately. If it was her husband, she wouldn't allow it, nor would he ask.

Jake was different in that regard. He got bored and restless, always looking for something to do, even more so in the last couple of years. We, as a group, kept chalking it up to his fear of getting old and assumed it was the start of a mid-life crisis.

Almost as if sensing he was going to be leaving, Bailey searched the area for her tennis balls and then dropped two at his feet.

"You want me to throw the ball?" He teased.

When he didn't immediately do so, she barked, making her wishes known, so he threw them down along the sand. She darted after them, returned, and dropped them again. We all watched for a bit, knowing the game would go on for a while.

Jim finished his pizza and walked toward his cottage to pour his after drink, then returned to join Jake around the fire pit. He added another log to the fire before sitting down. Ted followed and within minutes, the men engaged in a discussion about tools or the latest sale at the new hardware store that recently opened on the way into town.

Olivia and I started clearing off the table, washed and dried the pizza trays, and put them away. Madison filled three tumbler glasses with ice and poured in some *fireball*. None of us were heavy drinkers, but we liked to sip on the red hot cinnamon flavor once in a while when sitting by the fire. Sometimes we would overdo it and Olivia would tell everyone I said the f-bomb—since four-letter words didn't roll off my tongue as easily as it did for her. Drinks in hand, we joined the men by the fire, and all the dogs found their spots in the sand, except for Bailey, who was still retrieving.

It had been a few weeks since Jake was here with all of us by the fire. Everyone looked content, enjoying the teasing banter that passed between us, and the quick wit that we came to expect out of him over the years. He was infectious to be around when he was like that, even when he needed to be the center of attention.

And almost as if reading my mind, Jake retrieved a box from his sweatshirt pocket. "Since I'm going to be out of town for Kat's birthday, I thought she could open this now."

I frowned. "I thought we agreed to stop exchanging gifts for birthdays?"

He turned to face me and handed me the box. "This is special. Bet you don't remember, but it was twenty-two years ago today that we met?"

I gave him a puzzled look; leave it to Jake to forget our wedding anniversary, but remember the day we met. I had been researching first responders for a book and he was given the job of driving me around to various fire departments around the state.

"I was going through a nasty divorce," he continued, "my kids were angry and my finances were a wreck. Her support helped me through it. A year after the divorce was final, I convinced her to go out with me. We married a year later. My family said I'd be a fool if I screwed it up and I agreed… happy birthday, Kat."

The box was rectangular-shaped, wrapped in gold metallic paper with a crème velvet ribbon. I opened the box, stunned by what was inside: an emerald necklace, bracelet, and earrings to match; exquisite and very expensive. More expensive than we've ever spent on each other for a birthday present.

"They're gorgeous," I said, embarrassed by the gift and very public display.

"Oh, let me see," Olivia said.

I handed them to her as I got up to embrace Jake and whispered in his ear. "Thank you. You didn't have to do that."

"I wanted to … you deserve it."

Bailey didn't seem to appreciate her parents hugging and started barking.

"Are you jealous, Bailey? He threw the ball, again, to appease her."

Once we returned to our seats, he rejoined the conversation with the guys about tools, as if nothing happened, so I started chatting with the girls.

"Well, that was unusual," Olivia whispered, saying exactly what I was thinking.

"I know, right?"

Madison leaned over to look. "They're gorgeous, but so unlike Jake to do this in front of us."

"Maybe he's feeling guilty," I said with a shrug.

"Well, he is leaving on another trip," Olivia said while giving me one of her looks, intimating that I should stop letting him go.

That was the first time Jake ever made a public display of giving me a birthday present. Part of me wondered why he went to such lengths, but I was also grateful and it made me feel warm inside. Until a few moments later, a chill ran down my spine, causing me to shiver, and the feeling I had earlier in the day returned.

Somebody was watching.

I looked around, feeling silly because I was with my friends, but that stubborn intuition was telling me somebody was out there.

I took another sip of my drink and let the warm liquid run down my throat as my eyes discreetly perused the area so the others wouldn't ask questions. The other cottages in our little cul-de-sac were empty, and we did not expect the other owners to arrive until Memorial weekend. All appeared to be quiet, and I didn't see anyone out walking on the beach.

Olivia and Madison were in relaxation mode, talking about future scarves and blankets they wanted to crochet when they had the time. Olivia had been crocheting most of her life, but Madison recently picked up the hobby when she was having trouble sleeping and needed something to help her relax.

Jake, Jim, and Ted were still discussing tools and making plans to take a drive out to Jim's house to help with the upgrade of their in-ground pool in the coming weeks. He had plans to dig out the old platform surrounding it, put in concrete pavers, and then add a new fence to give them more safety and privacy. The guys agreed to help with the labor.

I observed both conversations, hoping they would get me out of my head and stop the unnerving feelings churning in my gut. If only I could have prepared myself for the events that were about to unfold over the coming days, and the secrets that would be revealed and rip my world apart, ultimately putting my life in jeopardy.

CHAPTER 6 – MY STALKER

Before – September 2017

I PARKED MY vehicle about a half-mile away from Jake and Katie Parker's cottage, headlights off and nearly hidden from view when the sun disappeared and the midnight sky blanketed the area into complete darkness. I was in the driver's seat spying through a set of night vision binoculars I purchased, dressed in a dark hoodie and black tights so that I could move around undetected.

Jake was on his shift at the firehouse, so it was just Katie and her two friends from next door. They were at the fire pit on the backside of the cottages, with no clear view of my location. I noted the day, time, and specific details about the area, and added the information into my memo app on my iPad, and then saved the file.

I learned about the cottage during the training class when a few of Jake's friends were chatting with him about his move every April. I eavesdropped on their conversation and learned that he and his wife close up their house to spend time at their seasonal site by the water. The conversation was a treasure trove of information; the guys asked if he minded the long drive, which he described, and narrowed down for me what part of the Cape the cottage was located when he named the nearby town. When they asked if there was a beach, I heard him say it was a private members-only beach. On a day that I knew he was working, I stopped at *Best Buy* for a few supplies and took a drive to see if I could locate it. There were only two private beaches near the town he named. One was exclusive to Kennedy-type residents and not an area that a first responder could afford. I drove around the other community for a couple of hours until I found the right cottage. I spotted his motorcycle trailer parked at the end of the driveway. I knew it belonged to him because of the decals lined up across the top. And so began my planned surveillance of Katie Parker.

After I finished writing in all the pertinent information that could come in handy in the future, I shut off the iPad and took another look through the binoculars: the three women were still sitting by the campfire, talking and laughing.

Katie was sitting in an Adirondack chair with her golden retriever lying underneath. Bitterness burned inside me knowing she had what I wanted; the hot guy and the perfect summer home. It was all so perfect. Then I smirked. Appearances were never what they seemed. Staring at the surroundings for a moment, my fantasy mind took over and my version played out in my head:

Katie and her friends were no longer part of the scene. It was me, there with Jake, only we were no longer sitting in Adirondack lawn chairs. We were naked and sweaty, standing next to the fire when he grabbed me by the back of my hair, pulled me toward him, and plunged his tongue into my mouth while his other hand explored my body. The kiss was fiery and made my body go weak at the knees, my nipples crushed into his chest as we fell onto the sand...

When I snapped back to reality, I realized I'd been so caught up in the illusion that my thong was moist. Had I also been moaning?

Even though the windows were closed, I could hear the ocean waves pounding the surf behind them. I did a quick perimeter search to make sure I had no peepers. Even though the other cottages were empty, a lone runner or walker could choose the cul-de-sac for their evening exercise, or a stray dog could meander into the area looking for scraps and might alert them to my presence.

Seeing no new obstacles, I opened the door to step out and quietly latched it enough to turn out the dome light inside. Looking around, I slowly crept toward the cottage. There were no lights, so I could walk around undetected in my dark clothing as long as I stayed in front of the house. The homes had lights over the front doors, but not bright enough to reveal my presence.

Motion-activated floodlights lit up the back decks of each cottage. The huge fire threw off red, orange, and yellow flames to brighten up the night sky, but that was further down on the sand and closer to the water. The only thing that concerned me was that the three women had dogs; were they trained enough to guard the area? If so, they could alert them to my presence. I didn't think so by what I observed when watching them. They remained by their owners the entire time as if the water tranquilized them or their owners had them chained.

When I arrived at the front of the cottage, instead of pushing my way through the tall seagrass that made up their yard, I tiptoed across the Caribbean beach pebbles used for landscaping the driveway to get to the front steps by the door. Once there, I crouched down low to remain in the shadows.

Not too long ago, residents in the New England beach towns felt safe enough to keep their doors unlocked. Since there was a deadbolt on the door, I didn't think Katie fit that category. I opened the storm door and allowed it to rest against my hip, and turned the knob on the door. It was locked. I reached into my fanny pack and grabbed a set of keys; Jake never even noticed I grabbed them from a cup holder in his Truck one morning when we went for coffee after the private training started. There were three keys, but only one of them fit the front door. One looked like it went to a padlock; the other was probably the key that went to the sliding glass door at the back of the house.

I slid the key in the deadbolt, turned it until it clicked open, and then did the same for the knob. I dropped the keys back into the fanny pack and very slowly opened the door. If the door creaked, that would be like using a dog whistle and I'd be discovered. I quietly slipped inside and remained in the shadows to avoid detection while I quickly surveyed the layout.

There was a low light on over the stove in the kitchen to help me see, so I kept my body down beneath the windows while I memorized the interior and mentally answered my questions. Was there any type of security system or cameras; even if there was, they wouldn't be able to identify me with the hoodie so large it nearly covered my face? I didn't notice cameras, either way. Where was each piece of furniture located? Did the windows have screens and did one of the keys in my possession also work for the sliding glass door? The front door had the typical Kwikset doorknob and deadbolt.

Everything in the interior looked brand new: stainless steel kitchen appliances; six leather barstools at the granite-top Island; burgundy leather sectional sofa with ottoman and recliners in front of a huge flat-screen TV; and real wood floors. I sat down in one of the recliners for a minute and imagined being the woman of the house. No wonder Jake chose to stay all season; there was a great view of the ocean. He must have put in a lot of overtime to afford a cottage right on the water in Cape Cod; the interior was incredible.

I couldn't convince myself to give wholesome little Katie any credit in such a cool cottage. I had already heard enough about her from the guys I worked with that it made me want to vomit.

I verified that the women were still at the fire and then set about completing the task I came there to do. Once I was finished, I locked the door and deadbolt behind me and armed myself with the knowledge necessary for a return trip. As I crept back across the street to my vehicle, they were still laughing and enjoying themselves, totally oblivious to the fact that they had an intruder.

What fools.

That gave me an immense feeling of power. I shook my head at their stupidity. People were so complacent. Tormenting Katie was going to be so easy. I added more notes to my memo so I wouldn't forget, and then slowly drove away from the area without turning the headlights on.

I'll be back…

CHAPTER 7 - KATIE

Present – April 2020

JAKE WALKED UP behind me where I was washing dishes at the kitchen sink, wrapped his arms around my waist, and rubbed his crotch up against me. "Want to have a quickie before I have to head out?"

"*Have* to head out?" I teased. "You don't have to go; you can always hang here and play with Bailey while I work. Besides, when have you ever had a quickie without the four-play beforehand?"

Hearing her name, Bailey picked up a tennis ball, walked toward the door, and stared as if that was her cue. When she realized we weren't paying attention, she stretched out on the cold hardwood floor and let out a heavy sigh.

He pulled away and playfully smacked my butt. "Try me."

"Hilarious. You've been teasing that for twenty years. Still hasn't happened."

He opened the refrigerator, grabbed an iced tea from the door, and guzzled half the bottle while he paused to pet Bailey. "Sorry girl, no time to play today."

"Guess that means the quickie's out, too?" I said, knowing he wasn't serious in the first place. It was like a dance he played before each trip.

He smiled as he walked down the hall toward the bedroom. Bailey followed him with the ball, hoping to change his mind.

"I marked this trip on the calendar, but you didn't mention how long you'll be gone."

"Not sure, yet," he responded. "I'm still waiting on Larry to find out how many bikes are going. The ride is on Saturday, so we'll probably relax at the pool after clean-up on Sunday. I won't stay long. I have the local ride coming up that I promised to help Steve with logistics. Since thousands of riders are planning to come there is a lot of pre-planning."

I remembered the red highlights on his calendar, mentally noting how much writing time that would give me. "Is Steve riding along with you guys on this trip?"

"He and a few others are meeting us there on Saturday morning."

"But you're not riding your bike there by yourself on the open highway like you did the last ride?" When Jake traveled to Missouri he took off on his Harley at 9 o'clock, rode the entire day, only stopping for food and gas, and then stopped at a hotel when it was dark; slept, and then repeated the process the next day until he arrived at his destination.

"No. Once I'm finished here, I'll take off and head over to Larry's. He's taking the trailer so we're going to load all the bikes on it and then I'll ride with him in his motorhome."

I only met a few individuals involved with the charity, but I knew most of them were either first responders or former military. I met Larry on a few occasions when he rode his Harley down to the cottage so he and Jake could go for a casual ride. It was a quick hello and handshake. Jake had told me previously that he was retired and had plenty of money to spend, so he went on most of the rides, especially those that got him out of the New England cold. I met a few others at a memorial lighting ceremony, but that was only one night two years ago, so I doubt they would remember me.

After everything was put away and the counters wiped down with disinfectant, I joined him in the bedroom where he was packing his shaving kit, bathing suit, and shorts into an overnight bag. His chaps and leather vest, covered with patches from previous rides, were lying on the bed next to his laptop.

"Hey, do you think I need a haircut before I go?"

I rolled my eyes. "You always ask me if you need a haircut before you go on these trips."

I noticed two of his Hawaiian shirts were poking out from underneath the chaps, which meant he would be doing some sightseeing.

"You know how I hate it when it's touching my ears and gets so thick. It irritates me when I sweat. I can hold off if you're busy—"

I wanted to say something sarcastic but held my tongue. Every time he was packing to leave for one of these rides we would go through the same spiel, and he always followed up with the 'if you're busy' line. I knew it was a form of subtle manipulation, that he wouldn't come right out and ask me to give him a haircut before he was leaving on a pleasure trip without me. It was like déjà vu for me, but I kept my thoughts to myself. There was no need for a discussion over something so trivial before he left. I had bigger fish to fry dealing with my outline. I walked to the bathroom closet and grabbed the haircutting shears and then set up the stool.

In less than an hour, I cut his hair; he was showered and shaved and was walking out the door. From the deck, Bailey and I watched him load his duffel and overnight bags into his side compartments, attach his iPod to the Harley speakers, and then put on his helmet.

"I'll text you when we're ready to hit the trail from Larry's house."

I nodded. "Be careful."

"Where's the fun in that?"

Typical rebellious Jake; doesn't want to get old.

He lifted his leg over the bike and adjusted himself on the seat until it was comfortable. He stored his chaps and vest in the compartment; for the trip to Larry's, he wore shorts and a Hawaiian shirt. He put the address into his GPS, turned the key, and then adjusted the volume for the music. Before he cranked the gas, he glanced over at me, smiled, and gave me his three-finger-wave salute—*I love you*—and then he was off.

After he was gone, I realized he left without giving me the itinerary, which meant I would get a text with the hotel information once he arrived at his hotel, as he did on previous trips. After two decades together, things became routine between the two of us, and I just trusted things were as he said.

Moments later, questions I had about his trip disappeared from my mind. I had priorities of my own. First, I needed to take Bailey for a walk and let her chase the ball for a bit. When she tired herself out, I would have a few hours of quiet time; I could check my emails and social media for anything pertinent, and then it was time to tackle that outline. Once I had that finished, hopefully, I would get a few chapters typed by the end of the day.

I had no way of knowing that my world was about to come crashing down around me in ways that would make a fictional murder plot for my book seem easy by comparison.

CHAPTER 8 - KATIE

Present – April 2020

WHAT THE HELL?

Was I losing my mind? Before I went to bed last night, I locked the sliding glass door, secured the dead-bolt on the front, and closed the Venetian blinds on the windows. It was the same routine I had followed since we arrived at the cottage on the first of April.

Yet, walking into the kitchen and family room this morning I noticed that somebody opened the blinds; the dead-bolt chain was dangling by the side of the door, and they opened the sliding glass door and left it open a few inches. Thankfully, not wide enough for Bailey to escape and have an adventure without me.

Slightly unnerved, I grabbed the baseball bat and walked through the cottage, searching every nook and cranny, closets, shower, and even under the beds, looking for an unwanted intruder, and then followed up to see if anything was missing.

"Some guard dog you are," I said to Bailey as she followed me around, wagging her tail, hoping we were playing a game.

On the other hand, if I did have an intruder, wouldn't she have barked to alert me?

When I returned to the kitchen, I stood by the island counter and looked around the room. Somebody had been inside the cottage. Then, as my eyes danced around the room, meticulously looking for anything out of place, I noticed what looked like a greeting card lying next to my laptop on top of the desk. I didn't put it there, and it wasn't there last night when I shut down the laptop. Jake was on his trip, so it couldn't have been from him.

I walked towards it, studied my desk to see if anything else was unusual before touching it. It was small, like that of a thank-you card. I picked it up and opened it, not having a clue of what it might say or who it was from. The minute I started reading I was more confused than before I started:

Katie, JR Harris, or whoever else you call yourself,

You are a 40-something-year old woman who acts like a 16-year old. You think you're all that, but you're not. I investigated you and know all about your "issues", and how you lie to the world. You don't deserve to live in his cottage.

Wow, have some respect for yourself and grow the hell up!

Oh, and P.S.: Obviously, I know where you live!

I sat down in my leather chair, taking a moment to read the card again. That was the strangest note I had ever read. I had no idea what this person was talking about. They had me investigated… for what?

His cottage?

Whoever wrote the note didn't know that it was my cash that paid for the down payment on the cottage, or that I transferred the monthly payments from my book account into the joint account. He merely wrote out a check. Besides, it was not their business. Who the hell wrote this?

Did somebody go through the trouble to break into my home just to leave this message for me? If so, I didn't know what to say about that, other than they might be delusional. Just like the phone call at the book store, they used my real name, but also the pen name. Why? One thing I did notice, both the note and the phone call asked the same question: *Why do you lie to the world?*

It had to be the same woman stalking me at my book signings. Was she stalking me at home now?

I reached into one of my desk drawers, grabbed an envelope, and tucked the card inside. There was no reason to waste time analyzing something I couldn't make sense of.

I grabbed Bailey's chain and opened the sliding glass door to lead her out on the deck and let her sniff detector do its work. After a few minutes, she lost interest in checking for trespassers, and instead searched for her ball. The deck had a layer of frost from the early morning cold and I didn't notice any footprints in the sand leading up to the deck.

I know I didn't forget to lock the doors. What was going on?

I tried to shake off the nerve-wracking feeling and continued toward the beach so Bailey could do her business, and romp around for a few minutes.

"Morning, Katie!" Madison yelled. She and Olivia were sitting on Olivia's deck at the cottage next to me, enjoying their morning coffee.

"Morning," I said in return and waved.

I gave Bailey a few minutes to do her business, picked it up in the doggie disposal bag I had connected to her leash then dropped it in the metal trash can at the steps leading up to the cottages.

"How was the walk?" Olivia asked when I reached her deck.

"It was a short one," I responded, giving Bailey a few minutes to get reacquainted with their dogs before I sat down. Olivia owned an adult brown lab and yellow lab puppy, but the brown lab usually went to work with her husband. Madison had two Shih Tzu's; one of them was still a puppy who loved Bailey.

"Coffee's on," Olivia teased with a smile; it was a joke between us because she knew I didn't drink it.

"I could use some fuel today."

"Didn't you sleep well?"

"I slept okay, but my morning has been odd. Something weird happened."

"What do you mean?" Madison said as she leaned down to pick up the puppy from trying to jump on Bailey's face, causing her to growl.

"Weird, how?" Olivia asked.

"Enough playtime, Bailey," I said and guided her away from the dogs and took a seat in the chair. "This morning I woke up to find the sliding door ajar, the dead-bolt was free, and the blinds were all open, yet I closed them and locked the doors when I went to bed."

They glanced at each other and frowned.

"That is weird," Olivia said. "Maybe your mind is so caught up with figuring out a psychological suspense plot for your book that you just imagined you did it?" The grin she wore let me know she was speaking in jest.

I rubbed my temples. "I may have plots on my mind, but my habits haven't deviated. I have the same ritual every night. Somebody is toying with me. And they left this."

I handed the envelope to Olivia; she removed the card and read it. "What the hell?"

"It's delusional, isn't it?"

"They investigated you?" She laughed sarcastically. "If they investigated you, they would have questioned us, your neighbors, who know everything about you."

Madison furrowed her brow and held her hand out. "What does it say?"

Instead of handing it over, Olivia read it in an animated tone to make it appear more menacing, which only made me laugh.

Madison said, "I don't know what to make of that."

"Welcome to the club," I said. "Odd though, that this card references me by name and pseudonym, just as the caller did when we were at the book signing."

"So you're thinking the caller is the same person who left this note in your cottage?"

"I think so."

"The woman?"

I shrugged. "No coincidences, remember?"

"How did she get in?" Olivia said, taking another sip of coffee.

"I could only speculate, but maybe she knows how to pick a lock. There were no windows open, nor any evidence of anyone trying to get inside through one.

The front door was still locked, only the dead-bolt was unchained. The sliding glass door was ajar, so it could have been their point of entry, but there were no tracks on the deck or sand."

Madison shook her head, confused. "Imagine going to all that trouble just to leave you that note. There's no way to make sense of that."

"Maybe that was her point," I said, and then I sat straight up in my chair. "Unless she only left that card to make me think that was her reason for entering."

Olivia seemed to sense what I was saying. "You mean she got inside for another reason, but why leave you a clue that anyone was inside in the first place?"

"To frighten me, keep me off kilter?" I said, shrugging, while I was deep in thought. "I don't know, I'm probably overthinking. It's just so weird. Oh well, I can't dwell on it or I will lose my focus. I have a writing schedule to keep. I better head back and get to it. I need to take advantage of the time I have while Jake's away."

"Remember what we've been saying," Olivia said, teasing.

I shook my head and smiled. "I know."

"Sex sells!" All three of us said simultaneously.

CHAPTER 9 – MY STALKER

Before – September 2017

AFTER MY SHIFT, I stripped out of my gear and stepped into a pair of men's boxer shorts left behind by one of my other playthings. I grabbed a beer from the case I bought and put the rest in the refrigerator, then sat down in front of the computer. After signing in, I opened the internet and went straight to Facebook; I needed information on Jake Parker and his perfect little Katie.

Jake was easy to find. I knew where he worked, what he looked like, and that he was a motorcycle enthusiast, specifically, Harley Davidson. What surprised me was that he had two pages. I scrolled through the first one I found. It seemed to be for personal friends, co-workers, and family. On that page, he shared information from the fire service, comical pictures, and now and then he posted an Amber alert or article about law enforcement incidents. Katie was a friend on that page, but she didn't like or comment on many of his posts.

The second page made me smile. Scrolling through posts, likes, and comments, it was clear that it was a page dedicated to a first responder motorcycle charity he was involved in. Most of the friends were either involved in the charity, attended the rides, or were volunteers. Most of his posts revolved around the charity, and sometimes, he'd post political commentary or information that occurred within the first responder community, just not the fire department where he worked. I read through some of the posts and viewed the comments; a lot of females, who were motorcycle riders or involved with the charity, liked and commented on his posts.

After a quick review, I realized it was a private page that he didn't want his personal friends to be a part of, and Katie, his wife, was not one of his friends. There was no mention of her or his personal life, at all. It was almost as if she, and that life, didn't exist. I also noticed the charity had a private group that he was a member of.

My smile grew wider.

I sent friend requests to both pages.

There were five choices for Katie Parker in the New England area, but three were eliminated from the start since they were not in the right age range. Of the other two, I had to click on the profile images and investigate the pages to figure out which one was the right Katie. I settled on the profile of a blonde woman hugging a Golden Retriever when I realized Jake was listed as one of her friends.

Spying on her page, I could tell Katie didn't share personal information. She didn't note whether she was married, single, in a relationship, or anything about her life at home; no address, birthdate, or phone number either. I didn't read anything into that, other than she was probably security conscious.

Looking through her photo albums, some of them irritated me. Wholesome was putting it mildly. She was a blue-eyed blonde, had a petite but athletic build, and seemed to participate in a few training exercises with first responders during the last few years. Why? Some of the images were taken at the firehouse; one was possibly Jake's, but no town or city was mentioned. Others were out of state, New York and California. In a few, she was decked out in athletic gear dangling from ropes off the roof of a building; climbing the Quarries in Massachusetts; rappelling off a bridge, and then posing with some of the guys who participated. That got my ire up. Was I jealous that she seemed so capable?

Bitch. The images portrayed her as someone who thought she was part of the first responder community.

I wanted to leave nasty comments on a few of the images but held off. I would deal with her in my own good time. Patience was the key.

Scrolling further I found an album filled with images of Katie's dog, Bailey, from the time she was a puppy, and learned that she was a member in several groups: a few writer groups; two political; and one for her high school graduating class. I couldn't help but be curious when I realized she wasn't a member of any group Jake was a part of.

What was going on there?

Katie listed her occupation on the about page; she writes screenplays and publishes books under the pen name, JR HARRIS. There was a link to her Facebook author page. I clicked on it. The first thing I noticed was a schedule for future book signings. That would come in handy. Looking through her posts, I noticed one that said she was working on a new book and expected it to be released soon. I sent links to one of my email accounts so I could check back from my phone.

I leaned back and smiled.

Book signings would be the perfect place to stalk a subject without them even knowing they were a target of one's attention. And Katie Parker was definitely in my line of sight now. Time was in my hands, but Jake would be mine. Wholesome Katie Parker just needed to be removed from the equation.

CHAPTER 10 - KATIE

Present – April 2020

OLIVIA SENT ME sent me an urgent text, using all caps, around six o'clock that evening. "IT'S HAPPENING AGAIN!"

My text back to her was also in all caps. *"WTF?"*

"Check out your Amazon book page. Some whack job is posting fake one-star reviews on all your books again. Madison and I will be over in fifteen minutes to discuss."

It wasn't unusual for Olivia and Madison to call or text me several times a day. They're not only my editor and publicist; they're also my friends. It was odd, however, when they texted and said we need to discuss this right away when they knew I was on a schedule. They wouldn't interrupt me when I was in the writing zone unless it was urgent. Normally, they were preparing the fixings for whatever dinner Madison planned for the evening. While doing so, they would enjoy a margarita or glass of wine on Madison's deck and commiserate that they hadn't purchased a spot for a waterfront Bed-and-Breakfast place yet. They knew it was just a pipe dream, but they relished the discussions. Madison would fantasize about the décor; Olivia designed the massive gardens in her mind, and both of them created personality traits for the eccentric guests they would have. Their discussion usually ended with a comment to me upon my appearance: I better write a scandalous bestseller so I could take part in their dream.

Bailey was devouring her food when they arrived and tapped on the door. She started to bark, but then seeing it was only them, continued to lap up her food.

"It's open," I yelled from where I sat at the kitchen island in front of my laptop, frustrated as I scrolled through the dozens of new fake reviews. A good number of them were attacking me, personally, not having anything to do with the book, and against Amazon review guidelines.

They rushed in with their drinks, Madison carrying her laptop. As my publicist, she would be the one tasked with writing posts on social media sites to alert readers of the hoax, and dealing with Amazon to get the fake reviews removed.

"I was sure we had this handled when it happened two months ago so that it wouldn't happen, again," Madison said, shaking her head with regret and feeling responsible for the continuation. "Maybe I wasn't authoritative enough with Amazon?"

"You're in no way responsible," I said, mentally imploring her to not give it another thought. "Amazon set up the review process. Anyone can log on to a book page and submit a review, even if they haven't purchased or read it. That's why it became necessary for those who received an early ARC were required to add the language that they received a copy from the author on the agreement they would offer a fair and honest review."

Madison placed her laptop down on the counter, opened it, and proceeded to type Amazon an email. "Maybe not, but you can be sure the techs are going to get an earful; anyone reading these reviews can tell that they are fake."

Bailey finished with her food and was now looking for attention. Olivia spent a few minutes encouraging her to do tricks for small training treats that she kept in her pocket to help train her yellow lab puppy. Once the treats were gone and Bailey realized we were in working mode and not there to entertain her, she found a spot next to the sliding glass door to keep watch.

"It's disturbing that Amazon hasn't been able to stop these idiots from doing this," Olivia complained when she joined us at the counter.

I nodded, but at the same time, I understood how difficult it could be for Amazon to distinguish a legitimate one-star review from a fake one right off the bat.

"The problem is there are millions of books for Amazon to watch out for. Unless they are specifically watching the one-star reviews to determine whether they are real or fake, an author is forced to wait until they do their routine review checks on IP addresses, algorithms, or the author physically alerts them. For me, it's not just about stopping the fake reviews. Most readers can tell; it's only a new reader who has no experience with Amazon that might be swayed and not buy a book. What I want to know is who is doing it, and why?"

"Early on, we thought it could have been other disgruntled authors trying to stunt the competition?" Madison said.

I shook my head, uncertain. "I'm not convinced. The last time this occurred, I assumed it could be a possibility because it was happening to other independent authors. In some of those instances, however, there were personal rifts between them. I've never had an issue with another author, and have been more than helpful in sharing others' books on social media, even those that were my competition. That it's happening, again, makes me doubt another author was involved. This seems personal."

"I have doubts too, considering what's been going on, lately," Olivia said.

Madison put her laptop in front of me so I could approve the email she was forwarding to Amazon. She was my publicist, but I still had to authorize anything she submitted on my behalf.

I read through it and signed my virtual signature. "Hopefully they'll remove them right away, instead of the week-long wait we had to endure the last time this occurred."

I walked over to the refrigerator to retrieve a bottle of water, grabbed the container of watermelon and cantaloupe I purchased on my store run, and placed it down on the island to share. I didn't want to waste time washing dishes, so I reached for a box of toothpicks and napkins.

"Didn't Amazon crackdown on authors posting fake reviews?" Olivia inquired while scrolling through the fake ones and grimacing at some of the content.

"Yes, they did." I sat back down, pulled a toothpick out of the box, and snatched a chunk of watermelon. "They sent threatening letters to authors through the accounts page, letting everyone know that Amazon IT specialists could easily verify the identity and that if it continued, their books would be pulled from the site. I think this is someone who knows me, but also knows how to open up fake accounts and forward fake reviews."

Olivia frowned. "I agree they need to be computer savvy, but I doubt it's someone you know. Who would do such a thing, to you of all people?"

"I must have annoyed someone."

Olivia cocked her head to the side, mocking me. "Ms. even-keeled… I find it hard to believe."

Madison said, "I do think it's someone that wants to hurt you, but I don't think you know them, personally."

The thought made me shiver, and I remembered my stalker's actions and her recent note. Who would want to hurt me? "Other things have happened that make me believe it could be someone I know, or that knows me. We should still look into it."

"Explain," Olivia said,

I walked over to my desk, grabbed my journal, and scrolled through the pages, looking for specific dates as I returned. "It's not just the fake reviews, or the incidents at the bookstore, or the note left on my desk; several odd things have occurred over the last couple of years. By themselves I didn't give them much thought but add them all together with what's going on now, they make me curious."

"Like what?" They both said simultaneously, staring at me.

"And why is this the first time we're hearing about them," Olivia demanded.

"We know a woman keeps showing up at my signings, but she purposely avoids getting close enough for me to get a good look."

Madison added, "Yes, and I scoured the author page and messages but couldn't find anyone with a profile that fit the description."

"After I received the note at the cottage, it reminded me of other instances. A couple of months ago, I got the feeling I was being watched at the gym, even suspected someone had been in my locker while I was working out; they had moved things around. Thankfully, I take nothing with me worthy of stealing and I keep my keys with me. I also had similar incidents when out and about doing errands. I kept getting the feeling somebody was behind me, but when I turned around, there was nobody there."

Olivia frowned. "So you chalked it up to your imagination?"

At first.

"A few weeks ago when I went to BJ's I thought a woman was following me. I didn't get a look at her from the front, only the back, and her hair was up in a ball cap. She kept showing up in every aisle I was in. When I glanced her way, she quickly turned and rounded the corner. I went to follow her, but she sped up. When I looked up into the security mirror at the end of the aisle, I saw her rush out of the store."

"The woman at BJ's, was it the same woman you've been seeing at the book signings?"

"I didn't get a good look at her face in either instance, but height and attire were the same: the tight jeans and tank tops."

"There's more, isn't there?" Madison said, sensing my unease.

I rifled through a few pages in my journal and read through my notes. "A few times a month I receive friend requests on Facebook from fake profiles. Sometimes I'm rushed and forget to do my due diligence before accepting. Then I'd immediately get chat messages with personal content, so I'd have to go through and delete. Other times, I got weird messages from profiles that weren't even on my friend list, which means they specifically looked for me. There are millions of profiles, yet they chose me?"

Madison nodded. "I get friend requests maybe once a year, but they're not fake profiles. It's usually someone who knows one of my friends."

"That was the original purpose of social media; to make virtual friends to get reacquainted with those from our past and to meet new people. But these were fake profiles set up just to friend me."

"Which means they wanted access to you," Olivia said.

I nodded. "Recently, when I installed messenger on my phone so I could respond to messages when I wasn't online, I started getting phone calls, even though I refused to post my number on the site. I received four from an unknown caller and then three designated as a private number. The unknowns were hang-ups. The private calls went to voicemail and each time I listened to the recording I heard the same song."

Olivia and Madison exchanged looks. "You haven't told us about any of those things. What song?" Madison said.

"I didn't say anything because I just chalked it up to the weird stuff that happens on social media. Some people pretend to be anybody they choose. I immediately deleted messenger from my phone and I no longer accept friend requests without a thorough check of who is asking."

I grabbed my phone, clicked on the first voicemail message saved, and typed in my password. The lyrics of the song *Believe* by *Cher* started playing:

Do you believe in life after love
I can feel something inside me say
I really don't think you're strong enough…

Olivia grimaced. "That's bizarre."

"That was left on the recording from each private call I received."

Olivia looked deep in thought and then started to repeat the words I just read as though she was trying to mentally remember the rest of the song. "It almost sounds like a spurned lover."

"That's what I thought when I analyzed it, which you know I did, but Jake and I have been together for over twenty years; twenty-two counting before we were married."

"Oh no," Madison said, interrupting us and staring at her laptop. "Whoever it is, they're not stopping."

Olivia and I moved behind her so we could look over her shoulder. She pointed to a post that just showed up on the JR Harris book page: "*Don't bother reading this author; she's a fraud and a whore.*"

"What the hell!"

Olivia draped her arm around me. "Katie, sorry to say, but you have a full-fledged stalker."

CHAPTER 11 - KATIE

Present – April 2020

I GRABBED MY laptop and signed into Facebook to view the profile image of the poster. "When was that posted?" I tried to remain calm, but my heart was pounding.

"Just a few minutes ago," Madison said.

"It looks like a stock photo; probably another fake account."

Madison had the cursor hovering over the delete button. "Do you want me to get rid of it before a fan sees it?"

"Before you do, make sure you screen capture it, along with the profile, and print it out so I can add it to my journal of notes."

Olivia took a long drink of her margarita and looked like she was getting into serious mode. "We need to go through recent and past comments and see if there are any other questionable responses. They may know Katie through reading her books but have delusional ideas in their head?"

"One of my readers?"

Olivia shrugged. "We have to start with that thought. Who else would be watching your author page and learning the dates of your book signings?"

"What would possess a reader, or anyone, to suggest I'm a whore? Or leave a note in my house?"

"There's no way to know why a stalker would do what they do," Olivia said. "I can't help but refer to the spurned lover comment I made listening to the words in Cher's song on your voicemail. For whatever reason, this person latched onto you. If it's not a reader, then it's someone who has access to you and your world, enough to fixate on you. Maybe you know them, maybe you don't. But their actions tell me they feel rejected or slighted."

Madison was shaking her head. "I don't think it's someone she knows personally. We've known her for years. Spend three seasons a year living next to her. There is nobody in her world that would feel the need to stalk her."

I nodded. "That's true. I have spent most of my time in the last decade with the people here at the cottages. We know them all. Readers I've met through signings or the fan page get maybe a few minutes of my time. I do not know the dark-haired woman. I've never seen her until she started making her presence known at book signings."

The owners of the other cottages don't arrive until Memorial weekend. We don't hang out with them, per se, but they have occasionally joined us by the fire in the past few years, or attended one of the holiday barbecues. Madison usually had a family gathering once or twice a year, and she invited everyone in our little cul-de-sac community. I couldn't think of a reason for any of them to stalk me. None of them fit the profile image, anyway.

"Which brings me back to a reader," Olivia said. "Could it be possible that someone who is not all there mentally, read your books and somehow latched onto a character, and then you because you created them? Calling you a whore could be just a method of lashing out. Or, maybe the reader met you at a signing, and you didn't give them the attention they wanted, so they left posts or comments on the author page, and the response wasn't adequate for them?"

Madison said, "Well, anything is possible in today's world."

I nodded, shaking my head at the absurdity of it all. "We need to do a review of comments, messages, or emails, and then look at any responses made to those who reached out in the last two years. The first emails and messages I started receiving were a little over two years ago."

Madison nodded. "That will take time, but I'm on it."

Meanwhile, I read the nasty post again and cringed, glad that we caught it before other readers could see it. The profile image was a stock photo of a female model, probably purchased specifically to open the account. I clicked on the image. Since I wasn't a friend with that account I couldn't see much on the page. They used a scenic ocean image as the banner—another stock image—and proved to me it was a fake account. The page also didn't have twenty-five followers, which was a requirement to make it a legitimate account.

"Just as I expected, it's a fake account opened just to mess with me. It could be anyone."

"We'll figure it out," Madison said, determined to find the culprit as she reviewed posts, comments, and responses.

"When is Jake due home?" Olivia asked out of the blue. "Isn't the motorcycle ride only a weekend thing?"

"It is," I said, glancing at the clock. "I assume he'll be back on the road Monday. I was hoping to spend the time writing until he arrived. As my editor, you gave me a deadline, remember?".

"We'll clear out of here then and let you get to it. Don't worry about the reviews and crazy stalker; we'll figure it out. Who knows what set them off? Maybe they sent you something and didn't receive a response fitting their expectations."

"Hopefully it's as simple as that." I nodded, but deep down I knew that wasn't the case. I also got the sense the stalking was just starting to heat up. Breaking into someone's home to leave them a message was not a small thing.

Madison closed the laptop and grabbed her margarita. "After dinner, Olivia and I will go through it all and see if anything unusual catches our interest. You just go ahead and keep writing and don't worry about all of this."

Easy to say, not as easy to do, I said to myself. My gut was telling me that whoever was playing these games would not stop, so I needed to be vigilant. "Thanks to both of you, I wouldn't be able to get through this without you."

"That's why you pay us the big bucks," Olivia teased.

I chuckled as I followed them to the door and grabbed Bailey's chain. "Bailey, let's go take a walk and get your energy out so mommy can stay in the writing zone while daddy is gone."

The four of us walked along the beach and parted ways when we came to the steps leading up to Madison's cottage, two doors down from mine. They headed up toward the deck while Bailey and I continued, oblivious to the fact that My Stalker was already scheming more attempts to disparage, only next time it would be more personal.

~~

Being an independent writer had some advantages. There was no publishing company telling me what I could or couldn't write, I made my own deadlines so I didn't have to worry about egos getting in the way or disrupting the writing goals, and I didn't have to share in the profits. That said, being independent also had a downside; you needed to be disciplined to meet those self-imposed deadlines to compete with the major players.

As my editor, Olivia gave me two months to develop a plot and complete a draft of my new novel, a timeline I agreed to when she and I were sitting by the campfire ironing out the contract for the untitled book. If I failed to meet the deadline, she was leaving to visit her son who graduated from the Air Force Academy and would be gone a few weeks helping him get set up the home where he would be stationed. That meant I would have to wait for her return or find another editor to complete the publishing and marketing timeline I had planned.

The latter option didn't appeal to me. She was so in tune with my writing style and grammatical misgivings that she could edit the entire novel and forward the first revision to me within a week. No, finding a new editor was out of the question. Madison helped me with marketing, but neither one of us was good at editing.

With Jake gone, I had solitude and needed to take advantage of it. I grabbed one of Bailey's bones out of the refrigerator and set her up on the doggie bed, then sat down in front of the laptop, where I planned to remain for the rest of the evening.

CHAPTER 12 – MY STALKER

Before – September 2017

JAKE PARKER ACCEPTED the friend request for each of his profiles on Facebook!

I was so giddy it was like drinking a shot of espresso and a surge of energy went straight to my brain. I was out running errands when my notifications pinged. I had my phone programmed into my vehicles, so I never missed a call, text, notification, or email.

Should I take a selfie and send a quick note to say hey? No, I should probably play coy and wait to see if he attempted to message me.

I wondered what he thought when he realized I added him as a friend. I bet he scrolled through my photos. A few hot images were added to an album just for him. It would be great if Facebook added a feature that allowed users to track when friends visited their profile or browsed their photos, especially those set up with specific titles just to lure them in. Instead, we had to wait for them to like an image or leave a comment. Jake might not be the type to leave a calling card like most of the guys I knew who did so in the past. They left ridiculous comments advertising their immaturity, such as: Wow, that's hot! Seconds later, they would either poke me or send a private message asking for a hookup, just like high school teenagers. Sure, I dug the attention; that's why I posted sexy pictures but their actions were so predictable they ruined the chase.

Now that I was a friend on both pages, it exhilarated me to know I had access to his private page yet Katie—his precious wife—wasn't on there.

Why would you block your wife?

I couldn't help but wonder if she even knew it existed? It was a useful piece of information that I could use to toy with her.

Won't that be fun?

I learned a great deal scrolling through the private page. I discovered he joined a motorcycle charity that had monthly rides. Katie knew that. Was she aware that single women attended the rides … groupies; the kind of women that latch onto men looking for hookups? I already knew he was part of the group page: FRCG. Bet she didn't know about that.

I browsed through his photographs. He had tons from the rides: motorcycles, scenic images, and tourist spots he took pictures of during the designated weekends. Nothing to indicate he hooked up with anyone, but I doubt he would post images if he did, especially since there were fellow firefighters on his page.

Through my continued prying, I did discover that there were images and videos of him posted to the FRCG page because his name was tagged. To get access to those images, I had to become a member. On the about page for the group, it said FRCG was specifically for supporters or followers of the rides. That meant anyone who attended or was considering attending could be construed as a supporter. I was considering, now that I knew.

I scrolled through my photo albums looking for images of me on my motorcycle. There were several of me in leather chaps and jacket; straddling the seat holding my helmet. I chose the one of me in my denim ripped jeans and a white halter top. Sexy was better than tough for my objective. I switched out my old profile image and replaced it with the new one.

Almost immediately, some of my male friends liked the image; some were bolder and added comments. Like I said…

I liked all their comments and responded to those that said: *Harley hottie.* or *you're smokin'*—as if that would get them a night in my bed. Well, never say never; maybe if I was horny and desperate.

The only comment I was hoping to see was from Jake. His opinion was the only one that mattered right now. I sent a request to join FRCG. There were over five thousand members in the group, so I didn't think Jake would know I was a member, as long as I didn't like or comment on any posts and converse with him. I could just observe and gather information.

It was such a thrill knowing that if they approved my request, I would take part in something that poor little clueless Katie wasn't involved in.

CHAPTER 13 - KATIE

Present – April 2020

I SPENT THE evening in the zone, putting in four straight hours of writing, finally figured out some things with my plot, and completed bullet points so that I could see if my idea panned out. Woke up early to get right back to it, but had to put my plan on hold when I received another urgent text: *"OMG, somebody started a trashy blog page about you... come here quick!"*

Now I was sitting at Madison's kitchen table with her and Olivia, horrified by the content that was posted on a blog in the middle of the night. They were images of me taken by someone in the privacy of my home, making it appear as though I posted selfies of myself. There were a few of me in the shower; stretching and doing yoga moves on a mat in my family room; images of me in various stages of undress in my bedroom, and when I was asleep at night in my boxers and tank top. They took all the images over the last two days.

Olivia put a wastebasket and a roll of paper towels next to me in case I got sick, and then placed a bottle of Ginger-ale down on the table.

She rubbed my back. "Katie, first things first; we have to figure out how to get this blog shut down."

"This is all so horrible," Madison said, noticeably distressed. "They will not stop."

Whoever created the blog page posted a link on my author page with a note: *click on the link to see the real JR Harris*. They posted the link from a fake account, and Madison deleted it immediately, but she had no way to know if anyone had seen the images before she did so.

It mortified me.

"Posting fake reviews, emailing you, calling and leaving you odd messages, and now this; it's criminal," Olivia said, her voice laden with as much anger as I was feeling about now. "Whoever is doing this is trying to sabotage and harm you."

Madison draped her arm around me; my body visibly shaking. "How'd they get the pictures? Could they have been images that Jake took? Were they on your computer?"

I shook my head, bewildered and distraught. "No, I have never seen these before. I'm not aware of Jake ever taking pictures of me like this. I sure wouldn't take selfies. It's like somebody was spying on me with a camera in my home."

Madison and Olivia looked at each other, and their eyes went wide at the same time as the realization dawned on me.

"Well, either Jake took them without your knowledge," Olivia said, "or the individual stalking you planted cameras inside your home."

My hand flew to my mouth in horror, stunned by the possibility. Would Jake take pictures of me without me knowing? Would he do such a thing? I couldn't believe that. Somebody had been inside the home. Could they have planted cameras? I shivered at the prospect.

I forced myself to snap out of the shock my body was in; there was no time to whine and feel sorry for myself. I had to take action. I scrolled down the blog page to find out who hosted the site. I was relieved to discover it was the same company I used for my websites. I knew from reading the original support information and agreement when I signed up years ago, that you could report a blog that abused user guidelines and terms of use.

"Posting illegal images of an adult nature violates terms of service," I said. "I also know, firsthand, that an actual human reads every report filed, so the blog page should be taken down fast for fear of a lawsuit."

"That's a relief," Madison said.

I clicked on the three dots in the upper right-hand corner to bring up the proper form, filled it out, and checked the appropriate boxes. Then I typed in my email address before forwarding it to support.

"One of their techs will contact me via email. When they do, I'll alert them that the images do not belong to the poster, and were illegally obtained. The adult nature of the content is reason enough to shut down the site, but the illegality factor could warrant law enforcement involvement which would be an incentive to do so immediately."

"I would ask them for a report to go along with your copy of the evidence; this has gone beyond posting fake reviews," Olivia pointed out.

Madison said, "In the meantime, I'm also contacting Facebook to alert them about the fake accounts that keep posting this crap on the author page. Maybe they'll offer advice."

"Madison, just go into the admin page and make the settings so that nobody, except the three of us, can post or comment until approved. That way, you can review anything before it gets posted to the page."

Madison gave me a reassuring smile and opened up her laptop. "Oh good, I didn't know I could do that."

Even though I hired Madison to help with PR, she wasn't computer savvy and we've had to teach her a lot along the way. She used to have her own business, though, so she knew all about marketing and PR. There were just times when Olivia and I needed to show her a few things regarding technology and social media sites.

"After she completes that step, we should probably go to your place and check for cameras," Olivia advised. "You should also file a police report."

I nodded. "If there are cameras that will give them something to physically look into," I said, hopeful. "The last time I contacted the local department they informed me that I needed more, that they didn't have the staff necessary to research social media to try and find out who might be stalking me. Since there was no physical harm or threat, they said it was considered more of an annoyance at that time."

"On the plus side," Olivia said in a joking manner, "look at that figure, you look like you're still in your twenties."

I inwardly groaned; too mortified to think about readers believing I was so arrogant that I would post suggestive selfies of myself.

~~~

After we completed the computer aspect, we hurried back over to my cottage where Bailey eagerly greeted us at the door. I gave her a quick rub behind the ears and filled her dish up with two cups of food to keep her occupied. "Go eat your food, Bailey."

I grabbed a box of latex gloves and handed them out. "If we find anything, we need to preserve any fingerprints he or she might have left behind."

Then I stood by the island studying the kitchen and family area, glancing down at my phone to view the images I saved hoping to narrow down where a hidden camera could be.

"The camera would have to be up high to get images of me stretching on the yoga mat. It looks like someone was standing over me, even though I was alone."

Olivia glanced up at the ceiling in the family area. "What about the ceiling fan?"

I grabbed the ladder from inside the kitchen closet and placed it underneath, stepping up high enough until I could check each blade, rubbing over the service to feel for anything I couldn't see. Then I checked where the light fixture was fitted into the ceiling. "I can't find anything here."

From my view on the ladder, I scanned the room. "The top of the TV?"

Madison, who was the taller one of the three of us, walked toward the sixty-inch TV and rubbed her latex-gloved hands around the top and bottom, and then both sides, just to be sure. "Nothing."

Then she looked up at the built-in shelf above the TV where Jake stored an antique replica of a New York Fire Department ladder truck. She ran her fingers over the antique vehicle, and a few seconds later, pulled out a mini camera that was small enough to hold between her index finger and thumb. They lodged it behind the right-front tire of the antique.

"Oh my, it's so small."

I got down off the ladder and joined her to look at it. It was cube-shaped. There was no way I would have seen it unless I was specifically looking for it. I did a quick internet search on my phone for mini cameras and found the exact image. "All they needed was an app on their phone. This is terrifying."

"Where are the baggies?" Olivia asked.

"Next to the refrigerator; third drawer down."

Olivia opened the drawer and retrieved the box of baggies, grabbed one, and opened it so Madison could drop the camera inside. "Whoever planted the cameras probably wore gloves, but we have to be sure."

Madison frowned. "This was diabolical. Do you think they planted cameras when they left you that note?"

"I don't know, but that would mean they were inside doing so while I was asleep in the bedroom," I said, suddenly feeling out of whack. "Unless they were watching me and knew when I took Bailey out for her walk. There's no electrical work to do, so they could program them before arriving, and then just put the cameras in place."

"Who would go to such lengths? What if it had been a predator?"

"So much for Bailey being a good guard dog," I added.

We continued our search. Now that we knew how small they were, we looked in tight crevices. We checked the entire family area with no luck, but I found one lodged onto the led desk lamp and portable phone charger I kept on my desk. They were watching me when I worked. Since the clock, date, and weather were digital, the light kept me from noticing the tiny blue light from the camera. Plus, it never occurred to me to look for one. I slipped it into another baggie, and we continued into the kitchen.

We found one on the refrigerator door; above the microwave; on the curtain rod in the bathroom—which was how they caught me in the shower—and there were two hidden in the master bedroom and one in the guest room. The one consolation I had was; if the individual planted the cameras when they broke in and left me that note, at least they didn't capture any film of me and Jake in the bedroom. That would have been disturbing posting sexual images of an unsuspecting couple. Thankfully, the only images posted on the blog page were of me. It was clear; they were stalking me intending to cause harm; but who and why?

"Who would go to such lengths?"

Three hours later, and most of that time spent sitting in the lobby of the local police department, with a quick stop at Home Depot, we were on our way back home. After hearing my story and seeing what little evidence we had, the officers mentioned they knew of two other authors who rented cottages by the water during the summer, and they had endured similar circumstances in the past.

I didn't think there were similarities between their cases and mine. The authors-named had major name recognition; one because his book was an international bestseller with movie rights. Millions of individuals knew his name, and he had a lot of fans, because of the controversial topic. With those numbers, it would be common to have at least one who crossed the line on fandom.

The second author tried to capitalize on the success of the Fifty Shades momentum, only she reversed the roles between the male and female characters. A small group of fan fanatics of the original accused her of plagiarism.

The officer said they would keep investigating, but it would take time since their department was small. He said I could change my locks, but I reasoned it wouldn't do any good if they knew how to pick a lock? I couldn't figure out any other way for them to gain entry. He recommended I keep up with the journal and said he would make a note for on-duty officers to canvas the area more to keep an eye out.

"Well, that was a wasted three hours we'll never get back and not very helpful," Olivia said when we pulled into our beach community.

"I suspected that's how it would go," I said. "That was the consensus the first time I called them; I can help in building a case if they ever caught My Stalker, but that doesn't help to identify them."

Madison shook her head, dismayed. "It almost seems like an individual can psychologically torment someone without repercussions."

I considered installing cameras myself, in case there was another visit, but after the reviews and research on the various brands and discovering how many residents had their home cameras hacked into, I decided against it for the time being.

CHAPTER 14 - KATIE

Present – April 2020

JAKE WAS TWO days late returning from his trip.

After visiting the police department and filing a report, things quieted down at home. Olivia, Madison, and their husbands went back to their homes on Sunday evening, as they usually did. I spent the next few days glued to the laptop, except for my time walking and throwing the ball to Bailey. I had ironed out all my plot points, nearly finished with the outline, and could complete several chapters. All I needed was an idea of how I wanted the story to end.

What I didn't immediately recognize while typing was that I had been basing my psychological suspense on what was currently playing out in my own life. Reading through my journal and viewing some of the images that were posted on the blog fueled my anger, and I just started writing. When I went to read back what I wrote, my subconscious had taken over and the words just flowed.

Now that I was taking a break, I found myself glancing at the calendar and realized that Jake was late in returning home. No calls. No text notifying me that he would be delayed. Most women would automatically assume something was wrong, and they'd be calling everyone they knew trying to track down their husbands.

I realized early on that I wasn't like most women. Since the day we met, I never demanded that Jake check in with me over every move he made, and sometimes, he would get lax in communication, especially when he was with his alpha male friends. After two decades together, there was a level of trust between us, so normally I tried to give him the benefit of the doubt.

And Jake, well there was no easy way to describe Jake Parker. As a first responder, he put his life on the line for others and as an instructor, taught others to do the same. As a man, he would drop everything to help one of his friends, stop on a highway to help a woman in distress, charm the pants off senior citizens with his polite yes sir or ma'am and witty conversations that kept them smiling, and he'd be the only individual at a party who could get babies to stop crying when the parents could not.

He could also be a selfish and arrogant rebel who bordered on genius, moody when he wasn't getting his way, and bucked against authority unless it happened to be an individual who earned his respect. Some of the latter traits became more evident over the last few years.

Sure, I was mildly concerned that he was delayed. Sometimes, the guys Jake rode with would do a sightseeing ride and visit military sites in the area or take in the scenery, but I also knew he could just be trying to push my buttons. Even though Jake was the one frequently absent from the home, he would also get annoyed when I wasn't readily available to him when he was, and I was currently working on a new book. When I cornered him on it, he just denied it, but his actions proved otherwise.

During the late summer of 2017, I was contacted by a producer who read one of my screenplays, liked one of my spy stories, and wanted me to help him develop a story from an idea he had. After conversing for a couple of weeks and ironing out a contract, I agreed. Over the next three months, I worked day and night writing the treatment and screenplay, a draft of a book, which wasn't part of the contract, and teasers to help with marketing; also not part of the contract.

We never met in person. All of our conversations were through email, texts, or phone calls with Jake nearby most of the time, but he still got jealous of the time being taken away from him. In retaliation, he started going out for drinks with a couple of friends. When I told Jake I knew what he was doing, he said I was just feeling guilty because of the time I was spending on the project and transferring that guilt onto him.

I never got the chance to resolve the underlying issue, because it was soon after that Jake had a heart attack and had to have a stent put in. The seriousness of the situation made him reflect a little more on his life, so he calmed down. At about the same time, a real estate deal I had been working on for a fixer-upper came through, so I started renovations to use it as a rental for another avenue of income. Since Jake was on medical leave, he offered to help with the electrical and plumbing issues. We seemed to be back to our routine, so I put the situation out of my mind, but I never forgot it.

It was also around that same time that I first started receiving some of the strange emails and Facebook messages from what appeared to be fake accounts. I didn't waste time on them back then, because I was busy with the house. Instead, I copied and pasted the messages, printed them out, and started the journal.

Even though that was some years ago, Jake's delay reminded me I had to stop being so complacent. Failure to notify me of his hotel information and not letting me know he'd be late getting home was disrespectful. I just assumed it was a bunch of guys out on the open road when it came to the rides; it never occurred to me otherwise.

~~~

On the third day of me calling and texting with no response, I started to take it seriously. Now, I was having visions of him lying on the side of the road somewhere. I had no choice; I had to become one of those women who I said I would never be. In all the years I had known Jake, I never spied on him, not even to look at his cell phone when it was left unattended in front of me.

I didn't have a suitable answer as to why I never asked more questions. I think it was partially because I was raised by a dysfunctional and insecure stepmother. From the day she entered our home when I was five years old, I watched her nag and obsess over my father's every move to the point of neurosis. It drove me crazy to watch her insane behavior over the littlest thing, which made him remain at work more, instead of coming home. Unfortunately, her insecurities and abusive behavior forced me to run away when I was a young teenager. I wound up living with another local family to get through school. It wasn't long after that my father asked for a divorce; he said he would have done so sooner, but thought I needed a mother. By then, her behavior was always in the back of my mind, so much so that I automatically did the opposite in my relationships. I never wanted to be like *that* woman.

If I couldn't trust the man I was with, there was no reason to be with him.

Problem was, I went too far to the opposite. I rarely questioned Jake. I was partially to blame for his come-and-go-as-you-please mindset, and he had been taking advantage of it. Things had to change moving forward, but first I had to find out where he was.

CHAPTER 15 - MY STALKER

Before – September 2017

WHEN JAKE PARKER showed up at my house a little before eight a.m., he believed he was there because I wanted private training. He was oblivious to the fact that it was just a ruse to get him there; wasn't the first time I tricked a guy into coming to my home. The minute he arrived and saw my attire, I knew the gig was up. I was wearing one of my thin-ribbed tank tops without a bra, and a pair of cut-off jean shorts that rode up my ass. He immediately grasped I had another plan, but he played it cool; he liked the attention.

He came straight from work so he was still in his uniform, work boots opened at the ankles, and in a relaxed mode. He walked around to the back of his truck and pulled out his rope rescue equipment bag, opened it, and unloaded various colors of ropes, carabineers, and anchors. He separated them by colors and handed me a thick manual with images and descriptions.

I glanced at his meticulous organization and realized he wasn't giving in to my ploy; he was there to train me. I pretended to review the first few pages and studied the images.

After he spread everything out, he looked over at me and frowned. "Are you planning on training in that?"

Penetrating eyes traveled down my body and settled on my nipples, which were calling out to be ravaged—at least that was my desire. Then they continued and stopped at the area above my vagina, where I purposely left the top snap open on my low-rise denim shorts. My body was screaming to be touched.

I smiled, hopeful. "I didn't think you really came here to train me."

"You asked me to," he said, with a slight edge of irritation in his voice.

"Right," I said, and my lower lip curved into a pout. "But I thought—"

"Thought what?"

He wanted me the same as I wanted him; I could feel it and see it in the bulge in his pants. The way he looked at me when my tongue danced over my lips, and the way he stared at my erect nipples. I knew he was just playing hard to get so he could pretend to be the saintly and happily married man. I also worked with a few guys he trained with, and he was probably afraid if anything happened between us, it would get back to them. I didn't want to push him away before I had the chance to have his lips on mine, so I agreed, for now. I enjoyed the chase anyway.

"I'll just go throw on a pair of work pants."

"You do that."

I went inside and slipped into a pair of loose-fitting sweats, but left the tank top on, and stepped into my work boots. When I returned, there was another row of gear laid out. He was serious about work.

The next hour he spent explaining each piece of equipment, what it was used for, and allowed me to study the manual as a visual aid. I learned through the discussion that he was the one who put the manual

103

together from rope classes he taught or incidents he dealt with on duty.

We discussed knots; tension rope systems; rappelling; lowering systems and safety factors. I was impressed by his knowledge and understood why he was so respected in the first responder community.

After an hour of training and another twenty minutes of allowing me to practice figure-8 knots, we agreed that was enough for the day. I offered to help him gather up all the gear and reload it into his equipment bag, but he declined my assistance. He was particular about who touched his gear, and I picked up on the fact that he liked things done a certain way. He was a perfectionist. I stood back and observed, trying to figure out how I would get him to extend his stay.

"Do you want to come in for something to drink," I said, hoping he would at least allow me the opportunity to pursue my desire. "I have coke zero and Lipton tea." When we first met, I picked up on his drinking habits.

"I could use a coke if you have ice, and your restroom, if you don't mind."

I smiled and led him inside, motioning toward the guest bathroom near the kitchen.

I lingered by the bathroom door for a minute, and then walked into the kitchen and grabbed two mugs from the cabinet. He joined me after he finished, smelling like the coconut soap I had on the bathroom sink. He leaned against my pantry while I poured us both a drink. I dropped cubes of ice into the mugs and then handed one to him.

"You didn't ask me here to train you, did you?" He finally said, taking a long drink and observing me over the mug.

I sipped my drink, savoring the cool liquid on my lips with my tongue, and relished in his eyes watching me. "No more than training me was your only goal."

"That's presumptuous of you."

My eyes met his and held his gaze. "I admit I invited you here, hoping to start something. I was hoping you came here for the same thing."

He cocked his head to the side with a curious look in his eyes. "When you say start something—"

I shrugged; I was taking a chance by sharing my opinion with him, but I've never been one to hold back. "I haven't known you for long, but it just seems like you spend most of your days working. When you're not working, you're looking to schedule a class. That sounds like the acts of a man looking for excitement. No offense to your wife."

He didn't look offended. He shrugged and then nodded. From my perception, it seemed like he agreed with me. "Katie works on her writing a lot."

I pretended to commiserate. "And she's not always available… I understand."

"So you think you'll bring me some of that excitement?"

"I can do more than that," I said with bold confidence. Then, I added, "I'm very skilled with a stripper's pole. You could merely watch if that's what you chose."

He raised his eyebrows and his face turned slightly red; embarrassed. "A stripper's pole?"

"My body can bend and do things in ways you can't even imagine."

He took a step back from me. "And you don't care that I'm married?"

I shrugged, dismissive. "What I offer has nothing to do with marriage."

"What does it have to do with?"

"Pure pleasure and fulfilling desires."

His eyes went dark, but it wasn't from anger. "Damn, you're bold."

"I just go after what I want. I think I've made it pretty clear that I want you."

I could tell he was battling his inner demons. He wanted to stay, but he finally pushed me away. "I can't. It would get back to Katie and I don't want to hurt her."

I leaned up against the wall and studied him. I knew I had to play this right. "You're nervous. I understand."

"It's not about being nervous. I'm married. I came here to train you, and you're offering something else."

"Go. I won't push. Just know that I want you. Bad. And if you change your mind, don't worry, I would never tell your wife. I don't even know her. It would just be between you and me."

He started toward the door, and I followed him. "You can stop by any time if you want to give it a whirl. See what my body offers. If you prefer to keep it professional, I can do that too. The training was great."

"Would appreciate it if you kept this to yourself," he said as he stepped outside. "I have friends where you work."

"Count on it," I said through the door screen. "You can have me anytime, without fear."

With that, he hopped into his truck and drove away. I didn't wallow or wonder whether I would hear from him again. I went through some of my old photographs, found a few sexy images of me with a firefighter I work with, someone he knew well, and posted them on Facebook, but clicked privacy to make sure they would only show up on Jake's timeline. The goal was to continue to let him know I had options; that I wasn't just pining for him. Jealousy usually pushed men into action. The photo would also let him know I could be discreet. The guy in the picture was also married. He couldn't hold my interest, but I didn't tell his wife or anyone else. He was the one with the big mouth; he bragged about it to his buddies. We hooked up during a weekend of training out of town. I lost interest in him after we had sex, though. He was a colossal bore.

CHAPTER 16 – MY STALKER

Before – September 2017

JUST A FEW hours later, Jake liked the pictures of me with the guy—just to let me know he saw them. Then he commented on a few pictures of me on my motorcycle. So predictable. I knew seeing images of me with another hot guy would pique his interest. Every guy wanted to think they were the only fantasy in our minds. I waited a bit, played coy, and merely thanked him, no different from the way I responded to any other guy who commented on my images. I didn't want him to know I was scheming over ways for us to get together. He had to go on believing I could be a friend; one he could talk to, train with, and one who wouldn't give him any pressure about a relationship. I was dangling the carrot; I wanted him to be the one to take the bite.

And he did…

A few days later, I received a text: "*Hey, just got done with a training class; you doing anything?*"

Subtle.

"*Just hanging out,*" I texted back.

"*Tell me more about that kind of sex you had to offer.*"

I didn't respond right away, but when I did I sent a selfie with the text: "*Better to show you.*"

"*What are you doing right now?*"

"*Playing…*"

"*Playing what?*"

"*Playing with my body to get it ready for you. C'mon over.*"

I didn't receive a text response, so I assumed my actions went too far with the selfies. It took me by surprise when his truck pulled into the driveway nearly an hour later. When he showed up at the door, he said he had been out training and stopped off at the pub with the guys. He was feeling no pain.

He followed me into the kitchen and leaned against the door frame while I reached into the cabinet for a bottle of my favorite liquor. I poured some into a tumbler glass, added ice, and then took a big drink.

"So," he said, not good with small talk and waiting for me to make a move.

I walked toward him, set my drink down on the counter, and started stroking his crotch. Even I knew that was bold. His arousal was immediate, but he backed away as if I came on too strong.

"Hold on," he said. "I need to be sure about this. It could get back to Katie. Like I said before; I don't want to hurt her."

He had every intention of doing this; he just wanted reassurance from me that I wouldn't blab. I kept stroking him, watching his body react in pleasure. "It won't get back to Katie; I don't know her, and I sure as hell won't tell the guys I work with. It's just between you and me. Believe me; I need to keep it quiet just as much as you do, because of work. I'm sure you've heard."

He knew I slept with a few guys at work. Gossip in the fire service was worse than a bunch of women drinking in a bar, but the talk wasn't started by me. I kept my mouth shut, even after they forced me to see the department shrink.

He studied me for several seconds; probably having a debate within his mind, and finally said, "I need to call Katie and let her know I won't be home for a while."

I moved to the side and whispered in his ear. "Go ahead. When you're done meet me in the guest house."

Just as I planned, he dialed the phone while I waited nearby and was able to eavesdrop:

Jake said, *"Hey Katie, what's going on? How's everything at home; any problems?"*

I could hear Katie's voice. Not clear, but well enough. *"Everything's fine. Bailey got bit by a bug. Her nose is all infected. I had to take her to the emergency vet hospital to get some medicine. They said it would take a few days for it to go away. She has to rest and no ball until she's better. How was the training? Are you on your way back?"*

Jake responded, *"The guys were thinking of having dinner and drinks at the pub. The training was intense so I might sleep at the firehouse instead of driving home. You okay with that, or do you need me to head home sooner?"*

Katie answered, *"No, go ahead. I'm just writing and tending to Bailey. Let me know when you're heading home."*

"10-4. See you in the a.m."

I listened long enough to pick up on the fact that he could stay through the night if I pleasured him enough to be interested. Katie Parker had no idea that by being too nice, Jake was taking advantage. What a naïve woman. She should have demanded he come home. On the other hand, if she did, I wouldn't have had the chance to make my move. Smiling to myself, I hurried out to the guest house to prepare.

When he stepped inside the front room, I had seductive music playing. Vanilla-scented candles lined the concrete floor to guide him. He followed them into the back room and sat down on the leather sofa, where they stopped and he studied the room.

Bump N Grind by R Kelly played in the background, while I seductively danced around the stripper pole in a fire-engine-red leather bra and thong set, wearing a matching eye mask. My bags of sex toys and lotions were on a table, and the video camera was running to film our entire night of debauchery.

I could tell by the look on his face, what I was offering was more than enough to replace any thought of Katie and their injured dog from his mind.

"This was just the icebreaker," I said to him, as I provocatively danced toward him and got down on my knees in front of him.

"Tonight I'm going to take you to places no partner has ever taken you before."

He looked at me with questions in his eyes. "How so?"

I reached for a black silk bandana in my tool bag, draped it around his eyes and tied it behind his head, and seductively whispered in his ear. "Have you seen any of the Fifty Shades films?"

He shook his head. "No, but we've had medical calls at the station from couples whose sessions got out of hand after playing out some scenes... something about a butt-plug."

I removed his belt and slowly unbuttoned his uniform shirt. "We won't need a butt-plug tonight... I'll be using my tongue instead."

His penis immediately responded and with that vow, I treated him to a night of pleasure in ways he had never explored, and would never expect to, with his wife. When he woke up in the morning, I pleasured him for another hour so that he wouldn't need Katie.

After that night, it turned into a fling with him lying to his wife. He would stop by my guest house at odd hours of the day, sometimes on his way home from work in the early morning or on the way to a class, so it was only an hour. He told her he was training or stopping by Home Depot or Lowes to look for something. Sometimes, he didn't tell her anything. I started pushing for more. He'd relent for a few days, say things like: "*if only we met at a different time before I met Katie, then things would be different*".

I knew he was telling me what I wanted to hear, but the way his body reacted to my touch told me everything I needed to know. I became his addiction, and he needed my touch. Anything he desired, I fulfilled, and a lot of time passed before we even realized it.

Eventually, it became too much for him to deal with. He was afraid the wife would find out and ruin his perfect little world, so he gave me the friend's speech. I dialed things back. We pretended we were pals who trained together now and hooked up when he needed what only my body could give. He didn't seem to have a problem with friends with benefits, as long as I didn't push. I had no intention of the temporary deal for long, but I knew the game pieces had to be in their proper place. He got inside my head, so now he was part of my soul, and playing pretend was merely the charade I was taking part in to achieve my goal.

PART TWO:

CHAPTER 17 – MY STALKER

Present – April 2020

WITHOUT WARNING, IN April 2020, Jake started making excuses not to see me during our designated times. We had been using training classes as an excuse on and off for nearly three years. It was never consistent, and most of those sessions turned into us having sex. The time we spent together consecutively was probably less than two years, one day a week, with a few months of not seeing each other in between because of his hectic schedule, and he had a wife at home. Each time I pushed back, he gave in; stopping by for a couple of quickies in between, too afraid to lose what fed his desire.

Then one day he sent me a cowardly text trying to break things off completely: "Hey, just to let you know I have to cancel the training. It's getting to be too much."

I gritted my teeth and held my tongue for a short time. I didn't want to let him know how much the statement angered me. He frequently attempted to put space between us, but never stopped the training altogether. He always came around, eventually. This time, I sensed he was rejecting me outright, and I didn't like it. Something was taking my place at feeding those inner urges. I did my best to hold my feelings in check.

"Oh, that's a shame … I always look forward to it. You've taught me so much.

"Sorry about that," he texted back. *"I'm headed out on a trip in a few minutes, timing's just not good.*

Katie has a few things lined up for me to do when I return."

Oh, perfect little Katie; figures. Of course, he blamed her and felt the need to remind me. Too late; he already revealed how little his commitment to her meant when he repeatedly gave in to sex. She never offered to do for him what I did, and nothing in my stalking her revealed she was doing so now. Something was up. His marriage was nothing but a piece of paper by this point, but it was a reminder that I needed to change my tactics. I tried to remain light-hearted.

"I didn't know you were going on a trip," I texted in return.

"One of the motorcycle charity rides. Going to D.C. with a group of guys. We're meeting at a convenient spot, and then heading out. Just waiting for a guy to arrive."

"Sounds fun. If I'd known, I might have signed up.

He didn't text back right away. When he did it was a quick message: *"It's a private group thing."*

I didn't know what to make of that; so I wasn't worthy of going on a motorcycle ride? Maybe he just meant it was a guy thing—that only his buddies were going. Katie never went.

The guy sure wasn't easy to crack. But then again, if he was, I would have gotten bored. That thought made me smile… I enjoyed the challenge.

I suddenly felt the need to know more about the ride and who he was going with. I signed into my *Facebook* account and stalked his two pages. There was a little back-and-forth conversation about the ride on his private page—the one Katie was blocked

116

from viewing—mostly others telling him they were also headed there and would see him at the meet and greet. I didn't notice any commentary from anyone who mentioned they were riding together; those conversations must have been private.

The charity group accepted me as a member not long after I joined, but I didn't consistently view the page because Jake had been coming around. Now, I knew I had been remiss. I clicked on the group and perused the most recent posts and comments. There was an entire thread dedicated to the ride; those who claimed to be going, and the hotel where they were staying. I looked for specific posts and comments from Jake. As he said, he was riding with a group of guys, but one post showed he was meeting someone who was flying in from out of state. Arrangements were being made via private messages, so I couldn't figure out who it was. That meant I had to do a little digging.

On the right side of the page, there were several links for photo albums of past charity rides. I clicked on the link for last month's ride which was in upper state New York. There were dozens of photos from the ride. Instead of wasting time browsing all the images, I just looked at those he was tagged in.

My face turned red from the fury that was suddenly surging through my body. He went on the motorcycle ride with another woman. I was so angry I kicked the coffee table in front of me and the contents scattered across the floor. Katie let this happen!

"He thinks he can betray me?"

My only pleasure came from knowing I had damaging info to hurt Katie without compromising my involvement with Jake. Since that was my original goal, I was able to pacify myself for the time being, but the anger remained. I made a file folder on my laptop and saved all the tagged photographs into that file. I was scheduled to be at work in an hour, so I set the group page as a favorite to make it easy to access later. I signed out and spent another ten minutes looking through the photographs. With each click, the rage reignited itself and I suddenly felt the need for revenge. Katie would have to pay the price for her complacency. Satisfied that what I had so far was enough to upset her perfect little world, I sent another message to her. She deserves everything that's coming her way. If she was a good and caring wife, she wouldn't have allowed him to go on the motorcycle rides. She was too trusting.

CHAPTER 18 - KATIE

Present – April 2020

UNFORTUNATELY, SOMEBODY ELSE did the spying for me.

Just as I was about to do an internet search for the First Responder Charity Ride, my phone pinged to alert me to a *Facebook* message. I was all set to ignore when I received another and another.

I opened my page and clicked on messages: my inbox was filled with photographs from the motorcycle ride. I looked at the sender's profile; another fake account. Curiosity got the better of me, so I started scrolling.

There were images of the various motorcycles lined up for the start of the ride. What caught my eye, though, was the number of groupies in attendance.

I came to a photograph showing a motorcycle that resembled Jake's. I zoomed in closer: a flag with the charity logo was on the back, and the first responder decals on the front windshield confirmed to me that it was his. I chose those decals. Seeing images of his motorcycle didn't send any warnings, but my instincts were telling me I wasn't going to like the outcome if I continued scrolling. I did, and my gut was churning. Whoever sent me the images did so for a reason.

In one image, the motorcycle was parked among others in a line at the starting gate of the ride. Occupants were chatting and prepping for the start time. Jake was standing with a few others, and a tall, dark-haired woman was standing to his right. She could have been someone's wife or girlfriend, or a first responder who was there with her bike; she had the look of a biker chick.

Then, zooming in, something else dawned on me... she also had the look of the woman stalking me at the book signings.

The physical attributes were similar: long, dark hair, tight jeans, and the revealing tank top. In this image she had a bandana tied around her throat and she wore a leather *Harley* baseball cap.

In the next two images: Jake was standing at the back of his motorcycle talking with a male rider while the woman sat in the passenger seat of our bike taking a selfie with her cell phone; and the next, he was leaning in close, whispering in her ear. The images were unnerving, but nothing compared to what was coming soon.

The sender also provided a link to a YouTube video. I took a deep breath and clicked on the link. It took patience and restraint, but I watched the start of the ride: flags flying, patriotic first responders riding past a long line of uniformed firefighters and police officers standing at a salute on the side of the road, as they traveled under the large flag extended off a fire department ladder truck.

I kept my eyes glued to the screen, watching for Jake's motorcycle, looking for the bright yellow and green decals. I didn't have to wait long. When his bike arrived at the front of the formation and rounded the corner, I saw him salute, and the woman who was sitting in my seat filmed it all with her cell phone.

*I felt like somebody just punched me in the gut...
silly as it may have been; it was like a dagger to the
heart when I realized she was wearing my helmet.*

CHAPTER 19 - KATIE

Present – April 2020

THE THOUGHT THAT Jake was lying on the highway somewhere disappeared the minute I viewed that video. What appeared in its place were questions: who was the woman, why was she riding on the back of our bike, and why was she wearing my helmet? When I came up with possible and hypothetical answers, more questions followed. The ride took place in D.C. Jake didn't know anyone there, other than introductions to riders who attended the *Rolling Thunder* ride to honor veterans last summer, and most of those riders came in from surrounding states.

There were only two logical answers I could come up with: that she was one groupie depicted in the images, or Jake met her locally and she traveled with him to the ride. The latter one was hard for me to wrap my head around. Where would he have met her? Between jobs and classes, he rarely had time off. Sometimes, he and the guys he trained with would stop by a pub and have a beer after class, but that was work-related. Jake rarely messed around where working relationships were concerned; at least not the man I've known for the last twenty years. He cared too much about the reputation among his peers.

Was I wrong? Was it possible that the man I've lived with for two decades was a different version of the man that showed up at motorcycle charity rides?

I opened my internet browser and typed in First Responder Charity Ride (FRCR) hoping to find a timeline of events. There was a website for the main local charity and links for the various rides in different states.

I clicked on the link for D.C. which took me to a *Facebook* page. I knew it was the right spot because the profile image displayed the same logo Jake had patched on the front of his leather vest.

I scrolled down until I spotted a flyer for the past weekend ride and clicked on it. The timeline was just as Jake said; meet and greet Friday, ride on Saturday, ceremony after. He would have stayed at the hotel on Saturday and Sunday night after clean-up. He said they might do some sightseeing on Monday, so possibly a third night's stay. Checkout would have been eleven a.m. unless he paid for a later checkout. Either way, that would have put him on the road sometime on Tuesday, with only an eight or nine-hour ride. It was now Friday.

I sat back in my chair for a minute, feeling a little guilty for spying on him, but I had no choice. All he had to do was call or text and tell me they were staying a few extra days. He deserved it.

Thinking about it, Jake had gotten a little lax about regular check-ins. He used to be anal about doing so; even checking in when he was at work for a twenty-four-hour shift. When texting came around, he chose that method of communicating; sometimes it was just a smiley face to let me know he was busy, but thinking of me. Admittedly, that had slowed down in the last two to three years, but to be honest, I welcomed it when he stopped texting so often. Sometimes, we'd be texting for over an hour, about nothing in particular, and I missed out on writing time. Time was money when you're an independent writer. *And let's face it; motorcycle trips out of state were not cheap.*

He still checked in when he was on his way home from work to ask if we needed anything, to let me know he was stopping by for a drink with his buddies, or picking up an overtime shift. It only takes a minute to type a text. There was no excuse to not keep me informed, especially considering he was the one always absent from the home. Not checking in at all was not the norm.

"To hell with it," I said to myself, brushing aside my anxiety and guilt.

I continued to browse, feeling like a parent checking up on a rebellious teenager. Just like the website, there was the main page for the local ride in Massachusetts, and then separate pages for rides in other states.

Steve Taylor founded the original charity ride after one of his fellow officers had been killed in the line of duty and he wanted to raise funds to help the family. He had the right connections to market the charity, and a slew of volunteers to make it a success by encouraging first responders to take part. He anticipated a few hundred motorcycles would show up for the first ride four years ago. There wound up being three thousand. The number doubled the second year, with a good number of them coming in from out of state. Word spread through the first responder community, and those that showed up for the ride liked the idea and wanted to do the same in their respective states.

Jake and Steve met when the local charity was on its third year, attracting thousands. They became

124

friendly because of their similar interests, which was how Jake got involved. He liked the fact that the charity donated all the funds directly to the designated first responder or family. Because of that, Jake accepted the invitation to be on the board two years ago. Since then, he has tried to attend every ride.

That got me thinking again, so I pulled up the charity website, studied the ride schedule for the last two years, and printed out a copy. The D.C. ride was held each year in April. The local Massachusetts ride was coming up; I had it outlined in my calendar. When Jake attended the Virginia Beach ride last year, he asked if I minded him using his vacation time for that trip. He said a few vets were going and they hoped to hit all the military sights in the area. I couldn't go because I was on a deadline.

Now that I've seen the images from D.C., my mind was suddenly clouded with suspicion. Was this the reason he spent a fortune on emerald jewelry for my birthday?

My fingers started typing before I knew what I was doing. I searched for the First Responder Ride, Virginia Beach. My mind was already muddled, but my hands shook the minute the page started loading. Out of all the riders that attended, my husband was right there on the main page.

The cover photograph was like the one on the page for D.C. except his motorcycle was the only one prominently depicted. And he was not alone; he was with the same dark-haired woman, and the image was well displayed for anyone who visited the page. The image wasn't just a gut punch; it had me kneeling over in pain.

What the hell was this woman doing on my bike, wearing my helmet in two different states? I tried to think back on his behavior before leaving on the trip; nothing out of the ordinary. He needed help picking out a piece of luggage he could stow in the side compartment, so I helped with that. I bought him a *GoPro* video camera the previous Christmas, so we looked for a camera case to keep it safe when traveling. I helped him pack, cut his hair—as usual— and we had a barbecue with our friends and sat by the fire the night before. He had worked a heavy schedule that week, so he fell asleep early, but woke me up early to have goodbye sex before he jumped into the shower.

Everything appeared normal.

I took a deep breath and let it out, and then my fingers started working the keyboard, again. I found myself searching through photographs, hoping I wouldn't find more, but instinctively knowing I would.

And, I did.

Jake and the dark-haired woman were in several photographs; there was no mistaking that they were there together. Two were snapshots of them at the start of the ride, a few others were taken of them mixed in with a group of riders, and the final two images had the two of them posing together at the meet and greet.

She was with him at the bar of the hotel. She could be a groupie, a friend, a fellow first responder, or another member of the charity who didn't have a motorcycle and Jake was friendly enough to offer her a ride—in two different states. Yeah, and I could be the next international model for Victoria's Secret.

He's cheating on me.

Two rides, two different states, and both times she was a passenger. I didn't care how many explanations he conjured up—and I knew he would have an excuse for every accusation I threw at him—the man I have been married to for over twenty years has been having an affair using the motorcycle rides to do so. I also knew he would lie with a vengeance if I confronted him.

~~

Jake would be home soon. I knew that now. He wasn't lying in a ditch. He wasn't having a problem with his motorcycle or delayed because of a problem. He was late because he was screwing around. Having just discovered the images and videos, I didn't know the extent of his cheating, nor did I know anything about the woman.

I might have bought an explanation for one ride, but in two different states with the same woman? That was a tough sell. Was she the one who sent me the pictures? Was she the woman who I had come to refer to as My Stalker?

My stomach was nauseous, so I looked through the cabinet for a bottle of antacids. My pride was telling me I had to leave and maybe stay at a hotel if only to escape for a while until I could figure things out. It was easy to talk brazenly about what one would do if ever faced with the situation, and I was always adamant that I would be out the door in a heartbeat. Unfortunately, the adult in me knew running away was not a straightforward thing to do.

When I was sixteen years old, I got into a fight with my stepmother. It wasn't our first fight, nor would it be our last, if I remained. We had been battling since she moved into our home when I was a young child. I also ran away when I was twelve, but the authorities forced me back home when she called the police. The woman loathed me because I looked like my mother and my father adored me. I had scars from her hitting me and scratching me like a feline to show just how much she hated me.

This fight was no different; it started over something stupid—like every other one—only this time I fought back with my words. She punched me and bit me, leaving teeth marks on my arm. That was the final straw for me. Even if it meant never seeing my father again, I had to leave.

I threw some belongings into a bag, grabbed the keys to my beat-up car, and walked out the door. The first two weeks I slept in the vehicle and showered at the YMCA, too humiliated to tell anyone what happened. I was still in school, so I just kept to myself. I knew my stepmother would lie to my father and wouldn't show up at the school looking for me. I was no longer the naïve twelve-year-old. She would have been too afraid I'd show them the scars. She was an expert at keeping that side of her persona a secret. I also needed a job to pay for a place to live on my own, so I had to lie on the applications. It was a struggle, and I swore I would never put myself in that position again.

No matter how much it killed me in the present, I had to stay put and think through my options before jumping into action. First, I needed the facts about what was going on, and not just images that showed a rider on the back of the motorcycle. If I had to make changes, I needed to make sure I was emotionally, physically, and financially prepared to do so.

After two decades, I wasn't just going to walk out the door, forced to be the one to sacrifice and start over. I deposited the money in our joint account from funds from my books and renovation projects. Jake had been spending his funds on his motorcycle trips. He traded in the motorcycle I paid cash for and bought a brand new one, which meant a large monthly payment. I put in my dues probably more than most women would.

When I was first introduced to Jake twenty-two years ago, he was going through a volatile divorce. Once it was completed, we hung out, and I helped with his two children. When we married two years later, I knew he was in financial duress, so I convinced him we should buy a fixer-upper, renovate it, and sell it to pay off his debt. Most of the work fell on me because of his irregular schedule. It also meant I had to put my writing on hold, but agreed to do so, because it was going toward our future.

No, I wasn't just walking out and sacrificing my efforts this time. Life needed to appear normal until I knew what to do, which meant completing my book.

CHAPTER 20 - KATIE

Present – April 2020

IT WAS JUST past seven o'clock. I fed and walked Bailey far enough to get her tired so she wouldn't need to go out until it was time for bed, and then I could just put her on the chain outside. That would give me a few hours of writing; if I could keep my mind focused and not worry about Jake or the deceptive life he had been leading. How was I supposed to be creative and develop a story when my mind was exhausted from learning about his behavior and wondering what my stalker might do next?

To be successful as an indie author, I had to keep writing, keep publishing, and keep up the social media marketing. Personal problems couldn't interfere. Now, more than ever, my livelihood would be affected if there was a pause in my efforts. Authors relied on name recognition. My books were garnering attention, and I needed to keep up the momentum. I would not allow a stalker or Jake's cheating to interfere with that goal.

I suddenly felt re-energized.

I grabbed the journal and outline I drafted earlier, opened my laptop, and clicked on my story notes to get into the proper mindset. For me, writing a novel took patience and the ability to focus by cutting out the noise from the outside world. With a folder full of screenplays and plot ideas I created over the years, I still struggled when it came to developing them into novel form. It was only recently that I figured out how to make the task easier; I followed the format I used for writing screenplays.

I started with a virtual vision board based on my outline, only a condensed version using index cards on computer software. I typed sentences to describe each scene. Browsing the internet, I chose images that fit my fictional ideas then copied and pasted them into my board to help with cover ideas. After that, I developed the characters and their background, using as much information as I could from reality.

Law enforcement and rescue personnel were prominent in my past stories, so I did ride-a-longs, in big cities and small towns to see them in action first hand, and I questioned them about laws and procedures. I even spent time with victims and perpetrators to get into the mindset.

A screenplay could be ninety to one-hundred-twenty pages depending on genre, and less time-consuming than a novel of three-hundred-plus pages. Using the index cards, I wrote out all the action sequences for several chapters like I was writing a script, and then went back in to describe the scenery, and added in dialogue. It was easier to get the story typed because I could visualize the action as it played out in my mind, and the adrenaline kept me moving.

By emulating that process, I should have a completed book in a brief time. I already knew most of the story, just not the ending. Sadly, I now had more of an understanding of the psychological torment a victim goes through, personally, because of My Stalker. I haven't suffered physical harm, but the stalker's actions consumed my mind.

Equally upsetting was that I knew I was being stalked and tormented; I just didn't know who or why, with certainty. Was it the dark-haired woman on the back of Jake's motorcycle? She resembled the woman, but I didn't know for certain. I couldn't get a restraining order based on my suspicions.

I saved everything and named the file for my new vision board: Unknown. I had a few ideas for a title, but until I knew the finale, I couldn't choose one.

I stretched my arms over my head and twisted from side to side; my body got stiff after sitting in the same position for so long. That's when I felt the presence of someone and noticed several flashes of light coming through the seagrass in the backyard, one right after the other. What the heck? I tried to act like I was unaware. More flashes. That's when realization set in: somebody was out there with a camera taking pictures of me.

I jumped out of my seat. Hit the switch to turn off the interior light enveloping me in darkness, and then grabbed a flashlight and the wooden baseball bat from a barrel I kept by the door. Bailey thought it was time to play ball.

"No play," I said to her, but she stuck by my side, tail wagging, knowing I was going outside.

I grabbed her collar, slid the door open, and then stepped out onto the deck. The motion detector lit up the area over the deck. When I waived the flashlight toward the seagrass, it revealed a figure in a black hoodie moving about. Bailey saw it too, freed herself from my grasp, and charged in that direction before I could stop her. Keeping their face hidden from view, the intruder gathered up a tripod and started running in the opposite direction.

"Bailey stop," I yelled as I ran after her, now worried more about her getting hurt than about learning the identity of the intruder.

I hurried down the deck steps into the sloping sand, where our large fire pit was centered between the three cottages. A stretch of tall seagrass continued and expanded, with paths in between where Bailey and I normally walked into the woods. Her paws pounded over the sand and she disappeared from my sight, getting too far ahead of me as she rushed after her prey. Once I passed the cottages of our private cul-de-sac, a wooden bridge and set of stairs veered off to the left, with the shoreline continuing on the right. Depending on the tide, we would sometimes discover remnants and treasures of the sea left behind. Time seemed to slow down until I heard her distinct bark; she had the enemy in her crosshairs. A deep, guttural growl followed, and then a blood-curdling yelp.

"Noooo," I yelled. "Bailey!"

I sped up my pace.

A couple of minutes later, I heard a car door closing out in front of the cottages, the start of an engine, and then tires squealed as the vehicle peeled away.

I yelled for Bailey, but she didn't return. All I could hear was the noise from the waves. The security light didn't reach down past the seagrass, so I used my flashlight to guide me.

Should I call the police? Would they be able to do anything? Probably not. It would just be another notation in my journal. My dog had better be okay. I called Bailey's name several times. I was getting scared for my dog.

"Bailey, where are you?"

Olivia and Madison were due to arrive sometime tonight, but I didn't see the lights on in their cottages yet.

Dogs were creatures of habit. Maybe Bailey was just wandering the path we normally walked. She could be sniffing new scents, or something could have been dragged in from the sea. I got a few hundred feet away from the house when I heard her whimper and my blood ran cold.

"Please, no ... not my dog."

My feet were like jelly and my body was shaking. Not just from the chill, but from the fear that something happened to her. It was hard to run through the seagrass on thick sand, but I followed her sound; though I couldn't hear much outside of the waves.

"I'm coming, Bailey; tell me where you are."

She must have heard me. She started a steady whimper to guide me, and I followed along. When I finally reached her, she was lying on her belly with her paws out in front of her, shivering, a clear sign she was scared. Bailey was always chasing after critters or dogs that wound up on our property, but the minute she learned they weren't friendly, she backed off. I moved the flashlight over her shaking frame. I spotted blood on the side of her neck. Kneeling next to her, I re-directed the light over the area. I didn't realize that the anguished scream echoing around me was coming out of my throat.

Hurt me, but never hurt my dog.

"Oh Bailey, I cried, petting her to let her know I was there.

What the hell!

There was a homemade fishing lure made with a beer bottle cap, a treble hook, and two split rings lying next to her. By the look of the wound and the blood on the lure, I realized it was used as a weapon and jammed a hook into her skin.

Bailey assumed the intruder posed a threat to me, chased after them, and My Stalker found the lure and used it to stop her. It was common to find left-over lures; owners or renters of the cottages fished in the area quite often. Sometimes, they got lost in the ocean, and the waves and seaweed brought them to shore. I checked her paws and the rest of her body for injuries; the stabbing was the only wound.

It took every bit of self-control I had not to lose it. My Stalker just went from a nuisance to pushing me over the brink. You don't mess with my dog.

"Come on, girl, we're okay now. Let's go home." I tried to encourage her to get up by petting her to let her know she was safe, and then gently pulled her by the collar to guide her forward.

It took me a short time to coax her, but she finally got up on all fours and we headed back home.

"You did good, girl, trying to protect your mommy." She finally looked at me, but her face was the sad Golden Retriever look that melted my heart.

I got her back inside and looked at the wound with better lighting. There was a lot of blood, but the wound didn't look too deep. I dabbed it with peroxide, washed around it with soap, and cut away some of her hair around it so I could cover it with a small bandage to keep out the dirt. I still had some of her pain meds from a recent hip injury so I broke one in half and put it in a spoonful of peanut butter. At least it would help her remain calm.

"What a good girl you are," I said, nuzzling her face, overcome with relief that she was wagging her tail and eyeing the cookie jar on the counter.

"Do you want a treat?"

The Golden Retriever dance began; she sat down and gave me her paw. When I didn't respond fast enough, she started talking to me and her eyes would veer toward the jar.

"Okay, okay," I teased her. She could yell at me all she wanted. It was just good to see she was okay. I gave her a cookie and filled up her dish with fresh water. After a while, she curled up in her bed and started licking her paws.

CHAPTER 21 – MY STALKER

Present – April 2020

KATIE DESERVED TO see her dog harmed. I just wanted to get the damn thing away from me. I wanted her to see me, but I didn't want her to catch me. Why would she let her beloved dog run after an intruder, anyway? She pushed me to act. If she had been a more demanding wife, Jake wouldn't be off on a motorcycle ride trying to fill his void. She was the reason he kept pushing me away and feeding his appetite elsewhere. He was afraid of getting caught, and I was too close for comfort.

I had been watching her for quite some time, not just when she did book appearances. I followed her when she ran errands. I borrowed my dad's dog and walked through the area, pretending I was a resident just out for a walk. I purposely dismissed the words of warning from my employer-mandated psychiatrist during our last meeting. Her expert diagnosis was to advise me that my behavior was obsessive and erratic. What did I care; I had an objective. Tormenting Katie was all part of the game.

I hunkered down low in the seagrass, wearing my black-hooded sweatshirt tight around my head so she couldn't see my face. From previous trips, I learned that her outdoor lighting only lit up the back deck but not further down on the sand.

I had my cell phone attached to an extendable selfie stick tripod to capture images of her inside the cottage. She was working at her desk, which was right up against a large bay window opposite her

137

kitchen island, giving her a view of the water. Her hair was in a messy bun on her head. She must have had eye trouble since she was wearing glasses to view the laptop. I could tell she became frustrated now and then because she would stop typing, lean back in her chair, and take a few minutes to pet her dog. She gave entirely too much attention to that animal.

I had the zoom feature on the camera in as far as it would go. The view was so close I could see every facial expression and the roots of her hair; dark blonde with highlights from so much time out in the sun. I wouldn't need to be here if she hadn't removed the cameras I previously installed. Now, I had to do the shadowing myself to keep learning what her vulnerabilities were to torment her. Didn't take long to realize the dog was her major weakness.

The psychiatrist warned me that if I didn't continue treatment and get control over my emotions that my symptoms would get worse and other character traits of HPD could take over. I laughed when she said my actions sounded like that of a stalker. If she knew everything I had been doing, she would have put me on a 72-hour psych hold to have me evaluated. Katie Parker had become my obsession. She was in the way of something I wanted, and I was prepared to do what was necessary to get it. What I learned in the process was that I was enjoying the game. It gave me a thrill. Jake said it clearly; if Katie wasn't around things would be different for us.

When the Chief ordered that I see the department shrink with the excuse that my sexuality kept the men I worked with from performing their jobs; I called them a bunch of pussies. The shrink became another obstacle in my way and turned out to be as neurotic as they were.

On my very first appointment, the crazy woman informed me that I had to wear a bra to work, not a push-up and that I had to stop wearing the white tank tops under my turnout gear during training. One of the wives put in a complaint.

I had them by the balls. They wouldn't fire me because they were afraid of a discrimination suit that would open up a can of worms they didn't want to deal with. They couldn't deny I had affairs with a few of the men I worked with. It was offensive that I was the only one trotted out for punishment. I knew the Chief wanted me gone, and I relished in the thought that he couldn't do anything about it. He was tired of hearing complaints from the wives and girlfriends about my provocative attire and sexual personality. The department's answer was to send me to the shrink, hoping she would diagnose me with a disorder, then claim I was unfit for duty, or prescribe meds that would alter my sexual proclivities. It was just another means for pharmaceutical companies and doctors to make money off of meds they created for profit. Disorder, my ass.

Was it my fault men wanted to have sex with me and were insecure wimps who couldn't say no? I was the single one. But they didn't have to worry about me anymore. I found the man that satisfied my interests and he wasn't an employee, so the Chief could pound sand. All I had to do was overcome the human hurdle in my path.

I couldn't fathom how Jake married someone like Katie. How did she keep his interest for the last two decades? What did she have that I needed to add to my persona? He preferred the type of sex I offered, which she wasn't willing to give. My stalking revealed a woman that was always writing, exercising, enjoying time with friends, or playing with the dog. Utterly boring. Where was the adventure for Jake?

~~~

"Here we go," I said to myself a short time later when Katie turned off the interior lights so that I could no longer see inside the cottage. Took her long enough; she finally spotted the camera. A minute later, the outdoor light suddenly lit up the back deck area. Before I realized it, she slid the door open and the dog bolted in my direction after spotting me moving around.

I grabbed my phone and stashed it in my pocket then folded up the tripod. I heard the ferocious bark as the dog charged toward me.

"Fuck!"

I wanted Katie to get traumatized by my presence, but I didn't expect to be chased away by her protector. Damn dog. As I turned to run in the opposite direction, I tripped over a thick batch of seagrass and face-planted onto the sand.

"Dammit," I said. Something stuck me in the arm and drew blood. I spotted a fishing lure with hooks and grabbed onto it. When the Retriever was at my heels, growling at me the way a guard dog would an

140

intruder protecting its owner, I swung around with the hook between my fingers and jabbed her in the neck. I doubted it would kill the dog, but hoped it would scare the shit out of her. She yelped and backed off, whimpering. She was a coward, just like her owner.

Her fear allowed me to get back up on my feet so I continued running. I cut through the neighbor's yard and rushed out to the front of the cottages. While still moving, I used the remote-key to start my SUV, hopped inside, and punched the gas to high-tail it out of there. As I rolled down the window, I heard Katie's anguished scream alerting me that she found the dog. That was exhilarating.

CHAPTER 22 – KATIE

Present – April 2020

"LADIES WE NEED to talk."

"What's the matter?" Olivia asked, seeing the troubled look on my face when I approached her and Madison lounging by the fire pit.

It was late afternoon, normally the perfect time to start a fire with the breeze drifting in off the ocean, making it more comfortable than sitting around in heavy jackets. As our token pyro, Madison was always good at starting one and keeping it loaded with wood. They didn't arrive at the Cape until late last night and I spent the morning checking on Bailey and writing a few more chapters.

"Did you hear from him?" Olivia asked, assuming Jake's continued absence was the reason for my facial expression.

I shook my head, frowning. "No, but I received a message with some interesting pictures.

"What kind of pictures," Madison asked. "Wait, I sense a discussion coming. Let me put some more wood on the fire so we're not interrupted." She got up to retrieve more wood and stacked it in the pit like a Jenga to let the air breathe through.

"He had a woman with him," I said, the anger in my voice unmistakable. "And she was wearing my helmet."

"Oh shit," Olivia said. "Let me see."

Madison joined us as we huddled over my cell phone while I scrolled through the images forwarded to me, and then I played the YouTube video.

Olivia let out a heavy sigh. "I think we need a cocktail before we continue. Have a seat, Katie and I'll go get us some beverages."

"Who sent them to you, another fake account?" Madison asked after Olivia departed.

"Yes, which is so irritating on one hand, but on the other, I know the person stalking me is not a reader."

Madison nodded. "That's true; it's someone who knows Jake, isn't it?"

"Otherwise, how would the person know Jake went on a charity ride? I have only discussed his rides with you and Olivia."

Olivia returned with three glasses filled with *fireball* and ice, handed us one, and then returned to her seat. "Okay, what did I miss?"

"We've determined that her stalker is not a reader."

"That's right," Olivia agreed. "How would a reader possibly know about Jake's rides? So what are your thoughts about the pictures?"

"I just don't know," I said, flummoxed.

"Is it possible she's just a friend of a friend?" Olivia asked. She held her hand out for my phone so she could view the images again and attempt to analyze their meaning.

Madison was contemplative. "I just can't picture Jake cheating."

"Me either," Olivia said, scrolling through my phone.

"Especially not with someone who looks like her," Madison added. "Sorry to say; but she looks like used goods."

"What's that saying?" Olivia mused.

"Ridden hard and put away wet," Madison said.

"Madison?" I said, shocked. The statement was something I would have expected Olivia to say, but not Madison, who we often referred to as a saint. Being the eldest in a Catholic family, she was always tending to others, professionally and personally. She was the one that made sure the other members of her family were okay, and if they weren't, she would rush in to help. Her marriage to Ted and helping him raise his three boys helped to bring her out of her sainthood through the years, but she still worried about everyone around her and wasn't content unless they were.

"She's right, though," Olivia said. "She looks rough. No way he's cheating with her. Besides, he's crazy about you. Remember when you were away, renovating that house and he had to stay behind because his knee went out? The way he talked about you, there's just no way. He has you on a pedestal."

She handed my phone back.

"And when would he find the time?" Madison added. "He's always working."

"I just don't know," I repeated. I scrolled through the images again. "I wish I had a close-up; she resembles the woman that has been shadowing me. And the images are from two different rides, in two different states. What are the odds of that and still being innocent?"

Olivia leaned forward in her chair, thinking. "Okay, so let's say, hypothetically, that this woman is a friend of a friend or a groupie and she follows the charity around. We know groupies exist and some women are not shy about flirtation."

"And most of them don't care if the guy is married," Madison added.

Olivia nodded. "It's possible that she fixated on Jake, asked him if she could be a passenger. Being the accommodating one that he can sometimes be, he said sure. Maybe she assumed more than just a simple ride on the back of his motorcycle?"

"Knowing Jake as we do, Katie, that is a possible scenario," Madison said.

I took a sip of my drink and let the hot cinnamon soothe my throat. "The fact that she showed up in two different states rips a hole in that hypothetical."

Madison nodded. "I can see that, Katie, but with all the time we've spent together, we've come to know each other pretty well. We know Jake is on the selfish side when it comes to these motorcycle rides; I just can't see him physically cheating."

"Nor can I," Olivia added, "and you know I'm tough on him. We know he gets bored and doesn't enjoy sitting around the fire with the group as much as he used to. He's always trying to find things to do to keep his mind busy, which is why he enjoys the rides. I could see him enjoying the attention from the woman, and maybe even milking it to a degree, but I can't see him following up on it."

"What if she's my stalker?" I asked. "Even if you two are right and it started innocently on his part, maybe it's different for her. Maybe she's after Jake and trying to cause a problem between us? Maybe hoping I'll just leave?"

"That is possible," Olivia said, "but we can't jump to conclusions, yet. You only have pictures of the rides; no intimacy. Have you looked into the other rides, or done any spying on him to validate your suspicions?"

I shook my head. "Until I received the images I wasn't aware there was an issue, but I started to. I just felt guilty doing so, even though I know he deserves it."

"Katie, you write about detectives and spies. You research them and know everything about how they operate," Madison reminded me. "You know how to find the truth."

I let out a heavy sigh. "I know. I just never wanted to be one of those women in my personal life. I guess I don't have a choice."

"You do have a choice," Madison said, "you can go about your business and act as if nothing happened, or you can use your skills and find out the facts so that you're prepared."

"Bottom line," Olivia said, glaring at me to make me pay attention. "If this woman is your stalker, she's trying to do some serious damage to you and your reputation. Remember, someone put cameras in your home to spy, but they only posted images of you. It was you they were trying to torment. I know it's hard, but you need to stop being nice and get mad for a change,"

"After last night, I am mad ... I'm pissed off."

"What happened last night?"

I had to give myself a minute to calm down; just thinking about Bailey getting hurt was making my blood boil again. "My Stalker was trying to torment me while I was writing. When I went outside, somebody in a hoodie bolted out of the seagrass and Bailey took off after them. Whoever it was stabbed her in the neck with the hook on a fishing lure, scared the crap out of her, and me."

"No f'ing way!"

"Is she okay?" Madison cried.

"She'll be fine, but that's why I didn't bring her over; she is anxious about going outside right now."

"That's all the more reason why you need to remain pissed off," Olivia said.

"I agree, but I'm going to do more than that," I said, watching their facial expressions change because I piqued their interests.

"What did you do?" Olivia asked with a wicked grin on her face.

"My journal was getting thick. I tossed out the original outline idea I worked on and started using my journal to develop a plot using My Stalker story."

"Yes!" Olivia said.

Madison said, "I'm sorry it's happening to you, but it's a great idea putting it into a book."

"It certainly has the psychological aspects," Olivia said. "And remember, sex sells."

I was contemplative. "Let's hope there's nothing to these images and I don't have to find out just how much sex sells."

As I spoke, my gut knew otherwise. It was telling me the girls were wrong, and that there was more to the images than just a simple situation involving a groupie. If this woman was MY Stalker, she made quite a few attempts to cause me harm. A woman wouldn't go to such lengths if she was just a passenger on the back of his motorcycle for a couple of rides. It was hard to wrap my head around the fact that Jake would cheat on me, and with someone like this woman, but a voice in my head was telling me I needed to prepare for the possibility of far worse.

CHAPTER 23 - KATIE

Present – April 2020

I DIDN'T KNOW what time it was when Jake rolled up on his motorcycle. Bailey and I slept through the noise, which was unusual for both of us. Normally, she would rush to the door when one of us returned. When I woke up in the morning and headed to the bathroom, I noticed Jake's boots by the door. When I glanced in the room, he was lying on his side, a blanket draped over his legs, and he was sound asleep.

I went into the bathroom to use the toilet, scrubbed my face and hands, then brushed my teeth. By the time I came back out, Bailey was in the bedroom whimpering, trying to wake him. I needed to prepare myself before dealing with him.

I walked to the door and whispered, "Bailey come, time to eat."

She whimpered one more time. When he didn't respond, she followed me out to the kitchen. I noticed the sweatshirt from D.C. on top of my desk, which meant he thought I needed a souvenir. Seriously?

I grabbed Bailey's bowl and filled it up with two cups of chicken, rice, and veggies, and then mixed her vitamins into the food. "Here you go, girl," I said, placing the bowl down on her elevated stand.

While she ate, I filled a small pan with water and placed it on the burner on high. When the water came to a boil, I cracked two eggs to poach them, and put two slices of raisin bread into the toaster. Ordinarily, Bailey would join me after finishing her breakfast, hoping I would share, but she went into the bedroom and whimpered a few more times instead. A thump on the floor and the heavy sigh that followed let me know she was lying next to the bed.

I finished breakfast and walked past the room. He was still in a dead sleep, which meant he had only been home for a short time and was in his REM state. I got dressed and went back into the kitchen to grab the leash, prompting Bailey to bolt out of the room, fearing I would leave without her. She wasn't as skittish now that Jake was home.

While taking her for a walk, I tried to prep myself for the wild story I was going to hear about his delay in returning. I knew it would be a fabricated excuse. I would want to call him on it. After going back and forth in my head, I realized that wasn't the smart thing to do. Instead, I decided not to mention it, and pretend as if nothing had happened. I wasn't being complacent. This time, I just wanted to prepare. Everything needed to seem normal.

~~~

Later that morning, Jake was sitting on the back deck, browsing through his cell phone and throwing two tennis balls down the beach for Bailey to retrieve and return. With him at home, she had completely forgotten about her injury. I finished my shower, put a load of laundry in the washing machine, and was now at the kitchen island making a fresh pot of tea. It was still chilly outside from the morning fog, but the sun was breaking through and would probably be blue skies within the hour. The tea finally finished

150

brewing, so I filled the pitcher with peach nectar, stevia, and ice, and then put it in the refrigerator. I grabbed a windbreaker from the storage closet and slipped it on just to keep the chill away. Then I snatched my cell phone from the counter on my way outside.

True to my decision, I managed to keep my mouth shut about his delay. He didn't bring it up either. I did plan to ask him about the YouTube video and pictures taken at the ride, but I wanted to do so without it coming off as an accusation so that he didn't get defensive. I didn't want a confrontation. I wanted him to continue thinking I was oblivious so that he wouldn't go on the offense and hide any evidence. As long as I kept my conversation low-key, he wouldn't suspect me of spying on him, and I would be free to do so.

I sat down in one of the lounge chairs and studied him for a few minutes. As usual, lately, he was restless and impatient when Bailey didn't bring the balls right back to him but dropped them about a foot away, forcing him to use the tennis racket to reach them. During the last two years, I couldn't think of a time where he just sat down to relax without getting edgy. He was trying to train Bailey to return and drop the balls at his feet, but with his many absences, she would get caught up in the excitement of him playing with her, and forget the drill until he corrected her.

Still, take a chill pill.

"Oh hey," he said, noticing me for the first time, "I didn't hear you come out. I thought you were working."

"Taking a break," I said, putting my face toward the sky to let the sun penetrate my skin. "Just finished making a pitcher of iced tea and put it in the refrigerator."

"Cool, thanks. What do you think about putting some pressure-treated wood railings around the deck? I know we talked about it, but I don't remember what we decided."

"We decided that it would look nice, but we also agreed you didn't have the time. Remember, you're in the midst of your hectic schedule and I'm preparing a book."

Jake would always reminisce about things he wanted to do around the cottage when he was sitting idle and letting his mind wander. I usually didn't pay much attention; with very little time off, it was futile to get excited about a project that he wouldn't get to for a while. If I wanted something done, I just did it myself.

"I guess that's true, though I might have some time after the Mass ride."

"Speaking of motorcycle rides... who was the woman on the back of our motorcycle at the D.C. ride?"

Where my chair was located I could see his eyes and study his body language, but I kept my voice even-keeled to not appear suspicious or upset.

I could see the wheels turning in his mind wondering how I got the images. He played it cool and tried to brush it off, but I caught it. "I don't know what you mean?"

He was stalling, asking a question so he could come up with a response that would suffice; a well-known Jake trait.

"You know what I'm talking about."

"Who have you been talking to?"

I recognized this stalling tactic too; trying to cast blame on someone else for outing his behavior. "I haven't been talking to anyone."

After a minute, he gave me one of his shrugs. "It was no big deal. She's just a friend of one of the board members who flew in for the ride. Since I was solo he asked if I wouldn't mind letting her be a passenger."

"Why didn't she ride with him?"

"He had another friend riding with him?"

I opened the image on my phone where she was sitting on his bike and he was leaning in close to whisper in her ear. "You looked rather intimate for a woman you just met."

He barely glanced at the image. "Intimate… that's bull".

Now his defenses were up, which I wanted to avoid, but I couldn't help myself.

He chuckled. "I was leaning in because that was the only way she could hear me. The noise from the bikes was so loud she couldn't hear a word I was saying. Where did you get the picture?"

I ignored the question. "There are several pictures. In a couple of them, she was taking selfies of herself on the back of *our* bike."

The anger revealed itself in my voice, so I tried to hold it off.

Tired from chasing the ball, Bailey came up on the deck to lie down next to me. He took that moment to get up and grabbed a bottle of flavored water from the refrigerator behind the bar that he built onto the deck. "Do you want anything to drink while I'm up?"

"No," I said, but the tone of my voice might have given my anger away.

"Katie, honestly, it's not a big deal. There are always people signing up on the charity page, those that don't have a bike, but they want to take part so they pay the fee and ride with someone who is solo."

"You mean groupies?" I said, sarcastically, "just like those that get themselves invited to fire and police department functions hoping to meet a man in uniform?"

He nodded. "I suppose, but you know it means nothing to me. Why would I be in search of another woman when I have you? She doesn't compare to you. Be serious."

He sat down in one of the deck chairs and stared at me. "That woman means absolutely nothing. She was a passenger for the ride. The minute it was over, she rejoined her friends. I'll probably never see her, again."

"So if I showed up at a ride and asked to be a passenger on the back of some guy's bike, you'd be okay with that?"

He smirked. "I know that would never happen."

"Why? Because I'm predictable? Dependable?"

"Yes, you are those things, but you also—"

"Wouldn't consider asking another man to ride on the back of his bike, because I'm married? That's right, I wouldn't."

154

Jake smirked, but the look on his face showed his guilt. I witnessed that behavior when he and his first wife battled when his children were supposed to stay with him for a weekend. She argued he would run in and out attending fire calls and *her* children would be left with me. She wasn't wrong about that; if there was a call or issue at the fire department; he was out the door, no matter what was happening at home. Anyone involved in Jake's life knew that when they got involved. But the court set up the visitation schedule so she should have abided by it.

"You're being silly, Katie," he continued. "A friend asked me to do a favor. Don't make it into something more than it was."

"She was wearing my helmet."

"I didn't think that would bother you. You're not the jealous type."

"Exactly; so if it was so innocent, why didn't you mention it to me?"

He shrugged indifferently. "This is the first time we've talked about the ride, and I didn't mention it because it wasn't important. I have you; why would I need to go looking elsewhere for a passenger on my bike? She's not even in the same league as you."

"There are no leagues, Jake. We just happen to be two different types of women, but that's irrelevant." I wanted to add that she fit in with his motorcycle buddies, and I didn't. The Jake I've known for two decades wouldn't date a biker chick, especially one who had a cigarette dangling from her fingertips. One of his attractions to me all those years ago was because of my conservative values and wholesome looks. My gut was sending huge signals.

~~~

When I first opened the images of the woman sitting on our motorcycle, my immediate reaction was the desire to flee. Any woman who has ever been in that situation knows the feeling of that punch to the gut and the humiliation. I wanted to put space between us. I read comments on the charity page that confirmed what he said; that some asked to be a passenger. While it could have been as simple as that, I just couldn't buy into it, not in two different states? Still, it was in my interest to keep my thoughts close to the vest. Olivia and Madison were right; I needed to put my investigative knowledge to use. I needed the entire truth.

CHAPTER 24 – MY STALKER

Present – April 2020

WHILE JAKE WAS away, I researched what I could find on the new skank he was playing fifty shades with. I looked through her social media pages and studied the images she uploaded into her photo album on Facebook. Did an internet search of where she lived, worked, and anything else I could find. Some people weren't smart enough to hide their personal stories from Google. She was no exception. I couldn't help but laugh at what I discovered. She didn't pose the same threat to me that Katie did. In fact, after scrutinizing everything I found, including the images I discovered of her inside the charity group, I didn't even view her as a competition. She was trying to be like me, but not accomplishing her missive. She was just a groupie who showed up at the charity rides and latched onto Jake. She was a rookie where I was the pro. It would be easy to get rid of her without Jake losing his shit over it.

When he returned from the D.C. ride, he ignored me at first. I called him and then sent him a text letting him know that I missed the training, and him. That I understood his concerns about the two of us together, but that I wouldn't push if he reconsidered. I knew that he would.

It was about a week later that he just showed up without texting me. He pulled into the driveway on his motorcycle, tanned and lethal—at least to me. I didn't wait for him to knock on the door. I met him outside. "This is a surprise," I said, wearing a smile and offering him a coke. I kept two-liter bottles in my refrigerator just for him.

"What's going on?" He accepted the coke and took a long drink, doing what he always does; ogling my body with his penetrating gaze.

"How was your trip?" I thought it was better to keep the conversation light and not bother to mention the tramp. Katie was the only complication of any substance.

He leaned up against his bike, casual. "It was good. Weather could have been better."

I stood opposite him and put my hands in my back jean pockets which pushed my chest forward. He noticed. I knew why he was here, but I didn't want to let on. "Did you bring your rope equipment to train?"

He smiled, reached for my arm and pulled me towards him, then moved around and bent me over the seat of the bike and trapped me with his hard body. Using his right hand he held onto my hair and his left hand moved down my shorts and in between my legs until I was quivering in anticipation. "I'd rather bend you over this bike and take you right here, right now. That's really what you want, isn't it?"

"Oh God, yes," I said.

And then he opened the bike compartment bringing me back to the present and out of the fantasy scene playing out in my head. He showed up to train me.

"I have about an hour," he said, totally in professional mode. "We can practice those knots you were having so much trouble with."

"Good," I said, pretending I was just happy he agreed to restart the training. "Then I don't need to change?"

He looked me up and down, and I knew he appreciated what I was wearing. "Not if you're comfortable."

We carried the equipment toward the backyard and set it up on the patio. For close to an hour, we worked on knots, with him grilling me on their purpose. Each time he moved in to correct one of my moves, his arm lingered near my chest. I could see that he was physically fighting himself to not give in to my illusions.

When we finished, he started folding his ropes and placed them back inside the bag. I walked toward the guest house and disappeared inside. After several minutes of me not returning, he came to see what I was doing. I knew he would. He knew exactly what I used the guest house for.

The candles were lit. I was sitting on the sofa, naked with a blindfold on, my hands semi-secured behind me, ready to play out a fantasy he repeated to me many times during our time together. When he walked toward me and unbuttoned his uniform pants, I knew he had to have me. I was the only one who could fulfill his craving, not Katie, and most definitely not some groupie that invited herself to his motorcycle rides.

That thought was so invigorating I nearly had an orgasm the minute he entered my mouth.

CHAPTER 25 - KATIE

Present – April 2020

I WAS AT the kitchen counter putting ingredients together for homemade meatballs and sauce to go in the crock-pot when I heard Jake's phone vibrate and a text message popped up on the screen. He left it sitting on the island when he went into the bathroom. Under the circumstances, I would have thought he'd be too paranoid to leave his phone lying around where I could get to it. Then again, I have never spied on him, so why would he suspect I'd do so now. Little did he know; I was going to do just that until I knew *everything*.

I tiptoed down the hall to make sure the bathroom door was closed, returned to his phone, and tapped on the screen. Both of us had Samsung phones we could open without a password so the message came right up on the screen: "*I get out of work early so I'll meet you at the hotel. Can't wait to see you xxx.*"

The picture icon was that of a woman's body from the neck down to the thigh; deeply tanned, wearing nothing but an apricot lace bra and thong next to the name of Stacy Levin. No innocent married man would have an image like that as a profile icon on his phone next to their phone number.

I wanted to click on the message to read the rest of the conversation, but then he would know I did. He needed to think I was still the unsuspecting wife at home. I kept up the façade on the outside, but my stomach was physically sick. Even without reading the other texts, I knew she was meeting him at the charity meet and greet at the hotel bar. According to the flyer, the founder of the charity would introduce the injured first responders chosen to receive the funds raised at the weekend's events.

I heard the toilet flush; the faucet turned on, and the bathroom door opened seconds later. Keeping my ear toward the hallway, I backed out onto the primary screen of the phone and placed it face-down on the counter where he left it, then hurried around the counter. When he walked into the room, I was washing dishes with him none-the-wiser. Out of the corner of my eye, I watched him pick up the phone to read the text, and not even flinch in a reaction. He placed the phone back down, walked up behind me, and wrapped his arms around me; playing the game like everything was perfectly fine between us. He couldn't see me clench my fists under the soapy water. It took everything I had not to turn around and punch him.

"Did you want to get that shopping out of the way before I head out?"

Even though we each had certain chores around the house, Jake always enjoyed food shopping together. He got a thrill from finding the best deal for the buck and refused to eat non-brand foods. Going together, he knew he could slip in a few items that I wouldn't necessarily pick up; such as the lemon poppy-seed muffins and chocolate cupcakes that he insisted were a nutritional breakfast. Didn't matter how many times I lectured him about the proper breakfast, or recommended a protein bar instead of chocolate, it fell on deaf ears.

I tried to respond like my heart wasn't being ripped out. "I thought you needed a nap before you go? You said it was busy last night."

He just got off a twenty-four-hour shift with calls most of the night. It wouldn't be wise to spend a weekend partying and riding after very little sleep. Not that I cared right now, but he would get suspicious if I didn't put on the pretense of concern.

"I could always forego the nap and we could fool around instead?" He nuzzled up against me, pretending that I was the only woman that mattered in his world. I used to believe that, before that text message and the recent images that I received.

I wanted to turn around and knee him in the balls, but I had to keep up the charade. I tried to think back to each time he left for one of his rides. Did he always ask me for sex beforehand? How many times had I given in, not knowing that he was going off to spend time with someone else?

"We could, but you know having sex depletes your energy. How many times have you passed out immediately after?"

"True, but I could take a quick cat nap."

"Or, you could just stay home and have all the time in the world to fool around."

"That wouldn't go over well with Steve; he's expecting me to help."

I knew a little reverse psychology would do the trick. "So that's a no?"

"Probably not, but it'd be fun." He released me and playfully slapped my butt and then grabbed a tea out of the refrigerator. "Guess you're right though, I should probably take a quick nap."

"Probably wise, since you'll be partying and riding without a partner to keep you awake." I glanced at him out of the corner of my eye. If she was just a friend of a friend riding as a passenger and it was innocent, this was the moment he could say so, but he didn't. Will she be joining him for the entire weekend?

He took a long swig of the tea. "What are you going to do while I'm gone?"

"Olivia is waiting for more chapters to edit, so I'm going to work on those, plus Madison asked me to make my meatballs and pasta for later, so I don't need a store run anyway."

"Cool." He grabbed his phone and walked down the hall into the bedroom. I heard him shuffling a few things around, and then heard him texting; probably sending her a response. "Don't let me oversleep, okay?"

"Okay." I looked at the time on the clock. It was nine a.m.; he was planning to leave by noon, allegedly to help Steve with setting up. Once he fell asleep, I would have a couple of hours to go through his phone and capture his texts, calls, and photos. Since this was a local ride, he wouldn't need his laptop, so I could go through his files. I knew I would figure out his passwords; he was a creature of habit. Since I never spied on him before, he had no reason to change them.

Fortunately, when Jake first falls asleep, he's in a dead zone. I knew I could sneak into the room and confiscate the phone without him noticing. The house could be robbed and it wouldn't wake him, but the sound of a fire alarm and he'd be up like a shot.

I finished the dishes and dusted the blinds while waiting for him to drift off. When I heard the snoring, I knew it was time. I peeked inside the room; he was lying on his side with his face toward the opposite wall. I looked around the room; where was his cell phone? I found it on my pillow. I tiptoed around the bed, making sure to use the rug so I wouldn't make noise on the hardwood floor. Better safe than sorry. If he caught me grabbing the phone I could say I was setting his alarm in case I didn't return from taking Bailey out for a run; something I did once or twice a day. He would have no reason to think otherwise.

Sitting at the island with the phone in my possession, I quickly scrolled through his recent texts looking for the conversation with Stacy Levin. It was gone. His other recent conversations were still there: three texts with his son, a conversation with a first responder in Kansas who was coming to the ride, and another with a guy from his tech team. Either he deleted the conversation with Stacy, or he stored the texts in a different location.

I kept my ears on the hall, knowing he could appear at any time. I plugged his phone into my laptop, went through his contacts: the Stacy Levin with the lacy bra and panty icon lived in New Mexico. So she was flying in for the ride? How did he meet her?

I scrolled through his downloaded files and found a folder with her name and forwarded a copy of the folder to my desktop. There was also a photo album with her name, so I forwarded that as well. When it was finished uploading I glanced at the clock on the microwave and realized how much time had passed. I exited out and checked the screen to make sure it was the same as when I retrieved it. Once I verified that he was still asleep, I snuck back in and put it back on the pillow. I had enough information for now.

Olivia and Madison agreed to help me with close-up surveillance; I planned to attend the weekend events to get more evidence, and then head back home with enough time to search his laptop, plus check images on the GoPro and digital cameras. The goal was to get everything I could find. When it was time to confront him I wanted to be ready so that when he got defensive and offered his lies, I could counter with the facts.

I also had another area of concern; I needed to look into the financial aspect. How much of our money had been squandered on this so-called friend of a friend. I would need to spend time online going through each account and credit card statement. The whole sordid mess was making me nauseous. I sat down in my desk chair and put my head between my knees waiting for my stomach to settle. After several minutes, I picked myself up, grabbed a doggie bag and Bailey's leash. Hearing the sound, she came charging down the steps from her hiding place by the side of the bed.

"Let's go, Bailey, mommy needs to get some pent-up emotions out of her system before she strangles somebody."

CHAPTER 26 - KATIE

Present – May 2020

I OFFICIALLY CROSSED over into the category of a woman choosing to physically spy on their husband. I wasn't proud of that fact, but he left me with no choice. My strategy was to follow Jake to the city; remain out of sight and capture images of him with Stacy Levin, so that I had irrefutable evidence. I hoped to verify that she was my stalker. I couldn't tell from the images.

In the pre-planning stage, I checked the functions on my android smartphone and discovered it was limited on zoom-in capability. That wouldn't be sufficient unless I could get close enough to my target. That might be ideal, but it wouldn't be smart. The last thing I wanted was to be in a position where Jake could catch me. The decision to confront him with the evidence had to be on my terms and my timeline.

That being the case, I did an internet search for a suitable digital camera with adequate zoom-in distance capability. Most of the cameras I read up on had double the capacity of my phone, but the Nikon Coolpix P900 promised eighty-three times optical zoom and double that with the Dynamic Fine Zoom super-telephoto lens. Once the decision was made, I ordered the camera with overnight delivery to Olivia's address. When Jake was not around, I packed a go-bag: camera, laptop, clothing, and items necessary to disguise myself, and hid the duffel bag in the bottom of the hall closet.

~~~

"Are you sure you can do this?" Madison and Olivia confirmed with me several times on Friday when we were preparing to go. They volunteered to help me, but they knew spying on Jake was out of my comfort zone. Madison was born and raised in the city, so she knew the side streets and alleys to avoid the thousands of motorcycles rolling in to attend the weekend event.

Jake left at noon and told me he was going to help set up for the meet and greet, but I did not know what that entailed. We kept our eyes alert, just in case. If he was riding his motorcycle through the city and spotted us; that would have blown the plan. The hotel across the street from the Harley dealership where the charity ride started, was offering discounts to guests attending the charity weekend. Jake had a reservation there, so I opted to get a room two blocks over, requesting a view of the area needed. The girls were going to drop me off, head back home to take care of Bailey, and then pick me up Sunday afternoon.

Along with the camera, I purchased a few other items to help with my deception. The first part of my surveillance could put me in close quarters with Jake and his fellow riders, so I needed to alter my appearance without looking ridiculous. I felt silly purchasing the items, but when Olivia and Madison's husbands didn't immediately recognize me, I knew I was ready.

At six o'clock that evening, I slipped inside the bar on the lobby level of the hotel hosting the meet and greet. I chose a spot where I could see both entrances, but not be in the line of sight of wandering eyes. I had an hour before it was to begin. Designated tables were marked, and they set up a booth with souvenir paraphernalia to the right of the bar.

I slid into a booth seat in the back corner on the left side. My back was up against the wall so I could see everyone who entered. When the server arrived, I ordered two appetizers and a glass of red wine. I informed her I was there to study and use the hotel Wi-Fi. I noticed others were there to do the same.

Once the meet and greet started, the bar would fill up with men and women wearing jeans and black leather vests with the charity logo over the left-front pocket. Since most of them were first responders or military, I suspected my petite frame and blonde hair would single me out—especially to Jake—so I opted for attire fitting of the area. I chose a Cambridge University sweatshirt, ripped jeans rolled up above my ankles, converse tennis shoes, and my hair was a shoulder-length, layered-cut wig with reddish-brown hair and wispy bangs to hide my blue eyes. Anyone looking would think I was just a Bostonian student there to study.

About forty-five minutes later, members of the group arrived, ordered drinks at the bar, and gathered over by the souvenir booth. Like Jake, they covered their vests with patches lined up on the back, representing all the rides they attended. Jake strolled in about ten minutes after, but he walked in alone. That threw me off. He approached the guy standing by the souvenir booth. I assumed it was Steve Taylor, the former Marine who founded the charity. He was

168

the only one not wearing a vest, but he had on a baseball cap with his charity logo.

Seeing Jake alone, I started second-guessing myself. Stacy Levin's text said she would meet him at five. It was after seven. Was I wrong? Was I overreacting? Could Jake just have been allowing a passenger to ride along, as he said? I reminded myself of the half-naked icon image on his phone, and the three xxx's in her text.

A few of the men joined Jake, shook his hand, and then several women—also wearing vests—joined the conversation as well. They ordered drinks and continued their chatter. I observed the camaraderie that I was never a part of. As a writer, I had an odd schedule, but I couldn't help but wonder why Jake never invited me to any of the rides. He used the excuse that I wouldn't enjoy a long ride on the back of a motorcycle. Even if that were true, it would only apply to the rides out of state, not the local rides. Was I too conservative? Both of my parents were in the military before they passed away, and my husband was a first responder. One would think I'd fit right in.

The bar suddenly went eerily quiet when three men walked in with their wives. They were the injured first responders chosen to receive the funds raised from the weekend ride. I couldn't identify the injuries on two of the men, but the third had been in a fire or explosion; the entire right side of his body suffered from severe burns.

I felt horrible. My whole purpose for attending was to catch Jake in a compromising position. The party was set up to introduce the three heroes to the attendees. What kind of person was I that I couldn't just believe Jake was being altruistic? I had to keep reminding myself about the text. After an hour of everyone buying drinks for the three men and their wives, and the group thanking them for their sacrifices; I decided it was time for me to call it a night. It seemed tawdry to be trying to catch a cheater under the circumstances.

Before preparing to leave the bar, I glanced toward Steve Taylor, the man responsible for the charity. His attention was focused on the three men being honored. I wondered if he realized he was also a hero for what he was doing to help the men and their families.

I logged out of my laptop and stowed it back in the case, left money for the bill and tip on the table, then slipped out the side entrance. As I was walking back toward the lobby, feeling stupid for jumping to a conclusion, I immediately stopped in my tracks and ducked behind a wall.

At that exact moment, Stacy Levin was walking through the hotel entrance carrying an overnight bag. Same clothing: ripped jeans, black boots, low-cut top, but she also wore a vest with the charity logo. Her arrival must have been delayed. I studied her as she walked toward the bar entrance. She resembled my stalker, but her mannerisms weren't as flamboyant; something was off.

I hurried back inside so I could catch the moment that she met up with Jake. I pulled the camera out of my bag and zoomed in until I had them in view. She walked right up to him as if he belonged to her and plunged her tongue into his mouth, not caring that anyone was watching.

It took everything within my power to remain where I stood instead of marching over, slapping her across the face, and doing the same to him. The minute their lips parted, the group welcomed her. The next thing I knew, Jake playfully picked her up and tipped her over his shoulder, just like he used to do with me, and carried her out of the bar. It was clear they were going up to his room; obviously, he would be getting his quickie in now.

I left the bar and sent a text to Olivia and Madison when I returned to my hotel room: "*There is no question about it; Jake is having an affair.*

"*Madison and I are together, so you can just text my phone,*" Olivia texted back. "*You saw her?*"

"*I saw her. She and I couldn't be more opposite. She came into the bar and staked her claim right in front of everyone. The charity group knows about them, but obviously, nothing about me. I'm exhausted. Going to veg out. Will check in tomorrow.*"

Madison texted, "*We're so sorry, Katie. I hoped you were wrong, and it was just a misunderstanding. Screw him; he doesn't deserve you. We'll talk tomorrow.*"

CHAPTER 27 - KATIE

Present – May 2020

SATURDAY MORNING I woke up to the sound of motorcycles rumbling past the hotel, causing the windows to vibrate. I jumped out of bed to look outside and was stunned to see hundreds and hundreds of motorcycles rolling down the street and pedestrians lining up with their lawn chairs to watch.

I woke up later than normal, but I didn't sleep too well, all things considered. After texting Olivia and Madison I took a long, hot bath and fell apart emotionally, crying and feeling sorry for myself. I finally dragged myself out after an hour and collapsed onto the bed. The night was fitful. I tossed and turned. What surprised me was how composed I was seeing her in person and being forced—like everyone else in the bar—to watch her stick her tongue down my husband's throat. Hearing the motorcycles was my alarm clock. I didn't want to miss the start of the ride.

I grabbed my essentials and rushed into the shower. I didn't worry about drying my hair, I just pinned it up and put the wig on over it. I was lucky enough to get a room that had a large window with a view of the parking lot where all the motorcycles would line up for the start of the ride. If the camera worked as the reviews promised, I could stay in the room and film. I had no desire to fight the crowd to find a spot along the street. Showered and changed; I had a couple of hours before it started, so I went down to the cafeteria to grab a plate of scrambled eggs, fruit, and two bottles of water.

In the room, I nibbled on the food and searched through the viewfinder to see if I could locate Jake. Since he was on the charity board, I suspected his motorcycle would be up close to the starting point.

A fire department ladder truck was parked and first responders were positioning the large flag over the street. Three convertible vehicles were parked at the front where a banner was draped across the street, each one designated to hold a first responder who was a recipient of funds raised at the charity. Then there were vehicles with company names on the doors honoring them as sponsors who donated large amounts for the fundraiser. All the motorcycles followed. Police officers and State Troopers lined up to escort.

I finally located Jake. He was standing next to his motorcycle, talking with a few riders. Stacy Levin sat in the passenger seat. I zoomed in closer to confirm she was still wearing my helmet. My husband was cheating on me, but her wearing my helmet seemed to make the betrayal even more personal. The anger surged through me again as if I just learned of the deceit. She was on the bike with her arm draped over his shoulder, as if the two of them were married, instead of the two of us for the last twenty years.

I heard the familiar sound of Olivia's ring tone on my phone and picked it up. "Hello," I answered.

"Morning, Katie," Olivia said. "Madison's here, I've got you on speaker. We thought you might need reinforcements."

I laughed with as much muster as I could. "Why, what did you think I was going to do, march down there and confront him with hundreds of bikers around?"

Madison said, "We thought, maybe. It is one thing to believe your husband is cheating, but when you see it up close, it would be hard to control the anger and not react. I'm surprised to hear how composed you are."

"I agree," Olivia chimed in. "You're doing better than I would be."

I sat down on the edge of the bed but kept my eye on the escapades outside. There had to be a few thousand motorcycles lined up already, and more were rolling in. "I'm not composed," I said. "My insides are churning. If I had a baseball bat, I'd march down there and beat the crap out of his motorcycle, but you know that would just land me in jail."

"Can you see her from your room?" Madison asked.

"Yes. I can zoom in. The ride hasn't started yet, but she's already in position on the bike."

I digitally transferred some of the images from the camera to my phone and texted a couple of them. "Check your texts, I just sent over a few of the images I took from last night and this morning."

Olivia put me on hold so she could check her text messages, then turned on the speaker again. "What is he doing with her? She's not even attractive. What the hell is he thinking?"

"You were right, Katie," Madison said. "You two couldn't be more opposite."

"She seems to fit in with the crowd though."

Olivia smirked. "She looks even harsher in these images."

"Something is going on with Jake," Madison said, clearly disgusted. "To ruin twenty years over someone like her, and the cigarettes, so disgusting and so unlike him."

"I told you what's going on with Jake," Olivia reminded us. "He's terrified of getting old and he's acting out because of it. That heart attack was a trigger. He started getting restless."

"Well, I hope it was worth it," I said, trying to keep my anger in check.

"What are you going to do?" Madison asked.

"I'm going to find every piece of evidence I can find, and gather it until I'm completely sure about my facts. I'm going to finish my book to make sure I keep income coming in for my security, and then I'm going to present everything to him when I tell him we're getting a divorce. I will not lose my cottage."

When we first bought the cottage and took on the renovation project, Jake loved it. We worked tirelessly to make it our seasonal home. We still had some work we wanted to do, but we completed the major construction. We enjoyed sitting by the fire at night and enjoying the water during the day, but we especially enjoyed our friends. Jake getting restless in recent years and choosing to take part in the charity rides limited his time at the cottage, which put a damper on those friendships. They believed he was being selfish, but said nothing to him out of respect for me.

The enormity of what was going on hit me like a ton of bricks, and I completely lost it. The tears flowed and I couldn't stop them. "Twenty-plus years of my life reduced to me using a camera to catch my husband throwing it down the tube because of a biker chick."

"Katie, we'll be there to support you all the way," Madison said.

Olivia added. "Absolutely; whatever you need us to do, just let us know."

I calmed down and grabbed a tissue to wipe my face. "Thank you."

"So what's next," Madison inquired.

"I'm going to film the start of the ride from the room. Once it's over, I'll slip into the crowd for the after-party and get more close-ups, and then I'll have dinner in my room and catch up on the sleep I missed from last night."

"We can join you," Olivia said.

"I would love that, but there is no way you'd make it anywhere near the area. There are thousands of motorcycles lined up and residents have their lawn chairs and coolers positioned on the sidewalks. It's like the 4th of July. Tomorrow is the better option."

"Sounds like a plan," Olivia said. "Our husbands will be here to watch the dogs, so we'll have plenty of time as long as we're home for dinner."

"Oh yes, heaven forbid my husband has to fend for himself for one meal," Madison said sarcastically.

Even with the turmoil going on within me, I couldn't help but laugh. Ted had many talents, but cooking wasn't one of them.

CHAPTER 28 - KATIE

Present – Sunday, May 2020

BACK AT HOME, I was ready to continue collecting evidence. Jake wouldn't be home until Monday, so I had the rest of the day to go through the info on his electronics and put it all together. A few of the questions I wanted answers to were where did he meet her, how long has it been going on, and how much of our money has he wasted spending time with her?

I had files from the phone, but I needed to check the bank accounts, credit cards, and search files on his laptop, GoPro, and digital camera. With someone like Jake, you couldn't just accuse him of cheating. He would argue against every point you made until you'd wonder if you imagined everything instead of seeing what you know you did. Jake had a knack for turning the tables. I wanted the proof.

Financial and property arrangements needed to be considered. If I were to just walk away and start over, the money coming in from past books and the rental income I received might not cover all the bills and provide for my future. Continued sales were never a guarantee, even after I published the next book. In a community property state, Jake could ask for half of everything. With evidence, I had bargaining power. It wasn't about making Jake suffer—though nobody would blame me—it was about security. As a full-time first responder and instructor with the academy, Jake's wages and pension were guaranteed. He would be okay, financially, no matter what personal choices he made. I had to be smart.

I opened my laptop and signed into the joint bank account. When I pulled up the balance, I went numb. The seven-thousand-dollar deposit I transferred from my book account to cover the cottage payments was gone. I clicked on the last statement to verify checks, deposits, and withdrawals.

"Oh, hell no," I said out loud.

Before moving our belongings down to the cottage for the season, Jake was away for one of his rides. While there, he asked me to transfer the funds to cover payments for the cottage. I did, but looking at the statement, it showed that he withdrew those funds. There was one withdrawal while he was in Virginia, and then another when he was in New York. Now I was in panic mode.

It was possible Jake needed some money in his business account for rescue supplies and intended to transfer it back to the joint account before the cottage payment was due. If so, why didn't he just tell me that? Withdrawing the funds without an explanation just gave me another reason to be suspicious.

I made a note on my calendar to check the account again. If the money didn't reappear, there would be hell to pay. He didn't have access to my accounts, but it was a reminder of why I needed to keep publishing books to stay ahead financially.

After Jake was divorced and we started dating he was living in a small two-bedroom apartment. The court granted his ex-wife permission to stay in his house for three years—it was his before they met— while she saved money to afford a home for her and the two kids. In the meantime, she demanded that he have a place that provided bedrooms for each of his children, so we moved into a lease-to-own house that had three bedrooms to satisfy her request.

Years later when the cottage deal came up, we agreed that Jake would maintain the payment on the lease-to-own, and I provided the down payment and monthly payment for the cottage. I also paid for the renovations, but we both did the work to cut down on the huge expense of a contractor.

Now that I knew of his deception I wanted to keep the cottage, which meant I would be solely responsible for the continued rebuild, the payments, and taxes, and he would remain in the lease-to-own house. He wouldn't easily accept that decision, so I was hoping evidence of his betrayal would help to convince him and avoid mega attorney fees.

Before opening the files from his phone I decided to search his laptop, GoPro, and digital camera first. Then I would save it all on my laptop to go through at the same time to understand the entire picture of what he was up to. If there was that much material on his cell phone, I was sure to find a colossal amount on the laptop; it was like an appendage he couldn't live without. I had the feeling I was going to find a treasure trove of unwanted information.

I set up my desk so that the laptops were side by side with a USB flash drive plugged in to transfer any files or images I found. I typed in the username and password I assumed he was still using. When it worked, I realized just how gullible he thought I was; it never occurred to him I would investigate.

He had no idea just how angry I was. I suspected a woman was having an affair with my husband; that she broke into the cottage, planted cameras to spy on me, and then posted those images online to harm my reputation and future sales of my books. I was beyond pissed off.

I started by scrolling through the folders on his desktop. There were over a dozen, most of them fire-service-related or training classes. He wouldn't include pictures of his affair in work-related folders, just in case he accidentally shared it with other first responders. He would set up personal files.

I clicked on the download file and hit the payload.

There were two personal folders named: #1 and #2. I double-clicked on #1. Inside, there were files for each charity ride he attended in the last two years, noting the location and dates. Since I knew about the D.C. ride, I clicked on that folder just for confirmation: all it contained were photographs and videos of the scenic sights he visited while there. I checked folders for the last few rides and they were the same: scenic images and videos. I realized doing things this way would take a long time. Instead, I tried to search for files for the name Stacy Levin. Two sub-folders showed up. One in the #2 folder and one in the recycling bin. I restored the one from recycling and opened it.

"Oh my God!" I suddenly felt sick.

There had to be over six hundred X-rated selfies of Stacy Levin. I didn't have the stomach to open any of them at the moment, so I made a copy of that folder and sent it to the flash drive to transfer to my computer. In that same folder, there were also a similar number of MP4 videos. I copied those and forwarded them to the flash drive as well.

I was thoroughly repulsed, but I still pushed myself to continue. I double-clicked on the #2 file.

"What the fuck?" I said out loud. The angry tone of my voice caused Bailey to raise her head from her nap, concerned. "Mommy's okay, Bailey, lay down, girl."

When she resumed her position, I went back to my task. This folder had over a thousand selfies, and nearly the same number of MP4 videos, which meant over 1600 selfies with the same number of MP4 videos, so far.

I copied them over, but after seeing so many, it occurred to me I should do some more digging into the motorcycle rides. There was no way Stacy Levin had only been around for the last two rides. She had to have been around for a while to create that many X-rated selfies and take the time to send them to Jake.

I opened my phone and looked for the schedule of charity rides for the last two years. In September 2018, Jake traveled to Colorado. Opening up the #1 folder filled with rides, I searched for the Colorado file. There were two trips: one in 2018 and another in 2019. I opened 2018 and scrolled through the images. WTH! Sure enough, a woman resembling Stacy Levin was riding on the back of the motorcycle. Similar to my feelings about her wearing my helmet, it was a deep sense of betrayal that she had been around so long, and welcomed by the Charity Group as if I didn't exist and it cut deep.

Knowing that I opened each file for each ride location. Stacy Levin showed up at every local and out-of-state charity ride that Jake attended; nearly two years. Gut-wrenching as that was to learn, I knew there was still more to find.

Social media was a good place to start. I searched for her name on *Facebook*. There were a few profiles with that name, but it wasn't hard to find the right page: she had a picture of her with my husband as her profile image. Twenty years together. But this woman had my husband's image plastered on her page. I scrolled recent posts. It was like taking a hit in the solar plexus, and I couldn't breathe.

In November 2018, she posted a photograph of her with Jake on her timeline. He was wearing his motorcycle vest, so I knew they were at a ride location. By viewing the dates in my calendar and seeing the ocean in the background, I realized it was North Carolina. The post read: in a relationship. There were twenty-six comments; most of them from members of the charity group offering congratulations; I could tell because they were all wearing the leather vests with the logo. Then there was a post from one of Stacy's personal friends: *congratulations, who is the guy*?

Stacy responded: *my first responder from Massachusetts*.

"Fuck, fuck, fuck..." As far as I knew, until viewing all the images, Jake had been my first responder for the last two decades. And now, a woman whom I've never met, nor had any of his family and personal friends, was declaring he was hers.

She had a link on the left side of her page for Pinterest. I'm not sure why, but I clicked on it to see her interests. She had two boards: Wedding and First Responder Gifts.

My hand started to shake when I clicked on Wedding: pins for possible wedding dresses.

My husband was living a double life and the biker chick he had been seeing one weekend a month was choosing wedding dresses. I stumbled out of my chair and rushed toward the bathroom, I couldn't hold the vomit in any longer.

CHAPTER 29 - KATIE

Present – May 2020

NEEDLESS TO SAY, I haven't had a good night's sleep since I first got wind of this whole sordid mess, nor has Bailey since she would wake up every time I did. The four-letter words coming out of my mouth were a clear sign of my uncontrollable anger; Olivia would have been proud. I was changing into a person I didn't recognize. It felt like I was the one living the double life, spying and gathering proof of what he had been up to, and then storing it on a password-protected hard drive I purchased. I didn't know there would be so much. I was going to play the game until I had it all; every obscene selfie, video, and scenic image of the two of them together—evidence to protect my future.

Jake could go on thinking I was oblivious; the more at ease he was, the more complacent he would be. He wasn't a man who was suffering from a seven-year itch who had a weekend affair. It took time to film thousands of sexual images and videos, and he saved them all, and I had no clue.

My stomach was so messed up I needed something mild for dinner, so I cooked a plate of scrambled eggs and sliced an apple. I filled Bailey's dish and then sat at the island to eat while she devoured her food, not understanding that her life would change too. After licking her bowl clean, she walked toward me, hoping I would share mine.

"You never share yours," I teased, rubbing her behind the ears.

She stared at me with her puppy-dog face, trying to break my willpower, but the '*Sons of Anarchy*' ringtone on my cell phone alerted me to a call and saved me from her glare.

Caller I.D. said Billy Parker, Jake's younger brother. The mere fact that he was calling put me on alert; we were friends on social media, but he's never called me before.

I tapped the phone icon. "Hello."

"Hey, Katie, it's Billy, how's it going?"

It was the same greeting he always gave me when we'd see each other at the fire department or family gatherings, no matter how much time passed in between.

"Hi Billy, what's up?"

"Jake wanted me to call and let you know he was in a motorcycle accident on Saturday."

"Wh - what?" I struggled to find my voice.

Billy was also a first responder, but he didn't work as often as Jake. They took motorcycle rides together, but as far as I knew, Billy never took part in the charity rides. Jake must have called for his help.

"He's okay; his injuries aren't serious, but he has to remain in the hospital until Monday afternoon."

I paced the kitchen, feeling a twinge of guilt; even though I shouldn't. The last time I saw Jake, he was on the other end of the camera when I was spying on him and Stacy Levin on Saturday morning. I couldn't find them at the after-party, so assumed he took her back to the hotel room. It was hard for me to summon compassion. "What are those injuries?"

He stopped talking for a moment. It sounded like he was holding his hand over the phone and talking to someone in the background; probably Jake, but I couldn't tell, and then he got back on the line.

"His ribs are bruised and he has road rash up and down his face and body, but no concussion, broken bones, or any long-term physical damage."

"That's a relief that there's no long-term damage," I said, trying to keep my voice neutral so my annoyance with Jake didn't come through on the phone. "Why am I just hearing about it now if the accident was Saturday?"

Billy sort of chuckled. "Jake said your number was programmed into his phone, but he couldn't remember what it was. The screen on his phone was shattered by the accident so we couldn't get into it. I took the phone over to Staples to have it repaired and just picked it up."

I glanced at the clock. It was after closing hours for Staples, but there was no point in saying anything; Jake pulled Billy into his web of lies.

"What hospital is he in?"

Before he responded, I heard Jake in the background asking for the phone, and then I heard a commotion.

"Hey Katie," he said in a low voice that made him sound very weak.

"Hey, how are you feeling?" I heard the words come out of my mouth, but since I just filmed him with another woman I wanted to say: who the hell cared how he was feeling?

"I'll be fine," he mumbled. "I'm just going to look like I went a few rounds in a boxing ring for a while. You don't need to come. It's a long drive and I'll probably be out of it, anyway. They gave me a pain pill that's making me groggy; can barely keep my eyes open. Billy said he'd give me a ride home Monday. I won't get out of here until after lunch."

"Are you sure?" I knew exactly why he didn't want me to come, because of Stacy Levin. He made it hard to feel any sympathy. Was she injured, too?

"Yeah, I'm sure. He's going to hang around here tonight so he can deal with the motorcycle in the morning. I have a towing company coming to take it to the repair shop. It will be there for a few days, but it's not that bad. One tire is bad, and I'll have to replace some of the chrome, but nothing mechanically wrong with the bike."

"So I guess you got the brunt of the damage, not the bike?" I recognized the statement as me trying to push buttons. I desperately wanted to ask about her, but I had to force myself not to. Bringing her up would only alert him I had been spying and that I knew she was at the ride. Now was not the time.

"Yeah, I took the hit," he responded in a monotone voice, which made it hard to hear him.

"How did the accident happen?"

There was another commotion, and Billy was back on the line. "Sorry Katie, he's dosing off. You don't have to come down; I'll take care of everything here. If I have any issues, I'll give you another call."

I stopped listening and stared out at the waves while my stomach churned. I couldn't help but notice how weird and evasive they both sounded. I assumed it was because of her. If so, she was probably on the bike when the accident occurred. Was she there in the hospital with them? Facts about the accident would be in the insurance report, which I suspect he would try to hide from me.

After disconnecting from the call, I went into the refrigerator and chugged down a cup of Aloe Vera juice. Then I grabbed Bailey's leash, the flashlight, and took her outside for a walk. I started the aloe regimen each morning since the first day I learned that a woman had been on the back of our motorcycle. I was trying to prevent any health issues from taking over my body from the stress that was invading my mind.

When I was a teenager, I wound up in the emergency room with the most excruciating pain and was coughing up blood. After various tests, the doctor informed me if I didn't ease the stress in my life, I would be in far worse pain from a bleeding ulcer. Growing up with a dysfunctional stepmother who hated me from the day we met affected my psyche and manifested itself into a disease that had been percolating in my body because I kept everything bottled up inside. On the doctor's advice, I did a complete overhaul of my lifestyle; changed my diet and exercise, and to this day, I have not seen my stepmother or any of her siblings.

When Bailey and I returned, I handed her a treat, and then went through my nightly routine: locked the sliding glass door, chained the dead-bolt, closed the blinds, and then went into the bathroom to step into a hot shower. As the water rained down on me and filled the room with steam, I allowed myself a few moments to cry and released the tension. I remained in there for a good twenty minutes, scrubbing the grit and toxins off my body until my skin was raw.

Refreshed and smelling like soap, I grabbed my down pillow and comforter and returned to the family room to curl up on the sofa, which I started doing once I discovered Jake's deception. Bailey hopped up and stretched out at my feet, then wormed her way up along my legs.

Within minutes, I started to dose off and hoped I could sleep through the night, but my nightmares played tricks with me and I woke up in a cold sweat at four a.m. Visions of Jake and the woman flashed before my eyes like a kaleidoscope of neon lights. Sensing my distress, Bailey whimpered and eased up closer. I assumed so she could comfort me, but she just wanted me to rub her belly.

"A little selfish, aren't you, Bailey?"

After trying unsuccessfully to fall back asleep, I gave up and turned on the Smart TV. Aside from Roku and Fire Stick, I had it set up to use as a monitor for my PC hard drive. It had been a while since I used the PC, and Jake never has, so it was unnerving to see it currently connected.

I opened up the desktop, browsed through my programs and files, looking for a clue why it was on. I lined icons for the apps and programs I frequently used on the left of the screen. Personal folders were to the right. I right-clicked each folder to check the date it was last opened. Checking properties on each folder, I determined someone accessed my files on Saturday night when I was in the city spying on Jake. I couldn't have opened the files, and neither could Jake.

Someone was inside the cottage while I was gone!

I clicked on start, pulling up my programs and apps then scrolled down the list. I paused when I came to *OneDrive*. WTH? I uninstalled that from Windows early on because I preferred Dropbox, and I wanted to free up space. Why would it suddenly reappear?

Curiosity getting the better of me, I clicked on it twice to open it. It showed two files: documents and pictures. My heart started pounding. My intuition was telling me I was going to find something I didn't want to. I took a deep breath, clicked on documents, and let out a sigh of relief when I saw that it was empty. I floated the curser over pictures, struggled to swallow, and forced myself to open it. Two more files: Camera imports and screenshots. I almost started laughing. It felt like I was in one of those horror films and with each action; the dun, dun, dun, dramatic music played terrifying the viewer. I clicked on screenshots; another empty. This time I laughed out loud. "Get a grip."

What the hell did I think I'd find? I finally clicked on camera imports, expecting it also to be empty, but there was an MP4 icon titled: watch me. That dreadful feeling seeped back into my body. The smart thing to do would have been to delete without watching and uninstall the program, none the wiser. Unfortunately, the masochist in me won out.

I clicked on the video and the content filled up the entire sixty-inch screen: a dark-haired woman was filming a sexually provocative video of herself with the deliberate intention to arouse sexual desire. She was lying on a bed, blindfolded and naked, with her legs parted, showing her completely waxed vagina.

One hand was holding a spray can of whip cream to draw on her body. She designed little flowers to cover her nipples and then wrote: *Jake is mine*, along with an arrow directed toward said vagina.

Confusion rattled my brain. I thought I was going to be physically sick again. I hurried up to the bathroom, put the toilet seat up, and threw up the bile that had been sitting in my stomach. The last thing I consumed was the Aloe Vera juice. When I had nothing left but dry heaves, I flushed the toilet a few times and poured lavender mix with peroxide to get rid of the smell.

A view of myself in the mirror frightened me. My eyes were red-rimmed and puffy from the crying I had been doing the last few days. I brushed my teeth and rinsed my mouth with cinnamon mouth wash, and then scrubbed my face and hands.

Bailey was sitting in the doorway staring at me, looking sad, as if she could sense something terrible was going on.

"It's okay, pup," I said, lowering myself to her level while I pet her. "Mommy's just having some bad days. We'll get through this."

She followed me out to the kitchen and sat down near the refrigerator. I shook my head at her. "Yeah, I'm onto you; you weren't coming to check on me, you just want me to give you some food. It's a little early, but I guess just this once."

She started doing the Golden Retriever dance; lifting her paw to say please as her tail whipped back and forth. I picked up her bowl, grabbed her food from the refrigerator, and filled it with two cups.

Then I opened the bottle of vitamins for her joints and placed one next to the bowl.

While she devoured her food, I grabbed the jug of Aloe Vera juice and returned to the TV with the video still showing. Yep, I was a masochist. I exited out of the video to turn it off and put my thinking cap on.

Since I uninstalled OneDrive from my computer, someone physically had to reinstall the program, which probably meant they used it on their electronics. Granted, I was discovering a lot about Jake right now that I never knew, but I just couldn't see him doing that. He never used my PC, but more importantly, why would he go out of his way to hide an affair, but then upload a video on my computer revealing that he was?

I checked the properties for the file uploaded to my PC for verification: the date and time showed it was transferred on Saturday night when I was at the hotel spying. But then another thought occurred to me; how could that be? Stacy Levin was with Jake all weekend, I captured them on film. There was no way either of them could be there, and also be on my computer loading the OneDrive file.

That meant it was somebody else.

I thought back to everything My Stalker had been doing and the reality that Jake had been living a double life with Stacy Levin for almost two years. Because of that, I assumed she was the woman stalking me. That she was trying to make my life a living hell so that I would just leave. This new revelation meant somebody else was stalking me. Who else could it be? What was I missing?

CHAPTER 30 - KATIE

Present – May 2020

THE FOLLOWING MORNING, Bailey and I were on our way back from a walk along the water; she was splashing through the waves and trying to convince me to throw some rocks. Jake started that habit when the three of us would walk together, but with his schedule keeping him away so often, she was always trying to convince me. She put her nose down into the sand and pushed a rock forward, and then glanced over at me, dancing in the water to encourage me to throw. I finally gave in, tossed one down the beach, and watched her race through the splashing waves to find it. She found the same one; returned and dropped it at my feet so the game could continue. I enjoyed the back and forth with her and how happy she looked, her tail wagging and her tongue hanging out in her smile.

The act made me wonder how Jake could participate in such a simple thing with us; walking and skipping rocks putting on such a good front like everything was normal, yet he was leading a double life that was so graphically opposite of ours—so scandalous? How could he carry on in the two separate worlds, without me, or any of our friends, realizing something was up? It never occurred to any of us that his mind was so unsettled that he needed to create an entirely separate world. The whole situation was beyond embarrassing.

I stopped for a moment to admire the sun off in the distance and noticed the way the water reflected the blue from the sky. It reminded me that there was beauty all around us, even when we were going through hell. All we had to do was open our eyes.

The sound of Bailey barking brought me back to the present. Seeing her reaction alerted me that someone, or something, was in our yard.

"Who's there, Bailey?" I teased, walking closer. A couple of seagulls chasing each other across the back deck could merely be the reason for her boisterous reaction. A sudden, deep-throated bark verified that her attitude had to do with something more significant than furry little friends. She was in alert mode, tail straight out, hair standing up, and guttural growls in between. Seeing what she was looking at, I was in a panic, too.

A male police officer stood in my driveway and appeared to be surveying the front of my SUV. A second officer, this one female, was knocking at the sliding glass door.

Why would police two officers be visiting me?

The male officer had dark hair, tapered at the sides with a little more volume and style at the top, tall with broad shoulders and long legs, definitely an athlete. He joined the female officer by the door. She, too, was tall, but still a head shorter than her male counterpart. She was fair-skinned with red hair, pulled back tight into a ponytail, and they both wore the mirrored sunglasses.

"Coming," I yelled to them when we reached the sand behind my cottage. As I neared, I could see the patches on their uniforms; Malden Police Department. I tried to think of the reasons MPD would visit me. It was a long drive from Malden to the Cape. Surely, they didn't come to discuss my attempts at spying; Jake didn't even know. And what interest would it be to Malden? Maybe Jake's accident was in Malden? Did the ride go through the area? That was a possibility, but wouldn't that be a matter for the insurance company?

When we reached the deck, Bailey barked and bounded toward them before I could stop her, tail wagging, hoping they were there to play with her.

Some guard dog.

"I'm sorry," I said, embarrassed she'd get hair all over their uniforms. It was a constant complaint from Jake when he dressed for work and headed out the door. "She thinks everybody is here for her."

The officer put his hand out to allow Bailey to get used to his scent and then pet her behind the ears. "I've got one of my own," he said, reassuring me he understood.

The female cop seemed to be more reserved about dogs. She allowed her partner to deal with Bailey while she made introductions. "Katie Parker?"

I nodded. "Yes, I'm Katie and the furry troublemaker is Bailey." I finally corralled her and ushered her inside when I opened the door. "Is something wrong?"

"Can we come in," the female continued "We'd like to talk to you regarding your husband's motorcycle accident."

"His accident?" I said, surprised. Maybe there was more involved. Jake quickly handed the phone back to Billy when I asked how it happened, so I was basically in the dark.

"Your husband informed you, didn't he?"

"He called me about the accident last night from the hospital; did something else happen? Is he okay?"

"It's better if we talk inside," the male officer interjected.

I had an uneasy feeling. Whatever they had to discuss was serious enough for them to drive the distance to the Cape instead of calling me on the phone from their station.

"I'm sorry... of course, come in."

I grabbed Bailey's collar and held onto her as they entered. The female officer led the way, and then I motioned toward the kitchen.

I put Bailey on her dog bed. "Lay down, Bailey... and stay." She observed for a minute to make sure all was okay, then circled her bed until she found the right position so she could still observe us.

"Can I get you something to drink?"

"No, thanks," the female said, speaking for both of them. She removed her sunglasses; her eyes which were in serious mode.

I motioned toward the island chairs, but they remained standing, so I did as well.

"As I was saying," the female continued, "my name is Officer Rollins and my partner is Officer Nichols, we're with the Malden Police Department. We'd like to ask you a few questions if you don't mind."

"Okay," I said, suddenly nervous, considering the circumstances.

She pulled out a notepad and pencil while her partner casually looked around.

"Nice place. Nothing like most of the cottages I've seen down here."

"Thank you," I said. "We knocked down the existing interior structure and rebuilt it."

He raised his eyebrows. "You did the work yourself?"

I shook my head. "Yes."

Officer Rollins frowned, obviously wanting to hurry things along. "Mrs. Parker, you said your husband informed you about the accident, is that right?"

"Yes. His brother Billy called me last night from the hospital. Jake got on the phone, but he was too groggy to say much. They told me it wasn't serious, that he had bruises and road rash, but nothing long-term."

The two officers glanced at each other, both with a look of surprise.

"They didn't say anything more," Officer Nichols asked, genuinely curious.

"No," I said, looking back and forth at both of them with a worried frown. "Is there more?"

Officer Nichols walked toward me, pulled out one of the chairs. "You might want to sit down."

My stomach started doing flip-flops as I sat down. Did Jake lie to me about the accident, too? The female seemed to be the one taking charge, so I kept my eyes focused on her, anticipating the obvious bad news to come.

"Mrs. Parker, were you aware that your husband had a female passenger?"

This was the part that I was dreading. Neither Jake nor Billy mentioned anything about Stacy, so I wasn't sure if she was in the accident with them or at the hospital. Of course, I knew she was with him on

197

the charity ride because I was spying on him, but I wasn't aware of when and where the accident occurred.

"So he wasn't the only individual involved in the incident?"

Officer Nichols was studying my face and body language, obviously to gauge my reaction. "You don't look surprised," he said.

It could have been my imagination, but it sounded like there was a touch of sympathy in his voice, as if he thought I was the lonely, naïve wife at home while the husband was out enjoying life with a mistress.

"Was she injured? Jake didn't say."

Officer Rollins looked toward Nichols again, and her expression seemed to say just how crazy is this woman before she looked back at me.

"Mrs. Parker, I'm afraid the incident was more serious than your husband let on. He may not have suffered any long-term physical injuries, but the woman who was the passenger... well, she died at the scene."

I was sure the blood just drained from my face. If I had been standing, my knees would have buckled from underneath me. "She's... dead?"

CHAPTER 31–KATIE

Present – May 2020

THE ROOM SPUN and my stomach felt like it was going to eliminate its contents, but I had eaten nothing to purge. I'm not sure why, but I kept shaking my head no, almost as if to will the officer to tell me there was a huge mistake. That she was wrong.

"But, how?" I finally said, trying to cling to my sanity, "if he only suffered road rash, what happened to her? I don't understand."

I felt their eyes on me, and I was more than intimidated by the scrutiny. It made me feel as if I had something to hide, which I did. I had been spying on them. They knew Jake was cheating? Was it morbid curiosity? How would the wife react when we informed her?

Officer Rollin's voice was monotone when she explained, "When the motorcycle was struck from behind and skidded across the pavement, it threw the female passenger from the bike into the oncoming traffic in the opposite lane. A truck that couldn't stop in time hit her head-on. She died on impact."

My eyes went wide from shock. "Struck? Oh, my God! Another vehicle hit them?"

Officer Nichols' scrutiny intensified. "Evidence collected at the scene points us in that direction, but the investigation is ongoing."

"There was also a witness who claimed to see a vehicle intentionally speed up before hitting the motorcycle," Officer Rollins added, her face a mask of stone.

"Someone purposely tried to harm them? Did they see the driver?"

"The witness said it happened so fast that they couldn't get a good look at the driver, only that the vehicle was a dark-colored SUV."

And I have a dark-colored SUV, I thought to myself, which would explain why the officer was examining my vehicle.

"There were cameras in the area, so we've got officers tracking those down," Rollins said. "With any luck, we'll get the exact time of the incident and one of them will have a clear image of the driver."

I rubbed my temples with my fingers; I felt a major headache coming on. I was suffering from the delusion that it was a minor motorcycle accident. Jake said a tire was flat and chrome would need to be replaced, but there were no mechanical issues with the bike. How could that be if a vehicle hit them? I also assumed it occurred during the ride when they were moving slow and that he just lost control or something. Barring that, maybe it happened after the ride when they were on their way back to the hotel they'd be staying at for the rest of the weekend. By the horrific scene the officers were describing, I was wrong, so, so wrong, and a woman was dead.

From the minute they arrived, Officer Rollins was the one who shared the information with me, while Officer Nichols paid close attention to my body language, eye movement, and he listened to the words I used to respond. The two of them planned how they would proceed with me before they arrived.

He would be the officer who pretended to be nurturing and caring, and she would do the q and a, and keep her voice monotone. Did he have a dog, or was that just part of the dance to make me feel comfortable?

"Mrs. Parker, when was the last time you saw your husband?" Officer Nichols asked, interrupting my thoughts.

First, I had to remind myself that it was now Monday. "Friday morning."

"Where was this?"

"Here at the cottage, before he left to help set up for the charity ride he was attending."

"I'm familiar with the charity," he said. "I know the gentleman who started it."

"I haven't had the pleasure."

He seemed surprised by that, and Officer Rollins made a notation in her pad.

"Your husband's accident didn't happen during the ride. It happened in our district sometime later. As I said, we're waiting for CCTV cameras to firm up the exact time. Do you know why he would be in our area instead of the after-party?"

I shook my head. "No, I don't. Jake does training in Malden, but I don't think he knows anyone there that he would hang out with."

He nodded, but he didn't seem to understand any more than I did. Now was not the time to admit that I knew she was from New Mexico, and maybe Jake was giving her a tour.

Officer Rollins said, "Mrs. Parker, can you tell us your whereabouts on Saturday, between the hours of three and seven p.m."

"May I ask why?"

She just glared at me, as if it was obvious.

And then it dawned on me; Officer Nichols was inspecting my vehicle when they arrived, and I'm the wife. Of course, they considered me a suspect.

When I still avoided answering the question, she threw in another. "Were you and your husband having marital issues, Mrs. Parker?"

I frowned. How was I supposed to tell them I didn't know we were and that I just recently discovered he had been living a double life? I was just the gullible wife at home, without a clue. I looked back and forth at both of them. "You're both first responders; don't you have marital issues now and then with the hours you put in?"

Officer Nichols held up a ring-less finger, but Officer Rollins averted her eyes; I must have hit a nerve.

She bounced back when she chimed in for the kill. "I'm sorry, but I have to ask; were you aware that your husband was having an affair?"

My eyes moved from his that seemed sympathetic to hers, which left me feeling empty and cold. She held my gaze, and I knew I was in a serious pickle here because I knew.

Officer Nichols seemed to notice my unease. "You okay, or would you like to take a break and come to the station later to finish up?"

I rested my elbows on the island and put my head in my hands. I was in serious trouble here. I didn't have an alibi. I was there during the early part of the day, spying on my husband to catch him having an affair. By early evening I was in the hotel room, by myself, with nobody to verify it. Since I didn't know the time of the accident, I was at a loss.

"You haven't answered my question," Rollins said, with an edge to her voice that let me know she was running out of patience.

"I was there," I said, raising my head back up and facing this head-on. I realized I was making myself look guilty, but I couldn't lie.

Officer Nichols looked at me, surprised. "You're admitting you were at the motorcycle accident?"

I immediately shook my head no. "No. No, not at the… I mean, I was at the charity ride that my husband attended with his, with the woman. Well, not at the ride, exactly, but at the hotel a couple of blocks over, the Hampton Inn."

"You were staying in the hotel?"

"Yes. I only recently learned he was cheating, because someone was sending me emails. I assumed the woman he was seeing sent them, but I needed verification, to see it with my own eyes. The only chance to do that was to show up at the ride."

I could see the wheels turning in their eyes, hers especially; it was almost as if I was making this too easy for her.

"I didn't go anywhere near them; I kept my distance and only used the zoom-in capability on the camera to get photographs and videos. There were thousands of bikers there; they did not know I was even there."

Rollins gave me a pointed look. "Why did you need pictures?"

I looked downcast, embarrassed. "I wanted proof, so when I confronted my husband I would be ready when he lied."

"What did you do after the ride?" Nichols asked.

"As you mentioned, there was an after-party with a band. I was there until the music started. I left because I couldn't find them, so I went back to the hotel."

Rollins glanced up from taking notes. "Can anyone confirm you were at the hotel? Did you order room service?"

I shook my head. "It was a long day; I was emotionally drained, so I remained in the room."

She looked skeptical. "When did you arrive home?"

"Around noon on Sunday," I said, motioning toward Bailey. "I left her with the neighbors, so I took her out to do a run and throw the ball for a while when I returned, and we were back inside the cottage by one o'clock."

"Just so I'm clear," Rollins said. "You knew your husband was cheating and that he was attending the ride with another woman?"

I nodded, but couldn't look her in the eyes; it was too humiliating. "Yes, but my husband didn't know that I knew. He still doesn't."

"You realize that gives you motive?"

I knew that admitting the truth would only make me look guilty, but I was hoping the fact that I was innocent would bear out in the end. "I know how it looks, but I did not harm my husband or that woman. I'm not capable of that."

Rollins dismissed my comment with a smirk and a wave of the hand. "It can push anyone over the edge. You wouldn't be the first woman to snap after discovering her husband was cheating and seeing it up close."

"Except I didn't," I said, my voice resolute. It surprised me how level-headed I had been under the circumstances.

"We follow the evidence."

I nodded. "I understand."

They walked toward the sliding glass door to have a private conversation. They periodically looked back at me, making observations in their minds. I did a few ride-a-longs with police officers and detectives when researching information for my books. I've seen them in action enough to know these two were just doing their jobs, that it was nothing personal. Still, it was humiliating to be the one accused.

"Mrs. Parker, we're in the preliminary stage of the investigation," Rollins said, walking back toward me. "If you're willing to cooperate, we'd like to take your car in to have it looked at… or if you'd prefer we could get a warrant."

Officer Nichols added, "It's also the quickest way to eliminate you as a suspect."

"So I am a suspect?"

Officer Rollins cocked her head to the side. "To be perfectly blunt, Mrs. Parker, you, yourself, established you had motive, and the front of your bumper has a huge dent in it."

~~~

I stared at the dent on the right side of my front bumper and the shattered headlight, probably more stunned than they were at the evidence in front of me. The driver of the police tow truck connected the vehicle, making sure it was secure, got out to check the brake lights, and then hopped back up into his rig and dragged my vehicle away.

Officer Nichols gave me a look of sympathy and handed me his business card. "My contact information if you can think of anything else that might be beneficial to the case."

"We'll be in touch," Rollins added as they both stepped back into their patrol car and pulled out of my driveway.

How did I get a dent in my bumper? I had not been in a motor vehicle accident since I purchased the vehicle, and I would remember if anyone or anything else hit my car. Something nefarious was going on, but it sounded so ludicrous, I struggled to even say it out loud. Could the same person who broke into the cottage and purposely placed the sexually explicit video on my PC also have stolen my vehicle and used it to crash into Jake's motorcycle, hoping to frame me?

CHAPTER 32 – KATIE

Present – May 2020

AFTER THE OFFICERS left, I sat down at my desk and stared outside for a few minutes. Sensing my distress, Bailey came toward me and placed her head in my lap. "I can't believe this is happening," I said out loud, almost wishing Bailey could respond and make the pain go away.

Things had gotten way out of control.

A woman was dead. The fact that I was questioned by police officers and my car towed because they thought I could have used it in an attempt to harm them was beyond crazy. Somebody dented my bumper and smashed my headlight, or they physically used my vehicle to make me look guilty.

This was no longer a simple case of stalking the wife to convince her to leave. Whoever was doing this wanted me eliminated on a long-term basis. Feeling another surge of anger coming on, I gave Bailey one last pet behind the ears and then stood up. "Mommy's got something to do, and then we'll go for a golf cart ride."

With Bailey at my heels, I grabbed the box of large trash bags from the kitchen drawer, walked into the master bedroom, and opened my closet door. Looking through the winter section of my clothes, I pulled all the Harley leather jackets off the hangers and dropped them in a bag. The storage container on the top shelf was full of tank tops, chaps, long-sleeve shirts, and scarves; I dumped all of them into the bag. Two Christmases ago, Jake bought me a pair of

Harley boots, so I grabbed them from the bottom and added them. I added anything in my closet that was given to me, or I purchased to wear when riding the motorcycle.

Next, I scoured the contents of my lingerie drawer. On Valentine's Day, Christmas, and sometimes on birthdays, Jake would buy me matching Victoria's Secret outfits, mostly thong and bra sets. I gathered them all up and, with pleasure, dropped them down into the bag.

I glanced around the room, noticed a picture of us hanging on the wall. We were both seated on the Ultra Classic Harley that I bought him before he got involved with the charity. We used to take it on rides to see the changing seasons. His brother, Billy, and his wife were with us; they snapped the picture on their digital camera and emailed us a copy. I removed it from the wall and added it to my collection. Then I thought better of it and put it back on the wall; he might notice it was missing. I filled up both bags, so I hauled them outside and put them on the back of the golf cart. I went back inside and was ready to toss the Harley cookie jar Jake bought for Bailey's treats but decided against it. Jake might not notice right away if my things missing, but he would notice if Bailey's cookie jar was, since he spoiled her with treats every day. I also held off on trashing the collar and chain he bought her at Christmas.

"Let's go for a ride, Bailey," I said as I grabbed the key for the golf cart and headed outside.

I made a left turn out of the driveway and turned right at the end of the cul-de-sac. I followed the winding road to the end, traveling as fast as the golf cart would allow, which was less than twenty miles per hour—5 when going over the speed bumps. When I reached the end, there was a recreation building and sports park for members of the community. They positioned four trash dumpsters off to the right, next to the public parking lot.

I pulled over to the side of the road, let the cart idle, but put the emergency brake on. "Bailey, stay," I said. Then I walked to the back of the cart and picked up both trash bags.

Standing in front of one of the trash dumpsters, I paused for a moment to analyze the events of the last two days: the feelings I had when I discovered Jake had been cheating, the stalking and images of me being posted, and the humiliation of being questioned by two Malden police officers. I took a deep breath and let it out, then tossed the bags into the dumpster and stepped back into the golf cart.

"Let's go to the park, Bailey." I stepped back into the cart, let out the emergency brake, and pulled into a parking spot for the recreation center. As I turned off the key, Bailey jumped down onto the pavement in a hurry to go. I grabbed the chain and dog bags from the compartment, pulled the key out and dropped it in my pocket, and then followed her to the track. For the first time since the whole ordeal started, a subtle feeling of calm washed over me. I knew the angst would return, but for a moment, everything was okay.

CHAPTER 33 - MY STALKER

Present – May 2020

I WAS PARKED two streets away from Katie's cottage and fast-walked the streets dressed like a jogger out for a morning run with my lightweight backpack over my shoulders. It was almost six a.m., not dark, but the fog from the ocean gave me the illusion of secrecy. Katie's neighbors were at their cottages this weekend, but I assumed they would still be inside for at least another hour or more. The cottage obstructed their view anyway.

I still had the keys I confiscated from Jake's truck to open the sliding-glass door. I only needed a minute inside. The spare key to Katie's car was right where I saw it last; dangling on a hook by the kitchen closet with other sets of keys. I grabbed it and hurried back outside, locking the door behind me. I knew Katie wouldn't catch me. I knew where she was; spying on Jake at the motorcycle ride. I knew because I went there on Friday to do the same thing. I saw when her friends dropped her off at the hotel and watched her walk into the bar where the meet and greet was scheduled wearing that goofy getup trying to look inconspicuous.

After seeing her there, I realized it would be smarter if I hung back and observed who came and went from the hotel lobby. I saw her again when she exited the side entrance of the bar hoping to leave and then happened to see Stacy Levin walk into the hotel. The stunned look in her eyes followed by the pain of betrayal was worth the trip. That was when I devised my plan. Both women were in my crosshairs now. Hopefully, I could knock them both out of the equation with one act.

I stepped into her SUV and turned over the engine; took a minute to check the fuel gage and odometer in case I needed to fill the tank or worry about the mileage. One last look to make sure the neighbors had no view, and then I reversed out of the driveway and made my way toward the city. It was early, hours before the ride would start, but that was okay. I needed to recon first.

I knew from reading Jake's private Facebook messages that he and his skank were going to do a little sightseeing after the charity ride instead of going to the after-party. All I had to do was scope out the area he mentioned, find the perfect spot to do what I intended, and then find an acceptable place to park until it was time to follow them.

They mapped the route designated for the ride on the charity website in advance. I studied it, checked the street names where Jake planned to go sightseeing, and then found a spot to park the SUV. It was perfect. I could hide in the crowd of residents viewing the start of the ride to see the skank up close, then jog back to the SUV and be ready to tail them when they returned.

~~~

It was late afternoon. The location where I parked and waited was a twenty-minute walk from the dealership where the ride ended. I could hear the sounds of the engines the minute they returned and felt the rumbling sensation from the thousands of

211

bikes that traveled the route. I kept my ears alert and added a few images and posts to Facebook, did some more spying on Katie and the skank, and then engaged in a conversation with an individual who could account for my time on social media if asked at a later date. I had my phone location turned off, so he would assume I was at home.

My blood was already boiling from seeing Jake with the out-of-town skank. There were so many similarities between us it was like looking in a mirror; which gave me a bit of satisfaction. He craved me; I knew that deep in my bones, but he also feared that I would upset his perfect little world. She looked like me, tried to act like me, and wanted to give him the sexual gratification that I did, but she was safe because she lived thousands of miles away. I knew what he was doing. I also knew he couldn't exist without me feeding his addiction. Katie could never do so. And this skank—no matter how hard she tried—would never replace me. I would see to it.

When the noise subsided, I knew the ride was over. Jake would hang around for the speech by the founder of the charity before they went sightseeing, so I resumed my social media posts and kept my eyes alert for his motorcycle. Reading the message he wrote to the skank, I knew what streets he would take to get to his first destination. When I saw them, I turned onto Eastern Avenue and followed them from a few car lengths back. Most of the residents in the surrounding towns knew of the major charity ride, so there were very few vehicles on the road, none on this street at the moment. That would change later in the day after they realized the ride was over.

When I first came up with my plan, the goal was to torment them and hopefully stroke a little fear in Jake's passenger, leaving him to assume Katie was responsible. Watching them at the start of the parade convinced me to revise that tactic. As we moved along, I observed the two of them completely oblivious to the fact that they were being followed, and the anger that had been percolating inside me turned into full-blown hysteria and I was about to explode. Stacy Levin had her arms wrapped around his waist and kept leaning forward, kissing his neck. It wasn't enough that she tried to seduce him with her selfies and videos. Now she was trying to entice him on the open road. It infuriated me, sending me into a fit of rage worse than I had ever felt before. Katie allowed this.

It was no longer enough for me to just scare her. I was crazed.

After two miles on Eastern, I knew they would make a left turn on Main just up ahead. Their first destination was not too far away. It was time to act. I looked in the rear-view and side mirrors. There was nobody behind me, and no one coming in the opposite direction. Fury was blinding me. The minute Jake got into the left-hand lane, easing out to make the turn, I sped up and followed. I took a hard left and pressed the gas pedal to the floor, then rammed the right side of the SUV into the motorcycle, and then continued into a U-turn to wind up on Eastern going in the opposite direction.

I slowed down to view the fallout of my deed through the rear-view mirror: the motorcycle skidded across the pavement with Jake trying to maintain control. What I didn't expect: Stacy Levin was thrown from the bike and rolled into the opposite lane. I heard the unexpected sound of squealing tires from a pick-up truck when the driver slammed on the brakes. A loud thud followed. I knew then that the results of my actions were far more serious than the torment I planned—and possibly even deadly—though I couldn't summon up a reason to care.

I did another sweep of the area. That's when I saw a vehicle sitting on the side of the road on Madison Street, the next street over. I didn't notice them the first time I looked. I shrugged it off. There was no reason to panic. If there was anyone inside the vehicle who happened to witness the incident the vehicle was registered to Katie. Same for the CCTV cameras that might have captured the vehicle in the area; the wig and clothing I was wearing were selected so Katie would take the fall. All I had to do was return the SUV to the driveway, wipe any fingerprints away, and make sure the gas tank was at the same level it was when I stole it. I wasn't worried about the odometer. After giving it some thought, I realized Katie wasn't the type to check her mileage; she wouldn't have noticed that someone took her vehicle and used it with the intent to do bodily harm. The further away I got from the scene, the more exhilarated I got. Jake could be mine sooner than even I had planned.

CHAPTER 34 - KATIE

Present – May 2020

I SAT DOWN on the back deck and draped an arm around Bailey when she sat at my feet. Golden Retrievers were very sensitive dogs, loyal to their owners. She sensed my anxiety and wouldn't leave my side. I kept my eyes on the ocean and watched the waves turn to luscious white foam as they rolled over the sand and allowed the calming effect to take over as they ebbed back out to sea. I was trying to come up with answers. If I turned off the pressure for a bit and allowed the questions just to flow maybe I could figure out what I've been missing.

If the woman Jake was having the two-year sex-fest with was killed, well murdered, according to the police; then who was stalking me? I was so sure it was Stacy Levin; that she was doing so because she hoped I would leave. That seemed to be the logical answer. From her social media announcement, she believed they were in a relationship, and her Pinterest account revealed that she planned on getting married. Jake already had a wife. That's why I assumed *she* sent me the photographs.

I knew I sounded cold dismissing her death and only focused on me. But to be fair, I didn't know her. I was sorry that she was killed, sorry for her family if she had one, but she was having an affair with my husband; a very obscene one at that. The fact that he had been married for two decades didn't seem to matter to her. Maybe sympathy would come later. Right now, I just didn't have the time.

If it wasn't her; then who was it?

Who would have had access to her photographs and videos, and felt the need for me to see them? The time stamp on the video revealed that it was sent during the motorcycle ride.

I changed tactics and viewed the situation like I would a plot for a book. Jake was a character. He was married, yet having an affair. Somebody was following and stalking his wife. If not the woman he was having the affair with, who else would feel the need? Someone purposely rammed a vehicle into his motorcycle, killing the woman. That sounded like the act of someone personally involved; a crime of passion, which was why I was under suspicion. If it wasn't the wife, the individual personally harmed by the affair, who else would commit such a violent act?

Then something dawned on me. I had been so focused on myself that I couldn't see what was in front of my eyes. This wasn't about me; it was about Jake. Whoever was stalking me; could have also stalked Stacy. According to Stacy's social media, she had never been married and a recent post indicated her ex-boyfriend just got married. That told me there could be another female involved in the situation.

"Okay, Bailey," I said, petting her for a few minutes to let her know she wasn't being neglected, "mommy has to do something disgusting to try and get the truth. You want one of your bones?"

She licked her jowls at the mention of a bone and stared at me with eager eyes; willing me to move. I got up and she followed me back into the kitchen, where I grabbed one of her marrow bones from the refrigerator. After cutting away the plastic wrap, she gave me her paw, so I handed it to her and she disappeared over to her dog bed, perfectly content.

Since this whole mess began, I started storing all the evidence in a portable safe I purchased at Home Depot. I grabbed the key from a paper clip container, opened the lock, and returned the key—making sure it was hidden from view among the clips. I had also purchased a cheap laptop so that I wouldn't have to view any of Jake's double life on the one I used for my writing. Even though I have the PC, I only used it as a safety precaution. I preferred the freedom of using laptops and not being confined to one location. Whoever uploaded the video onto my PC didn't know I rarely used it.

I retrieved the new laptop and portable hard drive from the safe, sat down in the leather chair at my desk, but positioned it so that if Billy brought Jake home earlier than expected he wouldn't be able to see the screen.

After typing in my new password and waiting for the drive to load, I opened up a folder that I titled: Gotcha. Little did I know; there was so much evidence I had to keep adding folders inside. Between Jake's phone, laptop, GoPro, word docs containing texts and emails, and the digital camera scan disks I found, there were over two thousand images and the same number of videos saved. There were more; I just got so disgusted by the content that I didn't open two scan disks from the digital camera or check his tablet. Though it occurred to me, I might find his text messages saved on the tablet if I felt the need to see the words he used to converse with her.

Unfortunately, now I needed to go through the smut to see if I could find the answer. Before I knew about Jake's sexual affair, I assumed the stalker had something to do with my books since they kept showing at signings. Now I knew better.

Stalking, breaking into my home, and terrorizing me with a motorcycle were fear tactics used when I didn't get the message. Now, it was obvious things had escalated. Whoever rammed into Jake's motorcycle was after me, too.

I breathed in and out; there was no time to dwell. I right-clicked on the first folder I created: double-life #1. When viewing the properties it showed there were sixteen hundred jpeg images inside the folder. Opening it, I scrolled from beginning to end, doing a cursory glance at the images, getting nauseous during the process. They were all images of Stacy Levin; selfies, she took on her cell phone. In some, she was naked, posing in revealing sexual positions or using sexual tools. In others she dressed in push-up bras and thongs, pretending to be tied up or in other sexually provocative positions. They were all sent to Jake's phone through text message.

Next, I checked properties for the first image: created in September 2018, the first month they allegedly met at the Colorado ride. I scrolled down and right-clicked on the last image in the folder to check properties. She created it two days before the motorcycle crash.

I couldn't wrap my head around that behavior. She had to have taken two or three sexual selfies a day during the time she knew Jake. And that was only from the images in this "double-life" file. From everything I've learned they only saw each other when there was a charity ride; one weekend a month—usually Friday to Sunday night, except for two occasions when he extended his stay. During their time apart, she felt the need to send the selfies and videos to keep his interest.

She took sexual images at the gym; in the tanning booth; in the shower; when she was at work as a hospital assistant in the bathroom stall—which was disturbing all by itself. Who does that?

Every image was sexually and luridly suggestive, bordering on obsession and maybe even a touch of voyeurism, similar to what I had been thinking about Jake since my discovery. They both became addicted like a magnet to each other.

Frustrated, I closed that folder and right-clicked on the second file: properties showed over two thousand MP4 videos. I opened the file: double-life #2. Since they were videos, I would have to view the content. Only a masochist could do so. But how else was I going to find what I was looking for?

Taking another deep breath, I right-clicked the first video, created in October 2018. That meant Stacy started sending selfies and then graduated to videos a month into their scandalous affair.

Was I really going to do this?

My mind was begging me to stop, but I pressed on. If I was a detective trying to find a stalker in one of my novels, this is what I would have to do. I was saving the real cops from the trouble.

I opened the first video and pushed play to view and then immediately closed it after a few seconds. I did the same for the first two rows of videos after seeing the content. They were all close to three minutes long. Each one showed Stacy in a different location: a bed; a shower or tub, floor in front of a fireplace, an outside deck, a bathroom stall at work, or a tanning bed. She was playing out lurid and raunchy sex acts like that of a porn star to keep the temptation alive in Jake.

I didn't think anything could repulse me more, but I would be wrong...

I chose an MP4 mid-page and right-clicked to see if the dates corresponded: this one was created in December 2018—three months after they met. Thinking back, this particular video was made during the time I was down at the cottage for several days painting the rooms after renovations were complete. Jake had to work and hated the smell of paint, so he stayed at the lease-to-own house. My heart started racing from the immediate suspicion that was going through my mind. Bracing myself, I opened it and pushed play.

I was certain I stopped breathing when the video opened on the screen.

This time Stacy Levin wasn't the only participant, and I recognized the room. It was my bedroom in my home. While I was down at the cottage painting, she flew into town so she and Jake could get a quick fix. She was lying on top of the brand new denim bedspread and duvet I bought myself for Christmas. She was blindfolded, hands and ankles tied to the bedposts, and the scene that played out was like watching a low-rated porn flick. There was no fore-play or romance. It was all robotic. No emotion involved. Just sex acts performed by two individuals who seemed to be void of feelings from the looks on their faces and a man who seemed to be the one in control—my husband, Jake.

I felt sick.

Disgusted and repulsed.

He did this in our home.

I viewed a few more videos and realized they were more of the same, just in different locations. The videos she filmed alone were all pornographic to feed his addiction when they were apart. The videos of the two of them revealed a man who was not the one I had always known. Viewing them had me more dumbfounded than ever.

Jake had never asked me to take sexually explicit pictures or videos, nor had he shown an interest in tying me up, blindfolding me, or needing to be in control. When we met, I was the more creative one, sexually, just not to the point of bondage, or needing to film raunchy and unemotional sex. For me, sex had to do with love and romance. There were no feelings or romance in any of the videos I viewed of the two of them. The only explanation that made sense was that it was just physical, sexual acts to get off on.

Then I remembered a conversation not too long ago. Olivia, Madison, and I had been sitting by the fire talking about the success of the *Fifty Shades of Grey*. None of us had read the books or seen the films, but as a writer, I was curious about the success when they first came out, so I read reviews on an author site. Most of the comments were like my own thoughts: I had no desire to be with a man that abused a woman or felt the need to be in control, whether in or out of the bedroom.

Jake had overheard part of our conversation when he was cutting wood, and he said: "One woman's revulsion is another woman's fantasy."

I didn't give it much thought, because I didn't know he was cheating. I thought he was just taking part in the conversation. Seeing the evidence now, it made more sense. Jake met a woman that introduced him to her lurid lifestyle. She supplied all the tools and paraphernalia to play out those acts, and the physical reaction consumed him. It became about control and power; an addiction, his drug of choice, and he had to have it. As an adrenaline junkie, he probably viewed our sex life as stagnant and boring after twenty years, but he wasn't willing to give me up because I fit the persona he wanted to create for his peers. Instead, he created a secondary secret life.

Since I didn't attend the charity rides, those that did would only know what Jake shared with them. Stacy Levin knew about me, but our twenty-year marriage didn't stop her. Nobody would know about her obsession with selfies and videos, because Jake would never allow them to. That would remain hidden from his actual world. He was all about appearances.

My curiosity piqued, I closed out that file and went back to the jpeg selfies. I scrolled through the dates and looked for those during December 2018. Sure enough, there were several. Jake had to work one of the days she was in town, so she spent the time taking selfies of herself in my shower, and in my bed. Nobody would ever understand the humiliation I felt.

There was no doubt in my mind; if Jake walked through the door right then, I would have kicked him in the balls.

As sick as all of that was to absorb, I was still no closer to learning who was stalking me. What didn't I know? There were two scan disks I hadn't opened yet, would there just be more content of Stacy Levin, or something else? Would the tablet answer my question? I reached into the safe, opened a small plastic container, and grabbed the two disks. Inserted one of them into the card reader on the laptop and clicked start. The minute it started to load, I sat upright; worried I might find something worse than what I discovered so far. I was right to worry: more selfies and videos.

My hands started to shake, almost as if my subconscious knew answers before my mind did. I opened one of them and pushed play.

OMFG!

CHAPTER 35 - KATIE

Present – May 2020

I WAS VIEWING another sex video, only Stacy Levin didn't have the starring role. I knew that because the woman in the video resembled Stacy, but this one had a tribal-design tattoo on her lower back which was visible due to the sexual position she was currently in.

The two women were similar in looks; close to the same height and body type, both had long, dark hair, only Stacy died hers in the bluish-black tint, and they both spent too much time tanning.

Jake had been living a secret life, two times over…

Every reason I conjured up for why Jake succumbed to the world Stacy invited him into now had to be discarded by the revelation of this other woman who seemed to be a little more on the naughty side than Stacy.

Who the hell was she, and where did he meet her?

Fuck!

I already had enough information to use against Jake, but for some reason, I kept going. There was something inside me that needed to know it all. As I continued to browse the images and videos, I saw one with this woman standing near the Harley Davidson Ultra Classic Electra Glide motorcycle—the one that I picked out and bought for him.

Son of a bitch!

During the early years of our marriage, Jake bought a Kawasaki Vulcan 900. It was great for traveling around town, just not on long rides. The furthest we could go was Vermont or New Hampshire in the fall to view the fall leaves and coastal rides during summer.

We talked about getting a touring bike, but he mentioned he didn't like the loud exhaust on most Harley's; my prerequisite was a comfortable back seat. I found the Ultra Classic online one day, viewed all the images then talked to the sales manager at the dealership about the noise. I didn't mention it to Jake until I knew it would meet both of our requirements.

We both loved the bike the day we went to the dealership to see it in person. His desire was fire engine red, but he liked the burgundy color when he noticed all the chrome, pinstripes, and added fixtures of the anniversary special. It was a classy motorcycle and garnered a lot of attention because of the design and detail. That was long before he got involved in the charity rides, and long before he was hooking up with Stacy Levin.

"Fuck, fuck, fuck," I said out loud, tormented beyond belief. How could I have been so stupid? Olivia would be so proud of my new language right about now.

I rested my arms on the desk and put my head down for a minute so I could regroup. Truthfully, I just wanted to curl up in a fetal position on the sofa and cry. I probably said the f-bomb once or twice in my life, both times when I was doing renovations— one when I came face to face with a copperhead snake. In the last few days, I couldn't stop them from flying out of my mouth. I sat back in my chair, frustrated, angry, oh so angry, and a whole plethora of other feelings that were running through my head.

How could I find out who she was?

Maybe she was on his Facebook. I didn't want to scroll his page using my profile, so I signed in under my pen name: JR Harris. I only used that account for book-related information so he wasn't a follower. I went to the search bar and typed in Jake Parker. It stunned me to see two profiles show up. One page he used for work and personal, so he and I were friends. The second page was private and used for his double life. He blocked me from access. What kind of man blocked his wife from his page; obviously, a man leading a double life who took intentional steps to keep it a secret.

He didn't know that I could view his private page using my JR Harris profile. I never spied on him, so he was free to behave like the scoundrel he was. I can't even fathom how stupid I must have been.

His privacy settings wouldn't allow me to see his friend list, but I could tell most of them were with the charity. Browsing posts, most of the profile images were of individuals wearing the leather vest and logo. The only way to track her down if she was a friend would be to read comments to some of his posts and see if anyone fit her description.

The very first post was a glaring reminder of just how morbid our life had become. It was a notice for a memorial service for Stacy Levin, posted by the secretary for the charity with Jake's name tagged so it would show up on his page. I couldn't help but wonder what excuse Jake would give me for needing to attend a memorial service in New Mexico, where she lived.

I looked through the images of those that responded; there wasn't anyone that fit the description, so I continued. I scrolled down the entire page and didn't get lucky until I came to an image regarding 9/11. Like most firefighters, that date meant a lot to Jake. When he saw the news and watched the towers fall, it coincided with his days off at the firehouse. Instead of picking up training classes, he packed a bag and drove to New York to help search for bodies in the rubble. It cut deep with him. Each anniversary he would post an image that he captured while there. It was a comment on that image I hit pay dirt.

Her name was Lexi Thompson, and the image in her profile was an outfit I've seen many times: ripped jeans with a revealing white tank top. It was uncanny how similar the two women were to each other. Stacy's hair was darker, but unless one had a close-up it was hard to tell them apart. I had been viewing them through selfies and videos, and only discovered they were two different individuals because of the tattoo on the lower back.

I clicked on Lexi's profile to view her page. This woman didn't care about privacy issues. Her entire life was advertised through photographs and posts, and I devoured it all. She was also more than a flirt. Her habit was to post provocative images to get a reaction out of the men on her page. It occurred to me that Jake was probably not her first patsy. When I finished scrolling and saving anything of importance, I did an internet search to see if I could find an address. Unfortunately, I couldn't find a listing for her. Once I did, it would be time to stalk the stalker.

CHAPTER 36 – KATIE

Present – May 2020

OLIVIA AND MADISON sat impatiently at Olivia's kitchen table, receiving the overdue update on everything that happened since our last conversation. When the police officers were questioning me my phone pinged a few times signaling they were sending me frantic texts, especially once they saw my SUV being towed. I was able to stall them for a bit, mainly because I was embarrassed to tell them everything I learned, but they kept up the pressure until I finally consented to sit down and tell them the awful reality. Learning the truth about Jake didn't just have an impact on me. Olivia, Madison, and their husbands had been good friends to us; it would impact all of us.

It wasn't easy to admit that Jake didn't just allow groupies to ride on the back of the motorcycle, or have a brief liaison. It would be just as disturbing for them to learn he was having salacious sexual relationships with two different women. And that he created a double life that we would want no part of, and worked hard to keep it a secret? I informed them he set up a private page where he communicated with those of his secondary world, but he blocked those of us in his normal world from having access. And now, one of those women was dead, and I was a suspect in that death, or at the very least, a person of interest.

I told them everything. That I found thousands of obscene images and videos, the majority of which the filmmaker participated in bondage, the use of various sex tools, and unemotional sex fitting of a low-rate porn film.

"Ohmigod," Madison said, her hands flying to her mouth in shock.

"You physically saw the videos?" Olivia asked, her eyes showing it repulsed her.

I nodded, tears welling up in my eyes, the humiliation palpable.

Madison sensed how distressed I was; she stood and wrapped her arms around me. "I'm so sorry; all of this has to be horrific for you."

Olivia sat in stunned silence. "I defended him. I couldn't fathom that Jake would even cheat; this is beyond the realm of comprehension."

I nodded. "It's repulsive and nauseating, not just because the man I lived with for the last twenty years is capable of doing this, but because I had absolutely no idea. I don't know what bothers me more; that he could do it, or that I have been so clueless."

"He kept it hidden," Madison reminded me.

"But how could I not know? Sensed it, or at least seen some of the signs?"

Olivia shook her head. "It's worse than we thought, so much worse. Katie, none of us knew. Madison and I were defending him, telling you he couldn't possibly cheat. We've been just as clueless."

"Yes, but I live with the man. He's never even indicated to me that he was interested in that lifestyle. How do you hide something like that and for nearly three years—that I know of?"

"What you're describing is so far from the reality of the person we've known," Madison added.

"Honestly, I'm having trouble believing it. I know it's true, you saw the images, but I can't process it."

"I researched the dates for when it all started and tried to think back to his behavior. Honestly, I can't pinpoint anything that gave me an inkling that something was up, or things were off between us. Between work and his training classes he was always gone, but that was the case even before I met him. The only change was that he added the motorcycle rides. His behavior toward me never changed. But now I know; every time he took off for private training or a ride, he was meeting up with a woman playing fifty shades, then returning home pretending we were the normal couple."

"He had us all fooled," Olivia said, her voice laden with anger.

"While I was at home taking care of the house, cooking his meals, and doing his laundry, he was viewing the selfies, porn images, and videos on his cellphone. Right there, with me in the room. When I was down at the cottage finishing up the renovations and painting, she flew into town and they filmed their shenanigans in our house, on my bed, with my brand new denim comforter. *My comforter*. Was it even washed before I returned home? So disgusting. She took images and videos in my home!"

This time, Olivia joined in with the embrace, and the three of us stood like that, soaking it all in. When we took our seats again, it was easy to see all three of us were confused and feeling foolish because we didn't have a clue.

"It's just so hard to fathom," Olivia said with a sigh.

Madison nodded, "He's acting like a man obsessed."

"Worse," I said. "I think he has a sex addiction."

"Is there such a thing?" Madison inquired.

"Oh, yes," Olivia said. "Search the internet. I remember some years ago when a few celebrities admitted they had a problem and went into rehab. And don't forget the recent admission by that golf pro married to the gorgeous wife with two children."

"Oh, right," Madison said, nodding, "His story sounds similar; he kept his many liaisons private."

"We only know about them because they're celebrities," Olivia added, "It's a lot more common than we know, but few admit it in public."

"The porn industry profits," I said.

My body suddenly went still, and a moment of gloom washed over me. "It just occurred to me; I have to get checked out. Get tested."

I had unknowingly been having sex with my husband of twenty years while he was having raunchy encounters with other women, and from what I saw in the videos, they were not concerned with protection.

"Oh, Katie," Madison said, her hands reaching over to cover mine. "I didn't even think of that."

"Shit," Olivia said, outraged. "You know nothing about their other partners or sexual habits. They're adults who should have known better."

I nodded, shaking my head in disgust. "And one of them is a medical assistant in a hospital who had the disturbing idea to film herself going to the bathroom. That was sick all by itself."

"Gross," Olivia responded.

"From what I viewed on social media, I know one of them slept around. I have no choice; I need to make an immediate appointment."

I didn't know about Stacy Levin's sex life; her bathroom behavior gave me concern, but it was pretty clear from viewing Lexi Thompson's page that she was not discerning about partners.

"Do you want to use my gun and shoot the son of a bitch?" Olivia said sarcastically. "I have a concealed carry and keep one in the safe here at the cottage."

"There is no doubt; Jake is pushing me."

"You would never do that; you're too level-headed," Madison said.

I smirked. "And look where that got me. Jake's lucky I haven't grabbed his gun and shot him. After what I've discovered, a judge might say I was justified."

While we sat there commiserating and discussing the situation, I saw Jake's brother, Billy, pull into the driveway to drop Jake off. Now I needed to prep myself to face him.

Jake stepped out of the passenger side, retrieved a duffle bag from the back seat, and shut the door. He waved to Billy, and then the truck reversed out of the driveway. Jake's movements were slow; he was still in pain. He walked toward the bar on the deck and reached into the refrigerator. I could see him clearly from the motion-activated light that lit up the area. His body took a beating.

"He was right, he looks like he went a few rounds in the boxing ring."

"Too bad it wasn't from you," Olivia said, dead serious.

Until I presented them with the facts; she and Madison hoped Jake wasn't capable of having a full-on affair. Even after I caught him with Stacy Levin at the charity ride, something still convinced them he couldn't go through with actual cheating. They thought he may have liked the attention he received from a groupie and enjoyed having someone on the back of the bike, but they still couldn't picture him having a sexual affair. His behavior didn't fit with the man we've known. They spent more time trying to reassure me he was so enamored with me so much that he could never do that, especially not with that type of woman. Come to find out, he wasn't just carrying on with one of those types of women.

"Two of them," I said, feeling the disgust resurfacing again. I would need to get control of my emotions before I went home.

Madison kept shaking her head. "We now know that it is true, but it is still so hard to comprehend. The Jake we know is all about appearances. How long did he think he could keep this hidden, and people in his ordinary life wouldn't find out; his family, work, and personal friends? He'd be mortified to know we discovered the truth."

"He methodically set up his double life," I said, saddened by the realization that I had been a fool. "If it wasn't for the stalker…"

I studied Jake's mannerisms as he moved about on the deck. Could the signs of malcontent have been there all along, and I just missed them? We all missed them? Or was he so good at keeping the two lives

234

separate that I could have gone on forever without ever having known? What if I didn't have a stalker, or receive those photographs? What if the motorcycle incident hadn't happened that took the life of another? Would I still be living in my bubble, unaware of what he was up to? The thought made me cringe from embarrassment.

I watched him pull a tea out of the refrigerator, open it and take a drink, then walk toward the sliding glass door. Was it killing him inside that a woman he was sleeping with was now dead? I couldn't tell. Like the police; did he think I might have something to do with it?

"I can already see the damage he's done to you," Madison said, wiping away a tear that escaped her eye.

"My heart is shattered, so much so, that I don't even feel sympathy seeing him injured. He didn't even bother to warn me about the police coming to question me; unless they didn't tell him. Maybe he doesn't know my car was towed, and just assumes I'm out at the store."

Olivia put her hand over mine; her own heart shattered over the agony I was suffering through. "We're here for you, Katie. Anything you need from us, just ask."

"Anything, Katie," Madison added, both of them just as unsure about my future as I was at that moment in time.

"I've been thinking… how do you feel about pretending we don't know anything, at least until I get the book done?"

They glanced at each other. "If that's what you want us to do," Olivia said, "but I'm not sure how you mean."

"I think we should continue to act as if nothing has happened; we know nothing about him cheating. At least give me the time to get the book done and handed over to you so you can edit it. I need to get all my ducks in a row, mentally and financially, before I confront him."

"That I can do," Olivia said.

"Absolutely," Madison agreed.

"I'm not sure how he will handle Stacy Levin's death; if he will tell me the truth about that, or if he will just continue to say she's a groupie. There's also a possibility that he doesn't mention it, at all. Like me, he might act as if nothing happened. No matter what he does, I need to get the book done before I have to make a life-altering decision."

Madison stood up and went to grab the bottle of wine and filled up her glass, then topped off Olivia's. "Wouldn't he think you know something since the police questioned you?"

"I'm not sure," I took another sip of my wine. "He didn't call or text, so I'm not sure he even knows. If they mentioned it to him, he probably asked them to use discretion where I was concerned out of professional courtesy. He might not bring it up, choosing to see how I handle it."

Olivia nodded. "I can see Jake doing that. He'll play it out; if you don't bring it up he won't."

"Exactly," I admitted. "He'll be evasive with me, until the memorial service. Then I'm guessing he'll ask permission to go, say she was a volunteer for the charity. He won't mention his ties to her. I will just have to put on my best performance and act like I don't know anything about it. Chances are, we won't have to do too much acting, because he's got a busy schedule coming up, and you know he won't miss work. The only time I'll have to spend with him is the night of the awards banquet at the firehouse."

"Oh shit, I forgot about that," Olivia said. "Anything you need us to do, we can do it."

"Thanks. I'll be furious with myself if I allow his crap to interfere with me getting the book released. I sacrificed my goals so many times in the past; I have to look out for myself now."

"So you've got the plot all figured out?" Madison asked.

"Jake figured it out for me; I'm taking dramatic licensing with my own story."

"I'm on board with that," Olivia said.

"Me too," Madison added. "You've got it all... salacious sex, murder, and hopefully a new beginning for the heroine."

"Leave it to Madison to be concerned about my future."

That statement made us laugh, if only for a moment.

CHAPTER 37 - KATIE

Present – May 2020

WHEN BAILEY AND I walked into the house, Jake was sitting on the sofa watching TV. Like the traitor dogs can be; she bounded over and jumped up to say hello.

"Hey girl, did you miss me?" He ruffled her fur and then swiveled around to look at me. "Hi. I didn't hear the car pull up."

He didn't know they towed it, which means he may not know the police were here.

"Wow, that must have hurt," I said, motioning toward the marks on his face. I needed to stall for a moment to figure out what I was going to say about the car. If I told him the police impounded it to check the front bumper, then the cat will be out of the bag, and he would know I discovered his disgusting life.

"Not going to lie; it hurt for a while the first night and the following day, but not as bad now. The doctor said I could go back to work in the morning."

I nodded. "Wow. I forgot you're back at the firehouse. Are you sure you can work?"

I reviewed the calendar earlier so I would know how much time I'd have to spend in his company. He was on a twenty-four-hour shift tomorrow, dive team the following day, the awards banquet that night—which I had already consented to attend, and then back for another twenty-four. There would be very little time to get into the reality that was now our life.

"Are you still planning to attend the awards banquet?"

I picked up Bailey's water bowl, re-filled it, and set it back down. "Yes, I already agreed to go; will be good to see everyone get their accolades."

Truthfully, I didn't look forward to the idea of pretending life at home was perfectly fine for all of his co-workers; I'll feel like a fraud. If I made an excuse now, he would get suspicious. He, and a few others, will receive awards for heroic actions they performed in the line of duty; Jake saved the lives of two children trapped in a burning building. I consented back when the awards ceremony was being planned—back when I did not know of Jake's philandering acts. He, and some guys he worked with, would ask if I suddenly decided not to go. It was easier just to make an appearance. I was prepared to play the game for as long as it was beneficial to me.

He stopped rubbing Bailey's belly, so she jumped off the sofa and walked over to get a drink. Then she parked herself next to the counter where her cookie jar sat and did the dance.

"You want a cookie?" Jake pulled himself up and walked toward the counter, opened the Harley Davidson cookie jar, and grabbed one of her treats to give to her.

"You sure you're okay," I said, noticing how he grimaced when he moved, and knowing he'd be suspicious if I didn't at least ask.

"Yeah, I'm fine. The scabs just get itchy when my clothes rub against them."

"Aren't they bandaged?"

He continued toward the refrigerator and grabbed an Iced-tea. "The deeper gashes are. The doctor gave me some salve and I have to check them periodically when I'm at work tomorrow."

Just as I said to Olivia and Madison, I suspected Jake would come home and pretend nothing had changed, nothing was going on, and a woman wasn't just killed on the back of his motorcycle. All because he wanted to keep his secret life separate from the one we had been living for two decades. He was too far gone from the good man I once knew.

He started down the hall toward the bathroom. "Do you know what I did with my set of keys to the doors and my toolbox?"

"The cottage keys?"

"Yeah, I haven't been able to find them. I have another set in my locker at work, but I wanted to grab some tools for trench training tomorrow."

Is that how My Stalker got inside because she was able to get his keys?

"No, I haven't seen them. Did you leave them in one of the motorcycle compartments?"

"I looked when I got into the city on Friday. It's no big deal; I'll just bring the set home from my locker. Just keep an eye out."

I sat down at my desk to review emails and work on a chapter or two of my book, trying to look occupied. "Okay, I will."

"I'm going to go lie down. Still groggy from the pain meds and I'll have to get up early so I can stop for gas before heading to work."

"I'm sure Bailey will follow you so you might want to put a pillow in between the two of you so she doesn't kick your sores."

"Good idea."

He disappeared into the bedroom, which gave me the chance to breathe. I was sure I had been holding it in, not wanting to say something I wasn't prepared to follow up on. Even though I expected it, it was disturbing to see that he didn't comment on anything, not even to mention the death of Stacy Levin. Either he was in total denial, or he did not know the police talked to me. If he did, it was strange that he wouldn't mention it, at least to ask what questions they wanted answers to. He seemed rather calm for a guy who just lost the woman he'd been having sex with for nearly two years.

CHAPTER 38 - KATIE

Present – May 2020

WITH JAKE BACK at work on a twenty-four-hour shift, there were two issues I needed to take care of today, both of which were necessary to do when he wasn't around. The first was to find a clinic where I could get tested; the second was returning a call to the Malden Police Department to set up a time later in the afternoon to meet with the Detective now handling the case. I received a call from Officer Nichols last night when I was chatting with Olivia and Madison, but by the time I returned home, it was too late to call.

I dialed the number for the Women's Health Clinic the minute their office opened at nine a.m. "I need an emergency appointment," I said to the young woman answering the phone.

She asked me a few questions, tried not to be surprised by my answers, and then informed me they could squeeze me in at ten o'clock. I thanked her and disconnected from the call, acknowledging to myself, that it was the most humiliating call I have ever made. Then I called and scheduled an Uber ride.

After I got off the phone, Bailey was staring at me expectantly, hoping I was going to give her a little playtime since she finished her food. I would have been a mess through all of this without her affection, so I grabbed the ball and bat.

"We can only play for a few minutes," I said to her as she bounded out the door. "Mommy has an appointment to make."

Fifteen minutes later she was happy, so I gave her a treat. Then I headed into the bathroom, put my hair on top of my head, and took a quick shower. After drying off, I stepped into a pair of jeans, a nylon athletic shirt, and a pair of *Adidas* tennis shoes over bootie socks. Strands of hair were sticking out, so I removed the clip and brushed it into a ponytail, and then put on a visor.

Who cared what I looked like for what I was about to do. I grabbed my handbag, reassured Bailey I would be back soon, and then I headed out the door to wait for the Uber.

There wasn't much traffic, so I made it to the clinic with ten minutes to go before my appointment. The Uber driver found a parking spot and promised to wait. When I entered the building, a security guard sat behind the desk in the lobby and asked me to sign. Then he directed me toward the elevator at the end of the hall and I headed up to the 4th floor.

The receptionist seemed to know I was the woman who bared my soul on the phone merely by the embarrassed look on my face. Hers was one of empathy, so I forced back tears.

"Katie Parker?"

I nodded.

She handed me a form to fill out. "You can follow me and fill it out in the exam room so you have some privacy."

I followed her down a hall, passing several exam rooms; white walls and ceilings, very sterile, but they made up for it with professional photographs of the coast. She opened the door to room number seven. It looked like an ordinary room in my gynecologist's office: a metal sink and counter, with industrial cabinets above and below, an exam bed with stirrups, and a bench against a far wall. Not a room you want to get comfortable in.

She motioned toward the gown lying in a plastic bag on the bench and handed me a cup, also in a plastic bag.

"Once you complete the form, you can change into the gown. There's a bathroom right through there for the urine sample. The doctor will be here in a few moments."

"Thank you," I said.

When she closed the door, I sat down on the bench and filled out the form, cringing from each embarrassing and personal question: *How many partners have you had in the last ten years? One, dammit.*

How could Jake do this to me?

Once it was complete, I went into the bathroom, deposited my urine, and changed into the paper gown; constantly maneuvering to protect my backside. The exam table was cold, but I had to suck it up.

When the doctor walked in, I was visibly trying to calm myself by breathing in and out.

"Hi, Katie… I'm Dr. Kingsley" She walked towards me, offering her hand in introduction, and smiled in a welcoming manner. She was young, possibly thirties; very fit with a golden tan. Not harsh like the tans on Stacy and Lexi. She looked like someone who spent her winters in warm-weather climates, instead of suffering through the New England cold.

"Nice to meet you," I said in a shaky voice. This was so humiliating.

She picked up the form and scrolled down the page, her expression neutral.

"You've never been a patient at this clinic, is that right?"

I nodded. "Under the circumstances, I wanted to go to a clinic where I didn't know anyone, and vice versa."

She glanced at me. "Oh, what circumstances would those be?"

She wanted me to say it out loud, instead of just reading it from the form. The humiliation resurfaced and made its presence known by the look on my face. Tears escaped from my eyes before I could stop them.

"I just learned that my husband of two decades has been living a double life with other women; I need to be tested for diseases."

"I'm sorry," was all she said, but to be fair, what else could she say? I'm just a new patient off the street?

"Have you discussed this with your husband? Did he use protection?"

Her words had an immediate impact on me. My body shook as anger took over and threatened to burst. I took a deep breath and let it out.

There were so many things to consider when I found out Jake was sleeping around. The women he cheated with had former partners, and could still have, for all I knew. The very thought of him sleeping with them and continuing to have sex with me just made me sick.

When we met, he had already been a first responder for a while, but his job also required EMT training. He dealt with diseases and knew the risks. He was trained on how to protect himself out in the field, yet he failed to use common sense in his personal life, which put me at risk by having multiple partners and failing to use protection.

What the hell was he thinking? I already knew the answer; he wasn't.

"I haven't talked to my husband, yet, but I wouldn't trust what he had to say regarding this situation if I did, for my safety."

After acknowledging that, I realized for the first time; I had lost complete trust in my husband and I didn't care if I was portraying him as the cad that he was. For anyone who knew me for any length of time; that was a huge admission. It was the first time I didn't come to his defense. Until now, no matter what behavior Jake had exhibited during our twenty years, I always defended him. It was a relief to know I was facing the truth.

"I understand." She sensed that I didn't want to keep talking, or I might lose it. "Let's get started then. Why don't you go ahead and lie back; I'll need to get a few vaginal swabs and then take some blood."

She walked toward the metal table against the wall, placed the medical form down, and grabbed the necessary items. While she did, she explained what tests she'd be performing and the statistics.

The minute she mentioned the vaginal swab, my mind zoned out and I barely registered the rest of what she had to say. It wasn't until she told me I could sit up and get dressed, that I realized she was finished. It was all so mechanical.

I wrote a check to pay for the tests, cursing Jake for the money wasted, but acknowledging I'd be embarrassed if it showed up on an insurance form. The receptionist informed me the doctor would notify me of the results in three days or so. I walked toward the elevator in a daze, hoping that nothing would come of it, and worried about what would happen if something did. I would have to tell Jake I knew, even if I wasn't ready to.

Please, let them all be negative.

On my way out of the building, I stopped by the security desk to view the list of doctors in the building. I scrolled the names and specialties and jotted the name down for Sarah Goldberg. Ph.D. Dr. Kingsley recommended I talk to someone about the anger that was sure to surface and gave me her name. I barely remembered the ride home, but when he dropped me off all thoughts of the degrading appointment disappeared from my mind and a new nightmare took over: a Malden Police officer was standing by his vehicle waiting for my return.

CHAPTER 39 - KATIE

Present – May 2020

I HAD BEEN in police stations several times in the past and took part in the ride-along program with officers and detectives in both big cities and small towns. On those occasions, I was there to gain knowledge of police procedurals for my writing and was granted the opportunity to observe officers out in the field. I was even fortunate to interview victims who had crimes perpetrated against them, hoping to understand the trauma and emotions involved.

Today's visit with the Malden Police Department was not a social call. They summoned me as a suspect in a crime. Since I didn't have an alibi, they had no reason not to consider me an actual suspect; not to mention the dent in my front bumper.

I had been sitting in the lobby for well over thirty minutes. I watched uniformed and plain-clothed officers come and go; pedestrians walked in to file a complaint with the Watch Commander. I even noticed local media congregating, hoping for a story. When they walked past me I was sure they were wondering if I was a victim or a perpetrator who committed a crime, though I doubt the officers would allow me to remain in the lobby if that was the case. The time ticked by slowly.

This was one of the nicer stations I visited. I could tell they had recently renovated it; it had that fresh look and was still clean. The dispatch area was on the bottom floor where I sat, conference rooms for community meetings, was toward the left with windows all around. Holding cells were in the back off the parking garage. A Watch Commander sat behind a mahogany wood wall and counter, in the direct path from the contemporary glass-front entrance, centered between two sets of stairs that led up to the second floor, which was occupied by officers and administrators.

I was staying at a hotel at the time of the motorcycle incident, and nobody could verify that, so I had no alibi. To make matters worse; I couldn't explain the dent in my right-front bumper or the broken headlight. I could swear the vehicle was fine when I took it grocery shopping the day before, but I have no proof. The vehicle was currently being analyzed. Knowing what I do about my stalker, I was afraid the investigators were going to determine my vehicle was used to commit the crime, only I wasn't the driver. Would I be able to prove that?

I know I parked my SUV in its spot when I left home on Friday, and it was also there when I returned early Sunday. I had no way of knowing if someone moved the vehicle during my absence.

I heard a voice that sounded familiar and saw Officer Nichols. He walked out with Steve Taylor, the founder of the motorcycle charity, and they shook hands. I recognized him from his image on the charity page. Since Mr. Taylor and I never met, I wondered what he knew about me. Did he know Jake had a wife? Was he okay with him using the charity ride to cohabitate with a mistress? Or, like me, was Steve Taylor kept in the dark about the double life? Did he also consider me a suspect? He and Nichols shook hands and Mr. Taylor paused as he passed by me, but thought better of speaking with me and continued on his way out. I couldn't tell if he registered who I was, or if it was merely a polite acknowledgment of my existence because I was sitting there.

"Mrs. Parker," Officer Nichols called out to me from behind the counter. "Can you come this way, please?"

I could tell from his body language that he was in professional mode, and not the same accommodating officer who pet Bailey to make her feel at ease. I took a deep breath and followed him behind the counter, up a set of stairs, and past several cubicles until he stopped at an interrogation room where an Asian-American man was inside waiting.

"Mrs. Parker, this is Detective Li, the detective assigned to investigate the case. He will be the one asking the questions today."

Detective Li stood up. He was not much taller than me, but built like someone who was a frequent visitor to the gym; the sleeves of his suit jacket were stretched tight over his forearms. He smiled as he extended his hand, which put me at ease, and it occurred to me that could have been his purpose.

Officer Nichols pulled out a metal chair with a cushioned seat. "Have a seat, Mrs. Parker."

"Thank you." I sat down and tried to get comfortable. I didn't want to appear too nervous, but I wasn't sure I pulled that off since my palms were sweaty when I shook Detective Li's hand.

"Can I get you a cup of coffee or water?"

I shook my head. "No, thank you, I'm fine." I could only imagine what drinking liquid right now would do to my stomach. I drank half a bottle of Aloe Vera juice and took an antacid trying to settle my stomach before going to the doctor's appointment.

Officer Nichols pulled up another chair to sit opposite me, and I could already feel his scrutiny.

"Okay then, let's get started," Detective Li said, with no trace of an accent. "Officer Nichols supplied me with his notes from your previous meeting, so I just want to touch on a few things with you. He is here to observe, but he may have an additional question here or there; if that's okay?"

I nodded. "Okay." I immediately tried to recall everything that was asked that day and how I responded. I told the truth, so there should be no inconsistencies—at least I hoped.

He placed a recording device on the desk in front of me and switched it on. They both studied me to see if it made me nervous. It did not. I expected it.

"Your name is Katie Parker, is that correct?"

"Yes. Though I do use a pen name for writing books, is that pertinent?"

"What is that name?"

"JR Harris."

"And that is strictly for writing; you do not use it in any other manner?"

"Strictly for writing."

"Okay. How long have you been married to Jake Parker?"

"A little over twenty years, but we knew each other for two years before that."

"And how would you describe your marriage?"

"How would I describe it?" I wasn't sure what kind of answer he was looking for on that one.

"Was it a happy one?"

He couldn't have known how difficult his simple question was for me. I always thought we were a happy couple, but it seemed rather ludicrous to say that now when Jake was living a double life. All I could do was answer truthfully, from my perspective. "I thought we were a happy couple, maybe not happy as in we couldn't be out of each other's presence happy, but happily content. Jake works more than most, but I learned to live with his schedule early on. We both wanted the same things in our future—at least I thought so."

He was taking notes, but put his pen down for a moment and read through Officer Nichols' notes to compare. "I guess what I'm trying to decipher here is; were you aware that your husband was having an affair?"

I looked down at my hands. I expected the question, but talking about it with strangers was more than embarrassing. "I became aware, yes."

"And when did you start to suspect?"

"To be completely accurate, I never suspected … do you mind if I look at my phone for a moment?"

He nodded, and I realized at that moment that Officer Nichols wasn't there in case he had questions. He was there to study my behavior, just like he had done when he and Officer Rollins visited me at the cottage. Maybe he had expertise in profiling.

I reached into my bag, pulled out my phone, and looked through the emails for the exact date. "I started receiving notes and emails in mid to late April, so I guess you could say I never suspected; I was informed."

Detective Li glanced over at Officer Nichols. "So that I understand you correctly; you didn't suspect until you received those emails?"

"That's correct."

"Who were the emails from?"

I frowned. "I assumed it was the woman my husband was having the affair with."

"You no longer think that?"

I shook my head. "No. If it was her, they should have stopped after she was killed."

Officer Nichols leaned forward. "You received more emails after Officer Rollins and I informed you about Stacy Levin's death?"

"To be accurate, it wasn't an email; someone broke into my cottage and loaded something onto my PC. I use it as a hard drive to store and save documents. Someone installed OneDrive onto it and uploaded a video."

A tear fell from my eye from the emotion of being forced to go through the humiliation again. Detective Li handed me a tissue.

"How do you know your husband didn't use the machine?"

"He never has in the past, and I checked the properties on the video. They uploaded it during the time of the charity ride. Jake and Stacy Levin were together. Neither one of them could have done it. It had to be someone else."

I was in a rather unfortunate situation here. I wanted to alert them to the fact that there was a second woman, and just give them her identity, but aside from the fact that it was humiliating, it would also mean they'd need to know how I discovered that. If I told them about all the sexually explicit images and videos, they would probably want me to turn them over as evidence. That could ruin Jake's career. He deserved whatever punishment I planned to dish out via a divorce and property settlement, but I didn't want to be responsible for him possibly losing his job over issues in his personal life. As far as I knew, he kept the secret life away from work, just like he kept it away from me.

Officer Nichols nodded toward Detective Li. "In my notes, you'll see that she mentioned a stalker during our visit."

"Did you file any reports regarding a stalker?" Detective Li asked.

"I spoke with the local police department on the phone when it first started happening. At first, I just assumed it was a reader who had an issue with me. She was showing up at book signings. Since I couldn't provide an identity, they admitted there wasn't much they could do. They suggested I keep a journal and call back if it escalated. When I discovered somebody hid cameras inside my home and then posted images of me on my author page, I physically went in and filed a report. By then, I assumed it was the woman Jake was having the affair with. I didn't call them again when things escalated. It was too humiliating by that point, though I did text the officer handling my case after a recent break-in."

Officer Nichols pulled out a small notepad and pen. "Can you give me the name and number of that officer?"

I showed him the information I had on my phone.

Detective Li reclined in his chair and latched his fingers together behind his head. "I need to be frank with you, Mrs. Parker. You were our number one suspect in the motorcycle incident. You had means, motive, and opportunity. You admit to going to the ride to catch your husband cheating. And you have no legitimate alibi. Who's to say you didn't see your husband with a woman on the back of the motorcycle, and you simply snapped?"

I wanted to yell out: No. But I knew what he was trying to do; he was pushing me to react, so I held myself in check and tried to remain calm.

"You captured video of him on the ride. Stacy Levin was a passenger on what you perceived to be your motorcycle. She was wearing a helmet that I assume was yours. It had to be humiliating for you to see that, knowing others were seeing them together. It was probably eating you up inside. So you followed them when they slipped away from the crowd and went for a joy ride. You had to be consumed with anger by that point; watching the two of them have a good time while you were home taking care of mundane duties and the dog. You waited for the opportune time when there wasn't a lot of traffic on the road. Maybe you saw her getting intimate with your man and you lost all control. You punched the gas and rammed your SUV into the bike. Maybe you weren't intending to kill her, only hoping to scare them. You didn't know the accident would cause her to be thrown from the bike and into the opposite lane just as a truck turned onto the street and killed her on impact."

To put the nail on the coffin, he placed a photograph in front of me showing the woman lying on the pavement, her body distorted and blood splattered all around.

I'm not sure when I started shaking my head no, no, no… probably the minute he started with his fiery description, suggesting premeditation. My eyes went wide in horror, and my hands covered my mouth to keep the stomach contents from polluting the desk. I couldn't control the tears raining down my face.

Subconsciously, I knew he was doing a bad-cop interrogation, but it was one thing to know they were in a motorcycle collision. Hearing it described so vividly and seeing the deadly result hit me like a ton of bricks.

I bolted out of my chair… "I'm going to be sick."

Officer Nichols jumped into action; his eyes had been glued to me the entire time to study my reaction and he realized I needed a bathroom, and wasn't trying to make a break for it. He ushered me down a corridor and led me to the female restroom.

"I'll be outside the door when you're done."

I hoped he didn't mean so he could cart me off to jail. I rushed inside to the nearest stall, put the toilet seat up, and proceeded to vomit, my stomach convulsing after each thrust. Most of what I threw up was liquid and tasted acidic as it came back up through my throat. When there wasn't anything left in my stomach, I sat down on the linoleum floor and put my head against the cold wall of the stall.

What a horrific way to die.

I put my head in my hands. How was I going to convince the officers that I had nothing to do with it when Detective Li clearly defined why they thought I would? Stacy Levin was traveling to motorcycle rides spending the night in hotels, and performing lurid acts with my husband; I had to be checked for a disease, and I had been stalked and humiliated. If anyone had a reason to come unglued, it was me, but I didn't. Remarkably, I was still holding it all together, but admittedly, I did worry that I would crack at some point.

I inhaled and pulled myself up on my two wobbly legs; I couldn't keep them waiting forever. I grabbed some toilet paper and wiped down the toilet then flushed. I opened the stall door and went to the sink to wash my face and hands, and gulped down some water. When I looked in the mirror, I was terrified by the image looking back at me. I was not the confident woman who could handle almost anything being thrown at her; I looked like a wounded and lost soul.

Officer Nichols viewed me with concern when I reappeared. "Are you okay?"

I nodded. "I think so. As a writer, I'm used to creating heavy stuff like this for the characters in my books. I'm just not used to it in my own life."

He gave me a sympathetic nod, but I knew it was just part of his job. He led me back toward Detective Li's desk. "Can I get you a bottle of water, and maybe some crackers?"

I nodded then returned to my seat. "Thank you."

Detective Li had put the photograph away and was now reading through a different report. He looked up at me, but his expression was hard to read. Playing bad cop, I'm sure he needed to keep a stony demeanor. "Are you okay to continue?"

Officer Nichols returned and handed me a bottle of water, and a small package of saltine crackers. When he sat back down, I leaned toward Detective Li, feeling some of the old me returning.

"In response to your very graphic narrative: no. I did not follow my husband. I did not lose my cool. And I most definitely did not attempt to harm them. I'm just not capable of it."

He smiled, but it wasn't a friendly smile. "Everybody is capable of harming another when they've been pushed to the brink."

I heard the same line of thought from Officer Rollins.

Officer Nichols cleared his throat, obviously trying to change the direction of the conversation. "What Detective Li means to say is; you have suffered major emotional trauma—"

"Let me stop you right there," I interrupted; I didn't just feel the old me returning, I could feel the anger coming on too. "I know what you're trying to do here; I do it to the characters in my books. But no, no matter how much I've suffered, and yes, I have: I'm humiliated, devastated, angry, and every other word you could use to describe the anguish I've been feeling after learning that the man I've been living with for two decades, has been living a double life. I still am not capable of physically harming them. I'd get a divorce and go to a shrink, but I wouldn't ram a vehicle into a motorcycle."

Both of them stared at me; Detective Li seemed surprised that I was being defiant, and it might have been my imagination, but I swear I saw a touch of admiration in Officer Nichols' eyes. The moment didn't last.

Detective Li picked up a manila folder from his desk; it wasn't there before I went to the restroom. "Mrs. Parker, we just received images from one of the CCTV cameras in the area during your husband's motorcycle incident. Can you take a look at them for me?"

I felt my heart speed up as he removed the images and handed them to me. Their eyes stayed focused on me as I studied. There were three different images. In two pictures, the camera seemed to be overhead, so it was looking down at the SUV driving down the street. I couldn't make out the street name, but clearly, it was following the motorcycle, about two car length spaces ahead. If these were the only images, they wouldn't be able to persuade me it was my SUV. But the third picture I held in my hand proved it.

Detective Li saw my body tense up. "Do you recognize the vehicle in that picture?"

In this image, the camera was up close and showed the exact moment when the SUV rammed into the motorcycle. The front-right side of the SUV connected with the back wheel, and the image distinctly showed Stacy Levin's flight from the bike at the moment of impact. Even though my vehicle had a cherry tint to it, which was hard to detect in the black-and-white photo, I could still verify it was my SUV. I had a clear vision of the personalized license plate on the front of the vehicle: Real Heroes Don't Wear Capes when the vehicle made its U-turn.

"That is my vehicle," I admitted.

The issue that threw me for a loop when viewing the image, however, was that the driver of the vehicle had blonde hair, like mine, not the long dark hair I expected. The image didn't show the face, but the hair, along with the fact that it was my vehicle; I couldn't prove it wasn't me.

"But that's not me behind the wheel," I said, my mind already analyzing how I could prove it, provided they let me go home. The only way to convince them it wasn't me would be to provide an alibi for the time on the photo, find CCTV images from another camera that showed the identity of the driver or, have an expert zoom in to get a closer look at the face and clothing. I knew it wasn't me, but that would not convince Detective Li.

I looked directly into Officer Nichols's eyes. I suspected he was there to observe me as a profiler. Surely he could see. "Do you think I did this, am capable of this?"

Detective Li said, "Mrs. Parker, I said it earlier; anyone is capable, depending on the personal harm they've endured."

"I would like to know what Officer Nichols thinks," I said as I continued to stare. "He is here to profile me, is he not?"

He held my gaze, but wouldn't speak.

"I know you don't believe I did this."

Detective Li put the photographs back into the envelope. "The mind is a funny thing, Mrs. Parker."

I might have smirked, not noticeable enough for him to react, but it occurred to me he didn't have a clue as to the harm I had endured. If he did, he probably would have judged me guilty right off the bat. "Are you going to arrest me?"

This time Detective Li looked at Officer Nichols, and I realized his opinion mattered in the decision. Which one was the boss here?

"Not at this time," Nichols said. "We still have other individuals to question and a few other things to look into. We might need you to come in again. We have completed the inspection of your vehicle, so you're free to drive back home today. The officer who picked you up will take you down to the garage."

"And don't leave town," I said sarcastically.

"Goes without saying," Nichols said, though my imagination was running wild again; I thought I saw a twinkle in his eye.

The uniformed officer dropped me at the garage and handed me my keys. He was polite and had me sign a document that they released the vehicle to me, and I was free to go. During the drive home, my mind was clouded with confusion. The beach was over an hour away from Malden, so I had the time to think about the interrogation, and tried to remember every detail of the photographs. But of course, it was the image of Stacy Levin's body that kept revealing itself in my eyes. Jake still hadn't mentioned anything about needing to leave for a few days if he planned to go to the Memorial. Maybe they were having a private service, locally, just for the group? I had a feeling when the time arrived for confrontation, all of that would be discussed.

When I finally reached the Bella Beachside Community, I could feel some of the tension drain away. As I passed the cottages on the first few streets, I realized summer was not too far off. Most of the owners already had their colorful beach décor on display. By the time I turned into our driveway, I was putting the stress behind me until I saw Bailey hiding underneath the stairs of the deck. My heart started racing. I had an intruder while I was away and they forced my dog outside.

CHAPTER 40 - KATIE

Present – May 2020

I GRABBED HER collar and eased her out, petting her until she stopped shaking to let her know she was okay. I peered through the sliding glass door, didn't see anyone, so I opened it and paused on the entryway rug, holding onto Bailey's collar to keep her from moving forward onto the hardwood floor.

"Bailey, sit … stay!" I whispered.

While I was sitting at the police station being questioned, someone was definitely inside the cottage. My senses alert, I noticed a slight aroma of a woman's musky perfume lingering in the air. My nose had always been sensitive to smells, which was a major thorn in Jake's side since I was constantly reminding him to keep the toilet seat down. I also kept a spray bottle of lavender and peroxide cleaning liquid on the tile floor and told him to spray after every use.

The next clues I noticed; both the wood chest I used as an ottoman in front of the sofa and a nightstand were moved and somebody messed with items on my desk. Thankfully, I started saving my documents on my portable hard drive and locked it up in my safe with both of my laptops.

My heart was pounding in my chest the longer I was inside.

I lowered myself down next to Bailey to keep her still and listened for any sounds, trying to verify whether or not anyone was still on the premises. Bailey would normally react, but something scared her so she was acting docile. At the same time, I reached into my bag and retrieved my cellphone to call for reinforcements, if necessary.

After almost a minute with no noise, I assumed the intruder was gone. I glanced around the living room and kitchen to see if I noticed anything missing and scanned for new cameras. Logically, I knew it wasn't a burglar; it had to be Lexi Thompson. After what happened to Stacy Levin, though, I had reason to worry? What was she doing?

As I started moving through the house, Bailey started to get agitated. Was I wrong; was somebody still on the premises? With her by my side sniffing at all the scents that didn't belong, she kept trying to pull me toward the kitchen cabinets.

First, I checked each window to make sure they were all secure. The windows had not been opened; there was no dust on the windowsills from sand that would have blown in if they had been. The front door was locked and dead-bolted. The only other way to enter was through the sliding glass door—just as she did when she placed the cameras, which revealed to me, once again, that she used a key.

After tossing that thought back and forth, I remembered Jake mentioning he lost his set of keys. My logical deduction was that Lexi got a hold of them. Now I wouldn't have to humiliate myself by saying hey, during one of your sexual romps did you leave your keys in a position where the woman could get to them? I already knew the answer. What other personal information or items did she have access to?

I opened cabinet doors in the bookcase, checked my safe, and looked inside the chest where I stored blankets and pillows. I didn't see anything missing or out of place. What I did notice and thought was strange: the CD and DVD cases had been opened and a few discs removed from the slips that were now lying free. I thought I knew why. Maybe it dawned on her that Jake had sexual videos of her that he saved on discs that could be considered evidence. Nope, he kept them in a file on his phone, scan disks, and his laptop, which I already viewed and saved. There could be more on his tablet or somewhere else, but what more would I need to see that could be any worse than what I already have?

Bailey was still pulling me toward the cabinets, so I gave in and followed her nose. She kept going toward the sink cabinet under the island, sniffing like crazy and growling at the door. I couldn't fathom what was making her act that way. That's where I stored the dish soap, sponges, and disinfectants.

When I reached for the handle her growling increased, and due to her reaction, I intuitively took a step back. When I looked inside fear surged through me. A long, thick snake was curled up underneath the pipes and it started to move.

Bailey was feverishly barking now, and I had to yank hard on the collar to pull her away. I did not know what kind of snake it was, or if it was poisonous. All I knew was snakes scared me and the intruder placed it inside my cabinet for that purpose. I slammed the cabinet door, pulled Bailey with me as I grabbed her chain, and hurried outside, closing door behind me. I quickly hooked the dog to the deck railing and kept my eyes on the cabinet while scrolling the internet for animal control.

265

~~

Bailey and I waited outside while the man and woman who showed up from Cape Cod Animal Control went about their business to remove the reptile. I had to avert my eyes from the whole ordeal, especially when I saw them scrambling in my kitchen with the net. The snake was not being compliant. Once I wrote out a check to pay for their services, I asked them if they could do a quick check of the rest of the house to make sure there were no other surprises. When they came back outside and gave me the all-clear, I couldn't help but wonder why the two of them were smirking as they stepped back into their vehicle. Was my fear of snakes that amusing?

After they were gone, it wasn't easy to go about my business. I had the uncanny fear that there was something inside every cabinet I opened. What possessed her to put a snake inside my house?

A half-empty bottle of water on the counter reminded me I hadn't completed my search. I walked up the steps and checked the main bathroom; all was okay in there. Nothing was out of the ordinary in the guest room or second bathroom, either. I continued into the master bedroom and my body froze: a printed cardboard image of a woman's nude body, from the neck down to her vagina, was lying on my white comforter. In the image, whipped cream had been used to write *Jake is mine,* with an arrow pointing toward the woman's vagina. The image was a reenactment of the video that was uploaded on my PC and titled: watch me. Now, I understood why the animal control employees were smirking. They thought the image was me.

What was even more jarring, and a personal warning to me; was the eight-inch chef's knife taken from my kitchen cutlery set and stabbed into the center of my pillow with droplets of blood purposely deposited onto the pillowcase.

The scene was unnerving. But the thought that was running through my head; she knew that was where I slept from when she planted the cameras. Two of the images she posted were of me sleeping with my head on that pillow. She was sending me a message.

I took pictures of the scene with my phone and scrolled through the numbers in my contacts. I opened up the text message box and selected the numbers for Officer Nichols and the local police officer, who took the stalking report. Then I opened the keyboard, forwarded the images with the added a message: *Thought you'd like to know I had another visit from My Stalker... Katie Parker.*

Once that was completed, I spent the next few hours creating a power-point presentation and uploaded some images and videos I collected as evidence. When the time came, the viewer was going to get an eyeful by me merely pushing play.

CHAPTER 41 - KATIE

Present – May 2020

IT WAS DISCONCERTING to attend an awards ceremony for first responders, forced to put on a supporting smile because my husband was a recipient, and I faced the prospect that the man standing up on the stage accepting the praise was no longer the man I committed to twenty years ago.

I listened to the words of the Mayor: "First Responders put themselves in harm's way each day they go to work, and these awards provide an opportunity to recognize their bravery and sacrifice. This year, we are proud to honor Jake Parker, his family, and his legacy of heroism and sacrifice…"

I tuned out the rest of the speech observing Jake now through jaded eyes as he received the award; heroic actions definitely, but he was no longer that man in my eyes. He then thanked the Mayor, his Chief, and first responders standing on the stage with him. He looked humble next to the other recipients; all of them in their Class A uniforms exhibiting a professional demeanor in front of their peers and supportive families.

I sat with his brother, Billy, and other members of the department from Jake's group. That was uncomfortable since Billy was at the hospital after the motorcycle incident that killed Stacy Levin. Did Jake admit the affair? Even if he did, I'm sure he left out the sleazy behavior.

I kept looking for Jake's two adult children, but they didn't attend. Jake might have failed to mention it to them. His daughter lived in the city and worked nights, and his son was a member of a band that toured local establishments so he didn't see them that much; the occasional dinner, holidays, birthdays, and father's day.

A while back, I remember talking about the incident that earned Jake his award; rescuing two young children from a dwelling that was collapsing all around them after a fire raged through the building. I remembered it well. The call came in the middle of the night. Jake was not on duty but jumped out of bed when the alarm sounded for all personnel and mutual aid. Our house was right around the corner from the firehouse. Fire engines and ladder trucks from surrounding towns lined the streets. The red lights lit up our home and I could hear the radios from the rigs. There was no way I could sleep, so I walked toward the firehouse to see the action. Police had yellow tape up to block off the perimeter, but you could still see from blocks away. It was a four-family apartment dwelling across the street from the firehouse. Flames engulfed the entire building. I was not aware that Jake was inside the building and only learned that fact the following morning.

He shrugged like he normally did, and said it was no big deal; he was just doing his job. The words most of them used when attention came their way.

That was the Jake I always knew, respected, and admired. I wasn't sure who this new Jake was.

When I met him over twenty-two years ago, I knew from day one that he was dedicated to the first responder community, and that duty would always be his number one priority. To him, it was never just a job, but his calling in life was to be part of the team of brothers. Because of the way we met, I came to understand.

Following first responders around, taking notes and photographs for my research, I was able to see Jake in his element where he thrived. I also witnessed his reaction when one of his brothers or sisters in the community had been injured or killed, and for him, it cut as deep as if it was a member of his own family.

When he and I started a relationship, I never felt threatened by his love of service. I never asked him to take a day off, not attend an incident when he was off duty and a call rang out, or ask him to give up an overtime shift, even though he had already been away most of the week as it was. I recognized he was an adrenaline junkie, and his mind needed a constant challenge. It was in his DNA; who he was as a person. Similar to dating a man who chose a career in the military, you knew early on they could be deployed. You also had to deal with the fact that each day they may not come home. That was the man I was willing to commit to. Instead of wallowing in pity about his absences, I became more independent and spent time doing what was in my soul, which was my writing and renovating homes.

Now, I faced the dilemma that the man I had known and respected was finding other ways to satisfy an addiction that his first responder community was no longer quenching. I also knew that if I wasn't careful about how I handled the situation, his behavior could have a catastrophic impact on his career.

~~~

"Congratulations," I said when Jake approached where I was standing with his brother after the ceremony ended.

"Thanks," he said, pulling me in for a hug, which took all my effort to pretend that everything was okay under the watchful eyes of others.

Billy pumped his hand and slapped his back. "Well deserved, bro."

"Thanks, Billy."

Jake put his arm around my shoulder as if we were a normal, happy couple. "The guys are heading over to Connie's Pub. Do you want to join us?"

I shook my head. "No, you go ahead. I'm going to head home and finish up a few chapters. I'm nearing the end."

"Really? That's great. I guess we'll be congratulating you too, then."

I smiled to myself. If he knew what my book was about, the last thing he'd be doing would be congratulating me. I wasn't worried about him finding out though; he wasn't a reader unless it was a fire service manual.

"Sure you don't want to join us, Kat?" Billy asked me, and I could see regret in his eyes. He and Jake were total opposites in several areas. Billy was completely loyal to his wife, could never cheat, nor could he spend that much time away from home. I could tell it was eating away at him, that he had to keep Jake's secrets. I didn't blame him, but I knew I couldn't trust him. His loyalty to his brother would come first. I smiled and reached out to hug him.

"I'm good, thanks. I have some writing to finish up. You know the conversation will be all about fire scenes anyway; go on and have a good time."

Most of the other firefighters and families were mingling and enjoying the desserts and coffee, which were set up on a long table. This was the first time I had seen most of them in a while. Spending seasons down at the cottage, I didn't get to the firehouse much. It was a long drive from the beach, especially during summer. I rarely made an appearance unless it was a special event, such as the fire prevention weekend where Jake's group put on a vehicle extrication show, or one of the family parties.

On my way out the door, the Deputy Chief, Larry Haggerty, noticed me and walked along with me to my SUV. "Good to see you, Katie. It's been a while. How are you?"

"I'm good, how are you?"

"Can't complain," he responded. "Are you keeping the boy out of trouble?"

That had been a standard phrase from the Deputy since even before he was in the position. He was old school and by-the-book type, so he collided with Jake on various issues because of Jake's risk-taking mentality, and that he thought he was always right. Yet, even though their personalities clashed, the Deputy consistently said if he was ever in a fire, Jake was the one man he would want in the building with him.

"Keeping him out of trouble is a full time job, as you well know, Deputy Chief," I said, trying to laugh it off as a joke, but not sure I accomplished it.

"Don't I know it," he teased. "I've always said you were a saint to be able to handle him."

I laughed, but the look in his eyes made me wonder if he knew.

"It was a nice ceremony."

He nodded. "That it was, made me proud. It was good to see them get their recognition along with the other mutual aid departments."

"Yes, it was."

We arrived at my vehicle so I reached into my handbag for the keys but noticed Deputy Chief Haggerty glance at the front of my vehicle.

"Looks like you had a little fender bender."

Can't imagine what he would think if he knew the truth; that it was recently used as the weapon in a murder. I had to lie, which I hated to do.

"Yeah, I just haven't had the chance to get it fixed yet."

He swiveled around to head back toward the building. "Well, I just wanted to say hello. I understand the sacrifice families make being married to first responders, so thank you."

"Thank you, Deputy," I said, sincerely. "It was good to see you."

"I can't leave as long as the Mayor is still on the premises so I have to head back. Take care."

"You, too."

I stepped into the vehicle, turned on the engine, and sat there for a moment, watching him go. It occurred to me that this could be the last time I would see any of them once I confronted Jake with the truth. The thought made me a little sad. That's one negative to come out of separations and divorces; only one member of the couple gets to keep the friends and co-workers in their lives. Jake was the one whose behavior caused the problem, but I was the one forced to walk away from anyone we've known through the years of our relationship, except for Olivia and Madison. Even if I couldn't make a deal to keep the cottage, they would remain in my life.

As I wiped away a tear, I noticed a group of firefighters exiting the building and head toward their vehicles. They were from another town and nobody I knew, but one female had me transfixed. She was in uniform with her Class-A cap over her hair, which was tied back in a ponytail. When she veered toward her vehicle, she removed the cap and pulled her hair free. It was dark, so I didn't immediately recognize her, but the minute she walked underneath the overhead light, my mouth dropped open. She had long, dark hair, not black, so it threw me for a minute, but it confirmed my suspicion when she started talking with the group. Her hair was swinging from side to side and her hands moved about, flamboyantly, like a woman flirting. The same actions of My Stalker the day she was toying with me at the book signing when she weaved and bobbed in between bookshelves with her hair and hands flying about. I could tell by their body language that she annoyed the other women in the group—probably wives or girlfriends of the men.

That's Lexi Thompson: the woman who has been stalking me and was trying to frame me for the murder of Stacy Levin. The realization hit me cold. She knew Jake because she was a fellow firefighter. I didn't remember seeing her before she started showing up at book signings. Have I attended firefighter functions when she was there? How long has she been watching me, stalking me?

PART THREE:

CHAPTER 42 – KATIE

Present – May 2020

I WATCHED AS she waved goodbye to the group then stepped into a dark-colored SUV. When she started her vehicle and drove out of the lot, it took less than a minute to convince myself to follow her, keeping back far enough so she wouldn't get suspicious. Connie's Pub was only a few miles down the road, so I assumed she was headed there to join the others, but instead, she drove past the lot and made a right-hand turn toward the highway.

I didn't follow her right away, pausing at the intersection for a moment. Traffic wasn't heavy and I didn't want her to catch on that she had a tail. When I did continue, I blended in with the other vehicles but kept my eyes on the SUV with the red light on top. The town she worked for obviously allowed emergency lights on personal vehicles when traveling to scenes while off-duty.

She drove about fifteen miles and exited off the highway into a town called Longview. She turned left at the intersection, continued for another five miles, and then turned right onto a street that led to a woodsy area with houses set back off the street. By that time I had turned off my front lights and just used hers to guide me.

About a mile in, she pulled into the long driveway of a white ranch house that was surrounded by trees and parked in front of a second dwelling that looked like it was once a garage, but had been renovated to resemble a guest house. I pulled off to the side of the road to observe. She stepped out of her vehicle, walked into the guest house, and turned the lights on. Was that where she lived? She remained inside for several minutes, so I took the time to study the area. There were a few hundred feet between each home, with trees all around to give the homeowner privacy. There were street lights on the main road turning in, but the front of her house was basically in the dark. How would she like it if I turned the tables and started stalking her, taking photographs when she wasn't aware? I doubted that a nosey neighbor would see me.

The lights suddenly went out in the guest house. When she walked back out, she was carrying a duffel bag, closed the door behind her, and entered the ranch house. I noticed she didn't need to unlock the deadbolt, so she wasn't as worried about security. I looked for cameras and motion sensor lights but didn't notice any. A light came on in the far end of the house, possibly a bedroom. About five minutes later, I could see her shadow in the front window when a light turned on in the back of the house; was probably the kitchen if they designed it like other ranch homes. Once she had been inside for about twenty minutes, I did a little investigating for myself.

I turned off the interior light in my SUV so that it wouldn't turn on when I opened the door and stepped out, quietly latching it behind me. Then I crossed the street, keeping my eyes alert in case she came back outside or looked out the window. The trees did a good job of hiding me, though.

I wasn't sure what my plan was, but it felt good knowing I was the one now invading her space. I sidled along her vehicle, staying to the left of her driveway. I peered over the hood of the car through the kitchen window. The curtains were open and the light was on. It was a farm-style kitchen with old oak wood cabinets. She had her back to me, so I quickly moved toward the guest house, where I was out of her view.

The door of the guest house was locked when I tried turning, so I used the light from my phone to peer through the window: the front room had a desk and bookshelves all along the walls. Seeing nothing of interest, I sidled up against the vinyl siding and veered to the side to look through the back window. This room was large and covered the entire back of the dwelling. A sofa, chairs, and a big-screen TV took up one section. The area closer to where I stood at the window had a fitness area with machines along the back wall. A stripper pole was built into the right corner with a video camera set up on a tripod. Seeing the camera was a stark reminder of the videos I viewed of her and Jake. It made me curious to know how many ScanDisk videos Jake had hidden that I didn't bother to search for. Her tastes were even more salacious than Stacy Levin's, maybe because she also liked being in control.

A large wardrobe cabinet was centered between the rooms and the doors were open, revealing shelves of clothing, leather motorcycle gear, and accessories. Then something caught my eye: two wigs; one with long, black hair and the other was long, blonde hair, layered, just like mine. I gasped and had to cover my mouth, fearing she might have heard me. A sick realization occurred to me and the truth was begging to be discovered; was this woman so obsessed with Jake she was willing to do whatever was necessary to remove the obstacles in her way?

Was she diabolical?

Did she don the black wig to make it seem like Stacy Levin was stalking me, and then put on the blonde one, steal my vehicle, and maliciously ram into Jake's motorcycle hoping to frame me for the death of Stacy Levin?

I was so horrified I backed away from the window and tripped over a pothole in the driveway, knocking myself off balance and dropped my phone. This was all so overwhelming.

I ducked down and remained immobile for several seconds to make sure she didn't hear me. It gave me a moment to take a deep breath. Once I calmed my heart rate I scrambled around to reach for the phone, and that's when I spotted a motorcycle parked at the back of the house and covered with a tarp.

"Oh fuck," escaped from my mouth.

I crawled toward it and raised the cover: it was the same Harley that tried to run us off the road. Using my phone I took a quick photo, making sure I had the license plate.

I should have returned to my vehicle right then, but a shadow moving around in the window above me caught my eye. Guts, or stupidity, I didn't know which was fueling me now. Staying low, I opened my cell phone and clicked on the camera. After I verified the flash was off, I set it to take a picture. I peered up into the room; it was another office. She was seated with her back to me viewing content on a flat-screen computer monitor. Anger surged through my body after seeing what was on the screen: images of me.

I lifted my cell phone and took a snapshot each time she pulled up a new page. They were photographs of me from her various spying trips: the night she stabbed Bailey with the fish hook; at book signings; when I went to the store; to the gym; hanging out by the fire with friends, but that wasn't the worst of it. To the right of where she sat was a corkboard wall. Nailed to it was a collage: images of me and Jake, together, over many years of our relationship, only every image of me was marked by red crosshairs … she wanted me gone.

A few hours ago, I sat with Detective Li and Officer Nichols and told them I wasn't capable of harming another human being. I meant it when I said it. But right now, I wanted to throttle this woman's neck, or worse, make her suffer. Nobody knew I was here. Neighbors were far enough away they couldn't see me. I had to mentally will myself not to do something, not to retaliate. If I did, I knew it would just land me in jail, and I would be just like her. I took a few more pictures, so I captured it all, and then I snuck back to my vehicle. I started the car and did a quick U-turn before turning on the lights. It wasn't until I was back on the highway and headed back to the cottage that I acknowledged the reality: I found the woman who has been making my life a living nightmare and I walked away without getting revenge.

First thing in the morning, I planned to type an email to Officer Nichols describing what I found. I didn't know if the motorcycle and the blonde wig would be enough to give him probable cause to get a search warrant. Images of her viewing me on the computer and a corkboard full of images proving she was My Stalker might help, at least enough to encourage Detective Li to question her as a person of interest. On the other hand, they'll also want to know how I got my information; I would have to admit what I did.

I stalked My Stalker.

CHAPTER 43 - KATIE

Present – May 2020

JAKE WAS HOME today, which I didn't expect. His schedule said dive rescue training. Maybe he needed a day of recuperation. After all, he was in a motorcycle accident. He would never admit it to me, but he had to be dealing with the emotional impact too. A woman he was having sex with was dead, surely that would do something to his psyche. The police had to have informed him that the accident was intentional. Did he feel any guilt?

I fed Bailey and then walked her until she tired from chasing the ball. Then I sat down and transferred the evidence I collected from spying on Lexi Thompson to Officer Nichols via email. I had no way of knowing how often he was online to see it, but there was too much to text. It might even take him a couple of days.

I was already at my desk with my headphones on and typing by the time Jake got out of bed. Headphones usually meant I was in the zone and I didn't want to be disturbed. Thankfully, he took the hint and occupied himself with chores. Around noon he apologized for interrupting me and said he had an appointment regarding his motorcycle and then he was going to take Bailey for a hike at the Knob. It was a good place to take the dog to get some exercise while enjoying the breathtaking views. I was grateful. It meant I would have a few more hours of writing time without Bailey interrupting me to play. I did wonder about his appointment. Was he meeting with the detective about the investigation? I knew he wouldn't tell me until he had no choice.

After he was gone, I tried to put him and the entire mess out of my mind. I was finishing up on the final chapters, hoping to work through any questions I had about the ending. I wanted to finish them in a draft and then print a copy for Olivia to continue editing.

Drawing inspiration from my journal and reviewing images I took at Lexi Thompson's house, I wrote the narrative as the drama played out in my life. The only difference was the names and locations had to be changed since I was writing it as fiction. If anyone was telling me the story and said these things happened, I wouldn't have believed them. It was too farfetched. Yet, they happened; the truth was often stranger than fiction.

~~~

The writing was moving along so well it was early evening before I allowed myself a break. I was happy with all I accomplished and thought I knew how the story would end; stepping away for a brief period would allow me to analyze it, to be sure.

I grabbed a Greek yogurt and a bottle of water and went out on the deck to get some air. While eating, I tried to visualize my scenes for accuracy, and pleased with my progress until Jake sent me a message through Facebook messenger on my phone:

Hey, sorry to bother you, but my knee gave out again, and I can't get it back in. Can you take a break and come help me get Bailey back to the truck? We're out on the Peninsula at the Knob.

I smirked to myself. Jake had been having a problem with his knee for a few years now. No matter how many times I suggested he get it fixed, he kept making excuses. The first time it happened he was on duty at the firehouse, but he didn't want to take the time off of work so he didn't tell anyone. After a while, his doctor informed him he would need surgery if he planned to keep working. Unfortunately, that coincided with the start of the motorcycle ride season, so he put it off again. It happened a few times since then, but this was the first time he asked for my help. That meant he was struggling to walk and hang on to Bailey at the same time and probably had trouble dealing with the pain. If it wasn't for Bailey, I would tell him to pound sand.

"Do you have a leash? Water?"

"I have water, but no leash. We'll be sitting on the stone bench on the lookout."

"On my way."

The minute we stopped messaging, I wanted to chastise myself: I was doing it again. After everything Jake did to me and our relationship, I was jumping to help. I reasoned I had no choice; he had Bailey. Oh, who was I kidding? There had always been something in my psyche that made me feel as if it was my responsibility to help when somebody had a problem. I needed to fix the situation. I had it so bad that I would stop whatever I was doing and sacrifice my time to render aid. I knew it was a quirk in my personality—one I had since childhood—only it never bothered me to the degree it did right now. I just wanted to say f-you to Jake.

But I gave in. Bailey was with him and it gets dark fairly early in April. Hobbling around with a feisty Golden Retriever near the lookout where the ocean was all around could get dangerous. When Bailey spotted the water, she thought it was time to dig up rocks. Without a leash to stop her, there could be consequences at certain spots out on the Peninsula. Hopefully, she was calm and lying at his feet until I arrived. Once the sun disappeared, he wouldn't be able to see too well unless he used his phone; there were no lights on the hiking trails.

I threw a few items into my backpack: my Etip gloves in case I had to use the cell phone when I was out there, and my battery-heated jacket. If his injury was bad, I would have to call for reinforcements. It could get chilly at night, especially with the sea breeze off the ocean. I had water in the SUV, so I grabbed two bottles out of the back and dropped those in the pack.

I would probably run into a little traffic going over the bridge toward Falmouth, but it shouldn't take too long to get to Woods Hole. Once my gear was in the car, I added a flashlight and the rope leash for Bailey. It wouldn't be too dark when I arrived, but by the time I hiked out to retrieve him and helped him back out, the only light would be from the moon and fireflies. There was lighting near the entrance where residents had their boats moored at the marina. There was also no security at night, only monitored video surveillance—at least that's what the sign said the last time I was there. The sign also said no trespassing after dusk, but I was sure they would understand, under the circumstances. Either way, I doubt they had full-time monitoring.

I joined the traffic of Cape Cod residents heading home after a day at work. I crossed over the bridge. It was a beautiful drive on most days and even early evening, with a view of the boats making their way through the canal. During the early years of our relationship, Jake and I took rides on his Kawasaki touring most of Cape Cod looking at waterfront houses. It was always a dream of ours to find something near the water. When his kids were with us for spring or summer visitation, we took them for drives along the coast and wound up spending time at a few of the beaches. I had two photo albums of pictures with them building sandcastles, body surfing in the water, and skipping rocks along the peninsula walkway at Scusset Beach at the end of a bike ride along the Cape Cod Canal. That was so long ago.

I had the music playing in the background, but inevitably, my thoughts drifted back to everything that had gone on over the last few days—years, really, only I just became aware. Not a wise idea, thinking about the madness while driving in Cape Cod traffic.

Remembering the moment I learned of Jake's deception was like reliving it all over again, and the disgusting images played like an actor's showreel before my eyes. The pain and humiliation would probably remain with me for a long time.

How could I not know, not see?

My father was a military man who taught me how to play sports when I was a child and educated me on the ways of the world. Before I met Jake, most of my friends were law enforcement of some form. I traveled, had street smarts. When did I become so complacent that it was easy for him to create a secondary world and keep its existence from me, his family, personal friends, and co-workers? I had been so wrapped up in making sure we had a good home, trying to guarantee our financial security with renovation projects and my books to provide for our future, that I didn't see what the hell was going on in the day-to-day realities?

The anger snuck back up on me and I found myself smacking the steering wheel with the palm of my hand. Along with the pain, an immense feeling of shame washed over me, knowing the depravity that has been going on. Sexual behavior that was never a part of my world, and as far as I knew, never a part of Jake's world?

Did I ever really know him?

Was it possible he had dual personalities; one that had sexual cravings a normal relationship wouldn't provide, but he tried to keep it in check because his need to be respected in the first responder community was more important to him? Yet at some point, those addictions took over? Did it become too much effort to fight his inner demons, and he let them win out when the wicked carrot was dangled in front of him via the raven-haired vixens?

I smacked the steering wheel again, frustrated. It was a waste of time trying to analyze why he created his secret world; I may never learn the answer. I shook my head, overwhelmed by the disappointment in myself. I never had a clue, nor did our friends. Not one of us believed he could cheat, let alone to the degree that he was. We thought his desire for frequent motorcycle trips was the early arrival of a mid-life crisis. The conservative façade he put on had been so believable it never occurred to any of us that there was another personality lurking inside of him. There's a reason *50 Shades* sold over 50 million books and the films were so popular. He met women that introduced him to a world of sex the likes of which he'd never experienced, and performing the acts gave him a sense of power and control. They introduced him to their world, and he relished in the discovery. It was like a drug he had to have, and he behaved horribly to engage in that lifestyle.

Unfortunately for me, I couldn't erase the images and videos in my mind. They would flash before my eyes and interrupt my thoughts several times a day and night. All thanks to a woman he rejected who turned into an obsessed stalker and wanted to see my demise. It was all just so sordid.

The sign for Woods Hole finally appeared on the right-hand side of the road and brought me back to reality. I was so engrossed with the analysis of the delusional world I had been living I didn't notice when 28 ended and 28A began. The road curved slightly and became Locust Street and then Woods Hole Road, which took me to the village. After Little Harbor appeared on my left and I saw the Coast Guard vessels, I remained to the right, passing the post office and Woods Hole Inn. I took the next left, and then another left, which brought me into the main parking lot.

As I suspected, there were only a few vehicles in the lot. I didn't see Jake's truck, but he could have parked at the lot for the bike path and walked over. The Knob was a well-known spot. Locals brought their children to play in the shallow water of the beaches on both sides of the marina. Some would hike up to see the views; following the trails of the twelve-acre spot toward the peninsula lookout. There was also a bike path that started further down the coast, continued through the entrance of The Knob, and went inland. Most of the locals were gone when dinner time rolled around. Sometimes, stragglers hung around to capture the views at dusk, but it was a rare occurrence.

Boulders protected the bottom and sides of The Knob from erosion, and in one area, extended higher across the top to secure people from falling over when they walked the peninsula. A granite stone bench was built around the perimeter in one area of the peninsula so guests could sit and look out at the ocean, but there were also spots without any protection, other than the vegetation.

I never heard of anyone falling from the lookout, but that didn't mean it never happened. Sometimes, tourists would sit on the edge of the cliffs to look out at the view, and I wondered if anyone ever slipped and fell. It could get slippery on the rocks when the mist from the fog rolled in from the ocean. I would cringe at the sight of a tourist wearing their summer flip-flops when they ventured toward the edge. I wore my hiking shoes specifically for that reason. I could already see a layer of moisture floating over the water. A deeper layer of fog would be hovering as I walked toward the peninsula.

CHAPTER 44 - KATIE

Present – May 2020

I STEPPED OUT of the vehicle, used the remote to open the rear hatch, and put on my gloves and jacket from inside my backpack. The air was already feeling cool. The battery for my jacket was in my pocket, so I plugged it in but didn't turn it on for now. No need to use up the battery time until necessary. I also put my cell phone in the left-front pocket over my chest that zipped up vertically but had a lining to protect the screen.

Then, I grabbed the flashlight and lifted the backpack over my shoulders. I locked the SUV, stuffed the keys in another pocket then zipped it up as I headed toward the main trail. A woman and her child were lingering on the sand, packing their beach bag, and were preparing to head home. A young couple took turns with their camera, taking selfies of each other using the boats from the marina as background.

The main trail would be about a fifteen-minute trek to the lookout, where Jake said he and Bailey would be waiting. Most of the trail was a dirt path that meandered through the seagrass with the ocean on both sides. The biggest concern I had walking the trail at night were the ticks and May flies I wouldn't be able to see to avoid. Before leaving the cottage, I doused my body with a lemon-grass spray that was supposed to deter them. I also rubbed Vicks VapoRub under my nose and on my cheeks. They don't like the eucalyptus, so hopefully, they would

291

avoid my face. My clothing was another layer of protection. It wasn't safe to jog the trail when you couldn't see what was in front of you, so I opted for fast-walking.

Five minutes into the hike I heard a noise behind me, like the sound of someone's footfalls crunching over the path—just like my footsteps, only some distance away. I paused, looked around, and waved the flashlight in front of me and behind me. It wasn't completely dark yet, but the mist made it difficult. I couldn't see anyone; so assumed it was just somebody walking one of the other paths inland. It could also have been the wind rustling the seagrass, or the waves crashing into the rocks underneath.

A few minutes later, I heard it again. Like before, it was quiet when I stopped and turned around, but the minute I picked up the pace the noise began again.

Snap. Crunch. Snap.

Louder this time.

After verifying that I was alone, I chalked it up to my imagination. My nerves were shattered. I pressed the button on my jacket to allow the batteries to turn on the heat; there was a chill in the air. I picked up the pace, keeping the light out front to see my way across the path. The fog was getting thick. I was just about at the end of the trail. Wild roses, hyacinths, and Stork's-Bill wildflowers lined both sides, and then I came to the stone steps that led to the peninsula point lookout. With the right weather, the view of the ocean from here was normally breathtaking. I could hear the waves crashing into the earth down below;

the calming effect was usually a highlight of the visit to the Knob.

I let my eyes dance from left to right. Stone blocks served as benches and wrapped around most of the perimeter on the left side and the center in front of me. They were great for sitting to look out at the view, but they had a dual purpose; they served as a safety precaution to keep hikers from falling over that section of the cliff since it was the high point of the lookout. Jake said he and Bailey would be at the bench, but I couldn't see them.

"Jake?" I called out. No response.

I walked toward the right side of the point. There was no stone bench there, just vegetation. You could walk to the edge and see the view of Buzzard's Bay from there.

"Jake! Bailey, come here, girl."

On the right flank, there was a large boulder with a narrow path behind where people would stand to look out and take scenic pictures. There were trees, brush, and more wild flowers planted in the earth around the point, with boulders and rocks that kept it standing over the years. That's where I saw Bailey's collapsible water bowl, the one we specifically bought to carry when taking walks. Oh no, please tell me Jake didn't walk her this way and something happened.

"Jake, Bailey!" I called out again, this time louder. I walked down the path and leaned over to pick it up, looking around as I did to see if I could see them. When I stood back up, something heavy struck me on the back of my head. Momentarily stunned, I instinctively put the palm of my hand on the spot, surprised to feel that it was moist. As I turned to see what it was, unsteady on my feet, all I could see was a blur of black before a set of hands pushed me forward.

I stumbled and fell forward with nothing to stop me as I lost control of my body. Then I was tumbling down through the brush, branches scratching against me on the way down. I cocooned my head between my elbows, trying to protect it from the blows as I plummeted down onto the boulders used to support the peninsula. My shoulders took the hits instead. Excruciating pain surged through me with each bounce, and then I suddenly stopped moving. My body was face-down between two boulders, blocking me from plunging into the ocean. I remained there without moving so the person who pushed me would think I was unconscious, or dead; undoubtedly the result they hoped for.

I wasn't sure how much time passed before I attempted to move. By the time I did, my joints were feeling the pain from being violently jostled about. Admittedly, it would be much worse if I didn't have on the heated jacket to keep the elements from seeping into my bones. I tried to remember the details of how it happened, to keep my mind fresh. When I make it back up to the top, the information would be necessary. All I cared about at the moment was; where was Bailey?

The sky was pitch-black over the water. I was wet from the waves crashing into the boulders. As long as it didn't short out the battery, my upper body was warm. The rest of me was battered. My head was throbbing, and the pain in my right shoulder was excruciating. I hoped it wasn't dislocated.

I maneuvered myself so that I could reach into my backpack. I pulled out the rope leash I brought for Bailey. There was no way I could just climb up the rocks without help. I used one end of the rope to form a Honda knot and then looped the other end through to form a lasso. Now, all I had to do was lasso a heavy branch firm enough to aid with the climb. I pushed myself up to a seated position. A simple call to the police would solve my problem and get me back home. I knew that. But then there would be an investigation, more questions to be answered. I knew who did this to me—who shoved me off the cliff and left me to die. I needed proof. For that, I was going to see this through. I was thankful for the boulders; they kept me from plummeting into the ocean. I realized that was her plan.

I viewed the terrain above and looked for a tree with thick branches or a narrow boulder that I could catch. I found a branch I thought might work and tried to get up on my feet. That's when I heard voices, but I couldn't verify where they were coming from. Were they saying my name? I didn't know how long I was down on the boulders; time just seemed to disappear.

"Katie!"

I heard the voice again. I forced myself to look up; the throbbing of my head intensified. Was that light up there on the cliff? It danced over the boulders. Then pointed right at me, disappeared, and returned.

"Oh my God, she's down there," I heard a voice say. It sounded like Jake. But then I heard other voices. I had to be hallucinating; Olivia and Madison? What would they be doing with Jake? I suddenly felt a chill and my legs felt shaky underneath me just as a humongous wave knocked me off my feet.

CHAPTER 45 - KATIE

Present – May 2020

THE NEXT TIME I opened my eyes it was no longer dark and I was no longer outside. I wasn't wet or cold. I looked up; the ceiling above me was white instead of the midnight sky over the ocean. My eyes roamed around and I realized it was my room, my bed. The blinds were open to let in the sun and the flat-screen TV that was mounted on the wall was currently showing an NCIS rerun. The clothing I wore to the Knob had been removed. Now, I was wearing a pair of boxer shorts and a tank top—my usual sleeping attire. A comforter was draped over my legs. Did Jake undress me? After everything I had learned that thought was unsettling.

When I tried to sit up, I felt weak, like I'd been lying in bed for days instead of merely overnight. My head was still throbbing; getting whacked in the head was real and not just a hallucination. I glanced at my reflection in the dresser mirror. I didn't recognize the woman staring back at me. Someone wrapped a gauze bandage around my head. My right cheek was discolored, adding to the dark circles under my eyes. There was a homemade sling around my right shoulder, and both elbows were in severe pain. That probably happened from using my arms to protect my head when bouncing down the rocks.

I recalled how I got home and changed out of my wet clothes. I remember hearing voices: Jake, Olivia, and Madison, and another voice I didn't recognize. Later I learned it was a homeowner who showed Jake the video surveillance of The Knob. There was no security at the park, just volunteers who agreed to keep watch.

Images passed through my mind: Jake rappelling down; his tech rescue gear was always in his vehicle. When he first approached, I was defiant. Screaming and yelling at him. My body took a beating, so I couldn't fight him off with physical force. I didn't know the extent of my injuries yet, but I felt the pain. He didn't know what to make of my behavior; it was so out of character. He excused it by saying I was probably in shock. I yelled I was fine, knew exactly what I was saying, and just get me back up. I was cold, but I knew exactly what was going on.

When I heard Olivia and Madison yelling down at me, I finally consented to him checking my vitals. I couldn't hear their words, just the echo of their voices; them being close was reassuring. He asked me some questions to check my cognitive awareness, asked me how long I'd been there and if I was awake the whole time. I took a beating, for sure, but I told him I could make it back up with his help. I informed him that I never lost consciousness; I was just weak from the cold and sore from the fall.

He put me in a harness and secured me to the ropes around his waist using carabineers, and then told me to wrap my arms and legs around him so his arms and legs were free to move. Before coming down, he had attached ropes to a tree making a pulley system, which he now used to walk us back up.

When we reached the top, Olivia and Madison hugged me and rattled off question after question. Some I didn't want to answer in front of Jake. I pretended I was too out of it to respond. When Jake was out of earshot, I told them I'd tell them everything when he wasn't around. Now, I just wanted to get home.

Thankfully, the homeowner in charge of video surveillance agreed not to involve the local police. I didn't want there to be a report, so I took the blame, claimed I was stupid and careless. I just wouldn't be able to visit the Knob in the future. After what happened, I doubt I would want to, anyway.

Admittedly, I was reeling from confusion. Jake was the one who sent me the message claiming he needed help. Instead of finding him, I was pushed off a cliff and left for dead. Did I think he was capable of doing that? No. I never thought he'd cheat on me or create an entire double life, either. My sense of judgment obviously couldn't be trusted, but I was pretty sure who was responsible for luring me to the cliff… it wasn't Jake.

I heard a noise in the hallway which brought me back to the present. A prescription bottle and ibuprofen were on the nightstand to the left side of the bed. I leaned over to pick up the bottle, but I didn't have my reading glasses to read the small print.

"Pain medicine," Jake said when he walked into the room and saw me trying to read the label. "Olivia had some left from her knee surgery and thought you might need one for your shoulder when you woke up this morning."

"So I wasn't hallucinating, after all." I reached up to touch the back of my head to see if I could feel a lump. I did a small one, and it was sore.

"Olivia and Madison helped me with the bandage and the sling. You refused to go to the hospital, got hysterical. Why were you even there? How did you get down onto the rocks?"

I stared at Jake, not shocked by his reaction. He was in the dark. "I received a message that your knee went out, that you needed my help."

He was shaking his head. "I never sent any message, Kat. I took Bailey there for a walk, but we weren't there for more than an hour."

Bailey heard her name mentioned; her head moved back and forth between the two of us, listening to the tone of our voices to make sure everything was okay.

"I was here at home when Olivia and Madison came looking for you," he said sheepishly. "They were worried because you didn't send over the last chapters. I didn't know where you had gone, but I searched for your phone. We're on the family plan so we can do that. It located you at the Knob. It was dark, so we worried something was wrong. We drove there, and I called the emergency number on the sign. One of the homeowners in the area answered, so I asked him to view the video from the monitored surveillance. It showed you walking the path, but then lost sight of you when you reached the peninsula."

"Did the video show anyone else walking the path?"

He frowned. "We saw dozens of people on the path, but not during the time you were."

I was watching his mannerisms; he was being sincere; he had no idea.

300

"The three of us walked the area. We were about to call the police until we did one more sweep with the flashlight, that's when we found you down on the rocks. Olivia and Madison kept watching while I hurried back to the truck for my gear. Then they helped me set up. When I rappelled down, you kept yelling at me and insisted you were fine, that we just get you home. I recommended we take you to the emergency room just to get checked and you went ballistic. You were very persistent."

Various thoughts ran through my head when I was down on the rocks, not knowing when I'd make it back home. They were coming to me now. Bailey kept whining, so I kept petting her to let her know I was okay. "Where's my phone? It was in the jacket I was wearing."

Jake walked back down the hall. I heard the clothes dryer open and close. When he returned, he handed over my phone and held up the jacket with the battery pack.

"The jacket was wet so I emptied the pockets, then washed and dried it. The pockets are waterproof so the phone was protected. Your jeans had to be cut off to get you into your boxers. Your legs are all scraped up. It was hurting you when I tried to pull them off."

I pulled the comforter off to the side and glanced at my bare legs. He was right. They looked like they went a few rounds with some rose bushes and lost. I had abrasions up and down both legs. It was surprising that I didn't feel the pain from those, but it was probably because my shoulder kept throbbing so my mind was focused elsewhere.

"I'm a mess," I said to myself.

"So, do you want to tell me what happened?"

I rifled through my phone, searched for the message I received from him, and then enlarged it on the screen to show him.

He shook his head, looking bewildered. "I swear, Kat, I didn't send that message."

I let out a heavy sigh. I expected that response from him. After everything that's gone on, it had already occurred to me that Lexi Thompson had more access to Jake than just getting his set of keys.

"When I received the message yesterday, I drove to the Knob to help you. You weren't in the location designated in the message, so I walked around and noticed Bailey's collapsible dish on the ground. When I bent down to retrieve it, somebody hit me on the back of the head. It didn't knock me out, but it hurt. I remember touching my head and feeling the moistness, which was blood. As I turned around, all I could see was a dark-colored, hooded sweatshirt, before two hands shoved me forward."

"Somebody pushed you?" His eyes went wide at the realization, and I could tell his mind was churning. He had to realize this was all about him. Stacy died because of him. Now, that same person tried to kill me. I wanted to unburden my soul and tell him I knew everything and see him panic about the future. Now that my anger had allowed me to come up with a plan, I wasn't sure if telling him now was the best course of action. Unfortunately, I couldn't stop myself... hell hath no fury like a woman scorned.

CHAPTER 46 - KATIE

Present – May 2020

"COULD YOU GET me a bottle of water; I need to take some ibuprofen."

"Why don't you take one of the pain pills?"

I shook my head. "That would just knock me out. I need to be present for this."

He had a concerned look on his face when he left the room. While he was out in the kitchen, I leaned back on the pillow and tried to think of the best way to proceed, tell him what happened, and carry out the next part of my plan. Once I started, there would be no going back. Ah, to hell with it; I can't keep stalling, hoping for the perfect time. There would be no perfect time. I turned on the flat-screen TV, hit the source button, and switched it to the PC component. Everything I saved on my portable hard drive could be accessed through the PC now with the right password. I entered it and then opened up the PowerPoint file I created, verified it would play properly, and then switched to a blank screen and hit pause. I didn't want it playing until I was ready.

Jake returned with the water and a plate full of fruit, yogurt, and crackers. "You should probably eat something too."

He opened the ibuprofen and dropped two pills in my hand. I downed them with a gulp of water, and then I got comfortable.

Noticing the serious look on my face, he asked, "Should I be sitting down?"

"You probably should," I said.

He sat down in the club chair next to the vanity and then called Bailey over; worried that she was rubbing against my wounds.

I took in a deep breath, let it out, and stared directly at him so I could see his reaction. "Lexi Thompson did this to me."

His eyes went wide and his expression went from surprise to horror, completely stunned by my statement. "Lexi Thompson? Why would she harm you? I didn't know you two even knew each other."

I shook my head, disappointed that he was choosing to act innocent, and denial was his first reaction. "The gig is up, Jake. I know everything."

He shifted in his seat. "What do you mean, you know everything?"

I hit the select button on the remote which opened the PowerPoint on the TV screen and then I hit play while he watched in confusion. A steady stream of the pornographic images and videos I discovered played one right after the other. "I know all about the secret lives you've been living... Stacy Levin and Lexi Thompson."

His face turned red and his head continued to shake in denial as sexual images and videos of him and Stacy, and then some showing him with Lexi played on the screen. After a few minutes, he looked downcast and kept his eyes averted from the TV; and me. He could no longer look at either.

"Kat, I'm not sure what you think you know, but you shouldn't jump to conclusions. Turn it off, please."

"Just stop, Jake!" I yelled. "Look at the TV. Look at what you forced me to learn. I found over two-thousand images and the same number of videos, and there are more that I didn't bother to look at. You and your women filmed every dirty piece of your sexual lifestyle. From the images and videos alone, I could probably recap every sordid detail. I know you met Lexi Thompson through work some years ago. You might have trained her for all I know. You hooked up, explored sexual games and bondage, filmed everything, and saved them for later viewing. Then, something happened. Maybe she wanted more, so you broke it off."

"Broke it off? We were never an item. It was just sex … you were busy with writing."

"DO NOT INTERRUPT ."

He rubbed his hands over his face, defeated. "Maybe Lexi was pushing for more; who knows? You stayed friendly, continued to hook up occasionally. Then, Stacy Levin showed up on a motorcycle ride nearly two years ago. She lives out of state but enjoyed the same lifestyle as Lexi. She also has an addiction to filming sexual selfies, which was probably a turn-on to you. The difference; she was convenient. She flew in and attended rides once a month. You could get your rocks off for the weekend. And then she headed back home. With her, the chances were better that I wouldn't find out; me, the oblivious and trusting soul. The fool."

"Don't talk about yourself like that. You're not a fool."

"I am a fool! I trusted you for over twenty years. I never spied on you, questioned nothing you did, and demanded nothing from you, and you got away with creating your secret world. I am beyond humiliated by how foolish I have been."

"Kat, this isn't about you. You're the best thing that ever happened to me, you know that. I just, I don't know. I screwed up. I can't explain it. They introduced me to their world… I don't expect you to understand, I just—"

I put my hand up to make him stop talking. "I understand it completely. We've been together for over twenty years. We had our passionate sex and romance, romps in odd places, and even some erotica. We were hot and heavy for years. But reality sets in. You were always looking for that adventure in the fire service that kept you away from home while I handled the everyday problems that occurred, paying the bills, helping to raise your children, taking care of the dog. I never knew when you were coming home. When you did, you were out of sorts, from whatever calls you handled that week or issues at the fire department. The simple answer is; you looked for an outside adventure that included bondage and control, something you knew I wouldn't take part in."

"I didn't go looking," Jake said as if that excused his role in the act.

"Right. Lexi Thompson made it easy for you. She introduced you to her unemotional sexual lifestyle without having to worry about the everyday life of bills, house issues, or responsibilities. You came to crave it. It was like the days when you got excited rushing into a fire. And like a fire that needed oxygen to burn, your body needed the sexual release to feed the addiction. Look at the TV, Jake! That was the world you desired. There's not an ounce of emotion in any of those sex scenes you're portraying. It was disturbing robotic porn. You have a problem… but you're right, it's not about me. It's a sick addiction you've been acting out because you're not happy inside."

He cringed, but I didn't know if it was from the words I was using or the sound of my voice. Seeing the compilation of images and videos was bringing the anguish to the surface.

"I'm not unhappy with you."

"No, you're unhappy with yourself. You're always looking for the next fix. Who spends every single day accepting sexual selfies on their phone? And you saved them all. You viewed them at work. Here at home, while I was in the same room with you. Some of them were downright disturbing. Sick, even. What kind of person films themselves going to the bathroom?"

His brows furrowed. He looked at me like I didn't know what I was talking about. "That's ridiculous."

"You saved the images and videos, Jake. They're all on your electronics."

"I've never seen anything like that."

I shook my head, disgusted that he thought dismissing the one type of photo would negate the thousands of others. "Well, I did, and it's just sick."

Jake leaned over and put his head in his hands. "I'm sorry, Kat. I don't know what I can say."

"You're just sorry you got caught."

He raised his head and looked at me, stunned by my cruel words. "Someone is dead, Kat, and it almost killed you. I'm sorry about all of it. What do you think I am, heartless?"

"Yes, Jake, I think you're heartless. You're not the same man I've known. One of your playthings is dead, and you didn't say a word. You let the police question me, mentioning nothing. Still, to this very moment, you haven't said one word about the fact that Stacy Levin was killed riding on the back of the motorcycle."

"I did that to protect you. Once the police got involved, I was afraid to talk about it with you. I was trying to give you deniability. If you didn't know about her, then—"

"If I didn't know you were having an obsessive sexual affair with Stacy Levin?"

He cringed again. "In my mind, if you knew nothing about her, then the police could rule you out."

"You didn't just have one sexual affair. You had two, at least that I know of. You set up a separate life and blocked me from having access. And you failed to take into consideration that Lexi Thompson has mental issues, and didn't like being rejected. Before I knew anything about your sexual affairs, she was making my life miserable. She's been stalking me for a long time. She showed up at book signings and tried to sabotage my appearances. She put cameras in our home and posted images of me on my book page. She's been trying to harm me, professionally, mentally, and physically. She's the one who rammed into your motorcycle, killing Stacy, but she stole my vehicle to do it. The police haven't been able to rule me out, because she's trying to frame me. Since I haven't been arrested, she's trying to get rid of me, permanently."

It was finally getting through to him exactly what his double life created. He looked distraught. "I had no idea, Kat. Why didn't you tell me?"

"Are you kidding me? Why didn't I tell you?"

He got up and started pacing. "I made a mistake and things… they just got out of control. Now, I don't know what to do to make it right."

"You can't make it right."

"You're angry, I get that—"

"I'm beyond angry. I wasted over two decades of my life. You had such little respect for me you lived a secret life instead of asking for a divorce."

"I didn't want a divorce! I never wanted a divorce."

I nearly choked when I spoke. Was he for real? "What did you think living a double life with two different women would lead to? You set all of this in motion. *You* did this, even if you didn't push me off the cliff yourself, you're responsible for it happening."

Jake unexpectedly rushed toward me at the same time I felt something dripping down the side of my face. "You're bleeding."

"Don't touch me!" I shouted as if his very touch were poisonous.

He looked hurt and backed away. "Okay, but you can't get yourself upset like that."

I didn't realize it, but the entire time I was unleashing my anger out on him with my words, I had been obsessively scratching my head. I irritated the wound through the gauze. "Just leave, please."

He shook his head. "I can't leave you like this. At least let me wipe down the wound."

"No. Just go." I turned off the TV, too sick to continue viewing the images.

He stared at me for a moment, unsure of what to do, then knowing I was stubborn and wouldn't change my mind, he walked toward the door with Bailey following him. Before closing the door behind them, he gave me a pitiful look. "I didn't mean to hurt anyone, Kat. You have no idea."

I just stared at him; there wasn't much I could say. Once I was sure he was gone, I eased out of the bed and slowly walked into the bathroom. Looking in the mirror, I looked like death warmed over. My right shoulder was still in pain, so I removed the gauze from my head with my left hand and placed my round portable mirror behind my head to look at the wound. Blood matted my hair. I used a terrycloth rag and washed the area with a mild liquid soap. Once it was clean, it didn't look too bad. There was a lump the size of a quarter and a wound that I opened by scratching. The bruise on my cheek and the abrasions on my legs looked worse, but it was my joints that were suffering. Between my elbows and shoulder, it was hard to move. Still, I was lucky. It could have been much worse.

After going to the bathroom and brushing my teeth, I walked back into the bedroom, stepped into a loose-fitting pair of jeans so they wouldn't irritate the abrasions, struggled into a long-sleeve sweatshirt, and my Adidas sneakers. Not a simple task when you can't move your shoulder too well. Before leaving the room, I put on a baseball cap.

When I walked into the kitchen Jake was sitting outside on the deck staring at the ocean, looking like a child who just lost his best friend. He did. Bailey was sitting on the steps with a ball in her mouth, hoping he'd throw it. He wasn't taking the hint.

With him preoccupied, I sat down at my laptop, signed out of my *Facebook* page, and signed into his account. I didn't bother to do so before, because I had access to that profile. Besides, he wouldn't have posted anything on there that he wouldn't want me to see. What I hoped to do, though, was get access to his private account, the one he blocked me from seeing. It occurred to me that was how Lexi Thompson and Stacy Levin communicated with him. He didn't know I was aware of it, so chances were good that he used one of his usual passwords. I just hoped I came up with the right one before they locked me out of the page.

After a few attempts, the page opened after I typed in the numbers of his daughter's first name and birthday. I didn't waste time scrolling the page; the content was irrelevant at this stage. I went straight to the messenger and searched for conversations with Lexi Thompson. When the dialogue box opened, the first thing that popped up was a selfie of Lexi straddling her motorcycle. It was time-stamped last night after she pushed me off the cliff. Her mental capacity was so bad she was still sending him messages. She wore a strapless, low-cut top, no bra, and jean shorts, wearing a big smile while showing off a bracelet on her left wrist: the same emerald bracelet that he gave me for my birthday. I didn't think his betrayal could get any worse.

It took everything in me to not grab the baseball bat, storm out to the deck, and crack him on the skull. Breathe in. Breathe out.

I had a method to my madness for being on his page. I planned to pose as him and send her a message. I read through some of the early messages between the two of them, not because I wanted to. I needed to understand the type of language spoken between them, the tone. Did he refer to her by name, or something else? To pull it off, I had to make sure the message sounded like him. It wouldn't be easy. Most of their messages were X-rated. Who the hell was Jake Parker?

Then I browsed through some of their recent messages. The woman truly was delusional. Jake hadn't communicated with her since Stacy was killed, but she continued to send messages, most of them sexual to try and persuade him. One message caught my eye and I realized I could use it in my fabricated message to her. In it, she reminded him of the many times he said they could be together if he wasn't married. In her fantasy world, she probably took that to mean: get rid of the wife.

I typed and deleted several sentences before I was convinced that what I wrote would suffice enough that she wouldn't see through my ruse. I reread it a few times to make sure: *Damn, that bracelet looks good on you. Next time, wear the bracelet and nothing else. ;-)*

Hey listen, Katie finally left and hasn't been home. Now, there's no wife to interfere. How about you bring that body over here tonight so we can act out that fantasy you mentioned… how's 7? Let me know as soon as possible. Have to head out for errands.

I felt so filthy and disgusted after hitting send, but it was necessary. Now I had to wait. I couldn't take the chance that he might see the messages. If she was as obsessed as I assumed, she would be eagerly waiting for news of my demise, and the reply would be quick. I glanced outside; he was still moping. Bailey gave up and was lying by his side.

Her first response was fast and just as I expected. She complied with the request in the message: she sent a naked selfie only wearing the bracelet. The next message said: *you don't need her. She doesn't know how to please you. I'll be there at 7 with my bag of toys.*

Bag of toys?

I typed a quick response: *If I'm late, the door will be unlocked. Let yourself in and surprise me. You know what I like.*

She responded with another disturbing selfie. I immediately deleted the entire conversation so he wouldn't see it. I shut off my laptop and locked it in my safe deposit box. Then I retrieved the security cameras I purchased from my bottom drawer. The Lowes employee told me they were easy to set up. All I needed was wireless internet and I could work them from my phone. All I had to do was get Jake to leave for an hour. I looked through the refrigerator to see if we needed anything at the store. I grabbed the jug of Aloe Vera juice, took a long drink, and then poured the rest down the drain. I walked to the door and slid it open, holding the empty container.

"Would you mind running into town and picking up another bottle of this juice? I need it to keep my stomach calm. I thought there was some left, but it's empty."

"Sure," he said, pushing himself up. "You need anything else? Want me to pick up something for dinner?"

Typical Jake, already back in the denial mode, acting as if nothing happened, all because I asked a favor. *Play the game, Katie, play the game.* "I doubt I'll be that hungry, but pick up whatever you want."

He nodded. "K. Be back in a few. I'll take Bailey with me. Come on, let's go for a ride."

His keys were already in the truck; he had a habit of leaving them there most of the time, and his money clip was always in his pocket. I watched Bailey follow him. He opened the back door and helped her up into the seat; the truck was too high off the ground for her to make the jump on her own. The minute I saw him hop in the driver's seat and pull out of the driveway, I got to work setting up the cameras and everything else I needed for later. When Jake returned, I would have to come up with another excuse to get him out of the house for a short time, so that he wasn't here when Lexi arrived. That was the only way my plan would work.

CHAPTER 47 – KATIE/MY STALKER

Present – May 2020

LEXI THOMPSON WAS punctual. I heard her SUV pull up, though she didn't park in the driveway. She parked a few cottages away and walked toward my cottage like a thief in the night. She came around to the sliding glass door and let herself in, just as directed by the message. I was viewing her every move on my phone from a hidden location via the cameras I set up. I parked my car a few streets over and walked back once I convinced Jake to take a drive to Lowes and pick up some supplies for the toilet in the main bathroom. I purposely clogged it, tossed the plunger and plumbing liquid from under the sink, and asked him to pick up more.

She was oblivious to the fact that I orchestrated him to be out of the home for her arrival. The store was fifteen minutes away. True to form, he would walk the aisles looking at the latest tool sale and then stop at McDonald's picking up a tall coke—a habit I could put a clock to, so it was plenty of time for what I had in mind.

She called out his name just to be sure he wasn't there. When he didn't respond, she set down the duffel bag she brought with her and started nosing around at my desk. I suspected she would. She wouldn't find anything. I put everything in my safe deposit box and gave it to Olivia, along with my completed manuscript for editing, and asked that she watch Bailey for a while. If she browsed through the story before she started editing, she would know the ending between me and the woman who has been stalking me before Lexi did. I added it after installing the cameras, then printed it and put it in a manila envelope. Now, it came down to whether or not I had the guts to pull it off.

Lexi used my husband's messenger account to lure me to the cliff. I did the same to lure her inside my home. Like me, she assumed Jake sent her the message. She also had no way of knowing whether I was dead or alive. She might be deranged, but she wouldn't have remained in the area after pushing me off the cliff for fear of getting caught—she had nobody else to frame for that hit job.

Once she finished snooping, she grabbed her duffel bag and wandered back into our master bedroom. The former white comforter that she defiled with the knife and blood had been tossed and replaced with an old one I would be okay with throwing out. She set the duffel on the edge of the bed and pulled out some supplies: a black blindfold, various vibrators, lotions, leather attire, a rope, a can of whip cream, a bowl of strawberries, and the blonde wig.

Then she started rifling through my drawers. When she came to my underwear drawer, she picked up a few garments and studied them. She must have taken a liking to a turquoise set I bought for myself because she started to undress and put them on.

I thought I was going to be sick.

She rifled through another drawer, saw my makeup, and selected a pink lip-gloss. Looking into the mirror, she seductively rolled it over her lips, leaned over, and kissed the mirror. Smiling at the imagery of the glossy lips left behind, she dropped the lip-gloss into her duffel, piled her brown hair on top of her head, and put the blonde wig on. Posing provocatively in front of the mirror, she used her fingers to maneuver the layers around her head until they gave her the look she was going for.

It was eerie watching a disturbed woman try to transform herself into me.

Then she sprawled out on the comforter, tied both ankles to the bedposts, and then put the blindfold on. She reached for the can of whip cream and proceeded to draw a line from her chin, in between her breasts, and continued down past her belly button then drew an arrow pointing toward the turquoise thong covering her vagina. Then she wrote out the letters EM just above the panty line. I didn't have to be a genius to know what they meant. Satisfied, she placed four strawberries, curved into a smile, just under the letters. She set the stage just as she described in her fantasy. For the final touch, she looped the rope around the right bedpost at the head of the bed and laid her head down on the pillows to give the appearance she was tied up and Jake could do as he pleased.

CHAPTER 48 – KATIE/MY STALKER

Present – May 2020

JAKE SHOWED UP twenty minutes later than I expected. I could see him from the spot I was hiding. He stepped out of the truck, reached into the back seat for the bag from Lowes, and entered the cottage. Once inside, he set the bag and his McDonald's drink down on the island then walked toward the bedroom.

When he entered the room and saw the vision on the bed, he stood in the doorway for a minute, stunned. For a moment, it appeared as if he thought it was me? She had on the wig, was wearing my bra and thong—which he had seen before—and my pink lip gloss. A frown suddenly appeared on his face as he walked toward the bed. Through the camera, it looked to me like he was inspecting the body and realized it was not me. I was shorter by a few inches. I have a golden-colored tan as opposed to a deep fake tan and I have a bikini line visible when wearing a thong. Lexi tanned nude.

"Lexi, what the hell are you doing?"

He looked back toward the door as if he thought I might enter the room at any moment.

"Giving you what you desire," she responded in a seductive voice. "We talked about this."

"I mean, what are you doing here?"

"Don't play coy, Jake, you wanted this."

"But not at my home, not now."

For the first time, her body seemed to react to the rejection. She pulled her left wrist free from the rope and removed the mask, revealing the anger in her eyes. "It was what you wanted. You told me to come here. Told me you were running errands, but to go on in. You said I know what you like."

He was shaking his head no.

An ugly scowl appeared on her face. "Don't try to deny what you did."

He kept looking toward the door.

"How many times did you tell me if Katie was not in the picture, then you and I would be together?"

"I never said that."

"Yes, you did. You said it was a shame we didn't meet first, that you couldn't live without my touch. Are you saying that wasn't true?"

Jake raked a hand through his hair, rattled. He feared I would walk it at any moment, but I could tell by the look on his face he also wanted to placate her, too. He wasn't aware I was watching through the cameras.

"I meant it when I said it."

"You don't mean it now?"

"As I've also said repeatedly, I'm married."

"Well, Katie's no longer here, and we both know the only reason you hooked up with that woman from New Mexico was because of the pressure I put on you. She was safe."

He looked dumbfounded. "How did you know about her?"

She laughed hysterically. "I'm on your private page, remember? Your biker friends shared pictures of the rides and tagged you. Now, she's gone and so is Katie, so what's the problem?"

His eyes went wide, finally seeing the truth. "What do you mean, Katie is gone? Dammit, Lexi, what did you do?"

Her smile was sadistic. "I did what you didn't have the balls to do."

That was my cue.

CHAPTER 49 – KATIE/MYSTALKER

Present – May 2020

I STOOD UP from the spot in the seagrass where I had been hiding and observing their actions from my phone. I padded across the deck and opened the sliding glass door. Even if they heard me, there was nothing they could or would do at this point. Before I did anything else, I clicked on the phone app for the security cameras and deactivated each one. What happened from here on out, I didn't want the images captured on film.

Before heading to the bedroom, I walked toward the bookcase and opened the cabinet to the right of the TV. There was a small gun safe where Jake kept the concealed carry weapons on the top shelf. I turned the combination and retrieved his Sig P365 9mm. I locked the safe, closed the cabinet, and strode down the hall with the gun out in front of me.

Jake's face drained of color the minute he saw me with the gun, but the look on Lexi's face when I pointed the gun toward her was worth my crazy move.

"Do you know what the laws are in Massachusetts for shooting an intruder who enters your home, illegally?"

"You don't need to do this, Katie," Jake said, stunned that, for the first time, I dared to have the courage to stand my ground.

Lexi was glaring at me in shock, but it quickly turned to defiance.

"What's the matter, Lexi? Surprised to see I'm alive and well?"

"What the hell are you doing here?"

I smirked at her. "I live here. It's my cottage. You're in my bed, wearing my undergarments, my lip-gloss, and a wig trying to look like me." I walked toward the right bedpost and retied the rope to secure her wrist.

She gritted her teeth and tried to pull it free, but discovered she couldn't. She jerked, pulled, and tried to kick her ankles, but none of them would loosen their hold. Angrier now, she hissed at me. "It's Jake's cottage, not yours. You don't even have a job."

I laughed. She wasn't the first person who Jake talked to that hinted writing was just a hobby. Because I worked inside the home, he was never great about classifying it as a job, either. I knew she got that attitude from their conversations. I know he painted himself as the poor, neglected husband, and she lapped it up.

"You won't shoot me," she said through clenched teeth. "You don't have the guts."

I moved back around to the foot of the bed and kept the gun pointed at her. "I guess your investigative skills aren't as good as you think they are. Jake hasn't paid one dime on this home, have you, Jake?"

She stared at him with questions in her eyes but quickly bounced back. "I don't believe a word you say. The checks from his business pay the payment."

I rolled my eyes. I would not debate our finances with her. "Jake, did you fill her head with stories to make yourself look good, or has she been snooping on your bank accounts?"

His expression looked like he was a deer caught in the headlights. There was no way out for him, so he remained silent.

The checks that paid the cottage payments were from our joint account. She wouldn't know that because it had the business name on the account that Jake used for his training classes. She had no way of knowing both names were on the business and either of us could sign checks. It wasn't her business to know.

"Believe what you want," I said, taunting her the way she'd been taunting me. "Most of what you say and do is delusional. And when it comes to guts, I'll just tell you what was said to me recently: *Everybody is capable of harming another when they've been pushed to the brink*. I think both of you would agree… you pushed me to the brink."

A moment of fear flashed in her eyes. She started pulling the ropes again, harder, as if she was trying to break the bedposts. "I'm delusional?" She mocked.

"The visual display on my bed right now is proof of that."

She gave me a hysterical laugh. "I'm not the one who goes around lying to the world, pretending she's got this great relationship, and meanwhile, her husband needs other women to fulfill his needs because his perfect little wife can't. It wasn't me he blocked from his social medial accounts. He did that to you. Tell her, Jake. You opened a fake account and wouldn't allow her to see what you were up to."

I admit those statements hurt, but I wasn't about to let her know that. I glanced over at Jake. He averted his eyes and seemed to have been stunned into silence and was allowing the two women to fight the battle for him.

"Say something, Jake," she yelled. "Man up and get the goddamn gun away from her."

I stared at Jake, defying him to take a step toward me. "Sit down, Jake. This discussion is just starting," I said. He wasn't quick to move. With his arrogance, he probably figured he would be able to talk his way out of this.

"Sit down, or I will put a bullet in one of her knee caps," I ordered, and this time he thought I was serious by the tone of my voice when I positioned the gun directly over her right knee. "You have no idea just how angry I am."

He reluctantly took a seat and kept his eyes on me, worried; he had never seen me out of sorts like this and had no idea what I was capable of.

Using my phone, I pushed the camera and hit record, but placed the phone on the vanity so they wouldn't know. I only wanted our conversations recorded.

"So, Lexi; what was your intention of coming here tonight? Were you hoping to play out some sick fantasy of having sex in my bed? After all, it wasn't Jake you had been stalking for months or more. It was me. Do you have some twisted crush on me, or are you just hoping to be me?"

She coughed up some phlegm and spit at me in anger, like that of an overgrown teenager or demented adult. "Why would I want to be you? You can't even satisfy your husband."

"And yet, here you are wearing a wig and my undergarments to look just like me."

"Go ahead and shoot," she said, brazenly. "You'll be the one going to jail."

I laughed, which she didn't like because it meant I was dismissive. Women like her didn't like to be ignored.

She glared at Jake. "Do something, Jake, or I—"

"Shut up!" I shouted at her.

"Kat, what are you trying to do?" Jake finally managed to ask.

"Don't call me Kat … you don't get to call me that ever again," I yelled, summoning up my own hysteria. I was tired of everybody else having control; I wanted to gain some back for myself.

"Which one of you wants to tell me the truth? Lexi, how about you? What were you hoping to gain by stalking me?"

She gave me a sarcastic chuckle. "You are so naïve. Don't you know you're just his patsy… perfect little wholesome Katie."

"Stop it, Lexi," Jake demanded.

Lexi leveled him with an icy stare. "Why, will it hurt her precious feelings? You don't care about her, haven't cared about her for a long time."

"I never said that," Jake said, his voice defiant.

"Then why'd you give in to me so easily?"

I kept the gun pointed at her, but watching the dialogue between the two of them, it occurred to me I could get more answers that way.

He raked his fingers through his hair. "You said you didn't care, that you were just having fun."

Lexi exploded. "That was three years ago when we were just fucking around. I told you at some point I wanted more. Sure, you broke it off and hooked up with that skank, but you kept coming back. I thought you understood?"

He stood up, and we both yelled at him: "Sit down!"

He let out a heavy sigh but sat back down. "Lexi, I never promised you anything. You knew it was sex, nothing more."

She let out a scream, frustrated. "That's a lie and you know it."

Jake got quiet. "I don't remember what I said all those years ago. Maybe I said something to keep things going, but I had no intention of leaving Katie."

The bed started rocking when Lexi went nuts, trying to break free from her ropes. "You lying son of a bitch!"

Things were not exactly going as planned. I hoped to get some confessions out of them, not push them into a fight against each other, though I was getting info. If she kept it up she could break the bed; she was much larger than me. "Stop it," I screamed at her, but her anger only intensified.

She thrashed against the bed and banged her head against the headboard.

"Stop it, Lexi. I'll let you free; just admit you've been stalking me and that you tried to frame me for Stacy Levin's death."

"Untie me now!" she hissed between her teeth, looking like a woman who was undergoing an exorcism.

The violent way her body was moving on the bed, I was afraid she was going to give herself a heart attack. She acted crazed. "Jake, untie one of her wrists."

Jake glared at me, but he did as he was told. He untied the wrist that was near him, and she immediately moved to untie her other hand. When both hands were free, she tried to slap him, but he backed away before she connected.

"Lexi, tell me why you were stalking me," I ordered, nudging her with the gun to remind her I had a weapon.

She laughed sarcastically and went about untying her ankles. "You won't shoot, no matter how tough you talk or threaten."

"She's right, Katie," Jake said, and held his hand out for the gun. "It's not in you to shoot her, no matter what she's done to you. So let me have my gun."

"It's his gun?" Lexi shouted hysterically. "You can't even get a gun by yourself?"

I looked back and forth between the two of them, battling the altering voices inside my head. One voice was telling me to just shoot her already. The other reminded me that wouldn't accomplish anything but bring misery to myself. I tried to summon up the fortitude, reminded myself of the humiliation I had felt when I discovered the X-rated videos of the two of them. I wanted them to hurt the way they've hurt me. I wanted her to feel the pain she put me through with her stalking. I wanted revenge, but I just couldn't bring myself to do it.

As I slowly lowered the weapon, disappointed with myself for not being able to summon a cold heart and do what was necessary, Lexi's ankles came free, and she positioned herself upright on the bed.

"So clueless," she said with a snarl. "You made it easy to stalk you. I've never seen anyone so complacent in my life. I stole your car without you knowing. I followed you out to The Knob without you knowing. I thought you might catch me, but you were too dense to realize I could stalk you there, too. What, did you think I only followed you to the stupid book signings? How did you ever get a man like Jake?"

I stared at her with a satisfied smile on my face. "As clueless as I am, Lexi, I still had the brains to record you admitting to stalking me and committing two major crimes. I might be dense, but I won't be the one spending my days in jail."

It finally dawned on her that getting her admission was my plan all along. Her tall frame lunged toward me in a fit of hysteria. We both fell to the ground. I bumped my head on the vanity. Momentarily disoriented, I didn't have a full grasp of the gun. Lexi scrambled around on the ground and snatched it from my hand. When I regained my focus and got back up on my knees, she was standing and had the gun aimed at my face.

"Even if I go to jail, I'll have the satisfaction of knowing you'll be ten feet under."

Jake grasped what was going on. He jumped to his feet. "Lexi, stop!"

When she glanced toward him, I took that moment and plowed into her before she had the chance to pull the trigger. I tried to tackle her, but my shoulder was still weak and I didn't have the strength to hold her down.

She wriggled free and pulled herself up so that her back was up against the bed, giving her support. When she aimed the gun at me again, her face looked like that of a crazed lunatic.

This time, Jake jumped from across the room. Before he made contact, she pointed the gun at him. I heard a gunshot. I looked toward Jake. A bullet ripped through his shoulder and stopped his momentum. Stunned, he stopped to put pressure on the wound.

She turned the gun back on me. This time, she was wearing a wicked smile. I thought my life was over. Visions of Bailey flashed before my eyes… another shot reverberated through the room.

I wasn't hit, so I looked at Lexi. Her eyes looked down at her stomach, clearly in shock, and the gun dropped to the floor. I saw blood oozing from where she'd been shot.

Who the hell shot her?

"Katie, are you okay?" I heard a voice say that sounded like Madison.

I followed the sound. She and Olivia were standing just inside the door. Olivia was holding her own concealed carry, a Glock 9mm.

"I had to do it," she said with resolve. "I wasn't going to let her kill you."

I snapped out of the shock I was in, picked up the Sig P365, and started to set it on the vanity when I heard Lexi's voice.

"You think this is over," she said, holding her hand over the wound to stop the bleeding. "It's not. You will pay for this. I won't let you rest. You will always be looking over your shoulder, wondering if I am there. I won't let you rest."

Everything I had suffered over the last several months came flooding back and I snapped. I leveled the gun on Lexi, ready to fire the fatal shot that I could tell she wanted when Jake stepped forward.

"Don't do it, Katie—remembering that I forbid him to call me by his nickname, Kat—she's not worth it. She's no longer armed. You won't be able to claim self-defense. Don't throw your life away because of my failures. I screwed up, not you. She'll go to jail for a long time, you recorded her admissions."

I kept the gun aimed at her for a full minute before my body slid down to the floor with my back against the vanity. I was visibly shaking all over from the enormity of what just happened and the inevitability of what I knew was to come—a very public trial.

No, it's not over.

CHAPTER 50 - KATIE

Present – July 2020

THE LINE OF customers attending the first book signing of Before She Knew was already two blocks long and local reporters had cameras set up across the street. From the excitement, it looked like they were expecting My Stalker to get out of jail and make an appearance. The story made the rounds before they even printed the book when a junior reporter heard about it at the local police station and then leaked it to other media outlets. They camped outside the Bella Beachside Community, hoping for the juicy details.

As my publicist, Madison used her PR skills to make sure only certain information was revealed. Since the first report, her phone had been ringing off the hook, not just from reporters, but from women and men who suffered in similar circumstances.

Unfortunately, the truth was also out about Jake now, since he had been shot. He got lucky, though. It didn't affect his job since he kept that life hidden from his work and fellow employees. He may have watched Stacy's sexual videos on duty, but there was no proof. All he had to deal with was the gossip. There was plenty of that to go around.

The night of the shooting, Olivia, Madison, and I spent hours being grilled at the police station. Each one of us was in a different interrogation room, so we did not make sure our stories were the same. They questioned Jake at the hospital, where doctors treated him for his gunshot wound. I told everyone to tell the truth. I lured Lexi to my home, and it forced Olivia to shoot her to save my life. She showed up at that precise time because she read the ending of the manuscript where I described shooting Lexi Thompson in an act of revenge. She didn't think I could live with that decision, so she brought her concealed carry in case Lexi came with a weapon of her own.

The local officers doing the interrogation were also the ones who took the earlier stalking reports, so they knew there was a history, but there was still a lot they didn't know. I supplied all the evidence, the camera footage, and the recording of Lexi's admissions. It was there that a junior reporter overhead the narrative and ran with the story.

They called Officer Nichols and Detective Li in to fill in the gaps so they could compare notes and share any information from the crime scene with the ongoing case of Stacy Levin. My phone captured Lexi's confession, but Officer Nichols informed me that his department had already been attempting to build a case against her. They discovered other CCTV cameras in the area of the motorcycle incident; one of them revealed the facial images and proved that I wasn't the one driving the vehicle. While I was being pushed off a cliff, Nichols was behind the scenes gathering evidence against Lexi.

Based on the evidence they collected it was clear to the officers that Lexi intended to harm the individuals on the motorcycle in a fit of rage. They considered Jake to have been one of the victims, in that particular incident. Her mental status became a major issue as the cases played out. After her arrest at the hospital, more information came to light. Namely, that she had been seeing a psychiatrist. Due to privacy issues, the officers would not elaborate, if they even knew her diagnosis, but they hinted that I was lucky. Unfortunately, Stacy Levin was not.

Jake and I parted ways. I knew that would be the outcome the first time I opened the images of his behavior, even though I took my time gathering evidence for a divorce settlement. When I presented all the evidence I collected, Jake admitted he was embarrassed by his behavior, but he couldn't explain it. He agreed, it became an addiction. In the end, I only asked for the cottage and full custody of Bailey. I was entitled to part of his pension which would have been a huge payout, considering we were married for over twenty years, but I settled on a small monthly payment toward the cottage instead. Olivia and Madison were quick to tell me that, in that regard, I was a fool—they wanted me to take him to the cleaners. I assured them that this was better for me. It would be years before he would retire. Settling on a monthly payment now assured me that I could maintain the cottage if future books failed to succeed as I hoped.

He begged and pleaded for me to give him another chance; said he would seek help, but there was no way I could stay with him after what took place. The trust was gone. He packed his things and left a few days after the horrible event in our cottage. I only asked that he not be at the lease-to-own home when I came to collect my belongings.

Some of his family and friends claimed to be shocked, others not so much. I wasn't aware, but there had been rumors. A few firefighters he worked with saw pictures on Facebook but kept it to themselves. I also learned that his daughter knew about Stacy Levin and even liked a few of the images that were posted on social media on his private page. That was another betrayal; knowing some knew and didn't think I deserved to know, and they so easily dismissed me. It wasn't their responsibility to inform me, but I couldn't help but wonder how they sat down at a dinner or family function with me and pretended things were okay.

Not long after he left, Jake sent me a check to cover the funds that were missing from the account and added extra. He said he owed me more. Yes, he owed me more, but after everything that happened, I just wanted to move on and the small payment would suffice.

They say we should try to forgive, maybe in the sense that we don't hold onto our anger, but I will never forget. As it is, I still wake up at night seeing the sexual videos of the man I was married to because they continued to invade my sleep. We had over two decades together. Trust was shattered. I couldn't just erase the pain; that would take a long time.

There was good news to come out of what happened though. To avoid being charged for my part in luring Lexi to the cottage and the ensuing actions that occurred; the local D.A. gave me community service and requested that I take part in group therapy on the subject. I was stunned by what I learned. I was aware that divorce rates were higher than they had ever been, and that cheating was the number one cause. But I had no idea there were so many others who went through similar issues of a spouse living a double life. Sexual addiction was becoming too common.

There was one woman in the group whose husband was in the military, had one family in the states, and another abroad where he was stationed. One of the men in the group admitted his wife had been living a double life as an undercover officer, but she failed to tell him, and he nearly lost his life when a drug dealer she got involved with came to their home. Another's story was eerily similar to mine, except for the financial status of the man involved.

During each group meeting, they asked a member to get up and share their experience. Olivia and Madison attended when it was my turn to share. After my story was told, a group member asked why I couldn't pull the trigger, knowing Lexi pushed me off a cliff and left me for dead. Didn't I want revenge?

I thought back to Detective Li's comment about everyone being capable of harming another when pushed over the edge. I agree to some extent; if it came down to my life or theirs, I knew I could pull the trigger. But when I first had the gun aimed at Lexi Thompson, she was tied up and all I saw was a demented soul. If I would have pulled the trigger, I would have been what she was: a psychotic killer. The second time, she was down and already suffering from a shot to the stomach. As Jake said, she wasn't worth it. That was not the type of revenge that would have made me feel empowered. Overcoming what I endured and making a success of my life, despite it all, was the type of revenge I was looking for. Jake created the problems; I shouldn't have had to pay for them.

~~~

Two days after that meeting of me sharing my vulnerabilities to the group, the prep for my book tour began. Madison met with the media. Book reviews were coming in, and readers were seeking me out on the author page. There were thousands of men and women scattered across the states and abroad who were just like those of us in my group. My book, even though I classified it as fiction, seemed to give them a voice, knowing I based it on reality.

Madison received tons of emails from people sharing their stories and thanking me for having the courage to write about something so personal, knowing the embarrassment that would come from admitting it in the public arena.

There were also messages from some who asked the same question I repeatedly asked myself; how could he have lived a double life for so long without you ever knowing? Some said I must have been naïve. A few went further, saying I probably knew but allowed and accepted it because he was giving me a good life. They were entitled to their opinions, but neither was correct.

When the morning of the first signing arrived, I was terrified. It was one thing to air the story in a private group where others went through something similar. I also didn't feel the angst knowing readers would be seeing the words on a page and posting their comments. It was harder to know I would be facing individuals who read the intimate details and now had the forum to judge me in person.

As usual, Olivia and Madison used humor to snap me out of my fear. Aside from reminding me that I survived with my head held high, Olivia went further.

"I didn't save your life from a demented stalker so you could wallow in this silly insecurity," she said. Of course, she followed it up with a smile to let me know she was teasing.

They both came in for a group hug. "The book is fabulous, Katie," Madison said. "So just go out there and be yourself."

The minute she said, be yourself, I started laughing and Olivia joined in and said, "Oh Madison, you used those same words when she had a stalker in the crowd, and look how that turned out."

"My new motto, be yourself," I said, and the three of us laughed. We walked to the front of the bookstore and looked outside to see the crowd had grown since we arrived and there were still more people coming. It stunned me to see Officer Nichols was standing in the line. At nearly six-foot-three, he was easily visible among the crowd, and his chiseled features stood out. He was not in uniform and appeared to be mingling with a few others in the crowd. I couldn't tell if they were friends of his, or strangers interested in meeting the author.

Olivia and Madison smiled. "See, having a stalker wasn't so bad after all. Look at the handsome officer waiting in a long line to meet you."

Madison winked at me. "Maybe he'll ask you to meet for coffee… baby steps, Katie."

After She Knew - Sex, lies, and betrayal brought them here… and a woman hell-bent on revenge. https://www.bklnk.com/B09VH3JVHD

CR HIATT writes action-oriented stories with strong female characters as the heroes, and a touch of romance. She also created the series featuring the duo, McSwain & Beck. When she's not writing, she's usually renovating houses, riding her e-bike and spending time outdoors with her Golden Retriever, daughter, and friends, usually somewhere near the water.

Dear Reader:

Thank you so much for purchasing and reading Before She Knew.

Readers and word of mouth are crucial to an author's success. If you read the book and enjoyed it, I would be honored if you would consider leaving a one or two-line review on Amazon.

Thank you so much.

For more information on CR HIATT:
Website: **http://writercrhiatt.com/**
FB Fan Page:
https://www.facebook.com/CRHIATT

Also, feel free to email me to receive updates:
authorCRHIATT@gmail.com.

Made in United States
North Haven, CT
18 September 2023

41708705R00209